THE MANAGER

K.A. BRAGONJE

For C.J.B.

Chapter 1

Another day at the office and Emily was still not accustomed to the Russian winter. Her fingers were trembling as she peeled off her fur coat when a light tap sounded at her office door. She ignored it and continued her morning ritual. Grabbing her coat around the neck, she placed it on the hook and dusted the snow off.

Tap-tap.

She continued to tuck her gloves and scarf inside her coat pocket when she heard her door creak open.

"Excuse me, Ms. Lee." Emily's assistant, Katinka, peered around the edge of the door. She acknowledged Emily for a brief moment before focusing on a spot on the carpet-tiled floor, a strand of her wavy hair sweeping over her face.

Emily placed her handbag on the corner of her desk.

Katinka continued, her voice shaking, "I know you're still getting yourself organized. But, your message. You said you wanted to see me first thing. Have I done something wrong?"

"Close the door, please."

"Whatever I've done, I can fix it." Pushing her hair behind her ear, she closed the door. "I need this job."

Noticing the notepad Katinka usually carried around was with her, as well as a plain manila folder underneath, Emily smiled and gestured for Katinka to sit down in the chair opposite hers.

While moving towards her mini bar, she replied, "You can relax, you haven't done anything wrong."

"I... I don't understand."

Her back to Katinka, Emily twisted the lid off her already half empty bottle of vodka. Picking up a nearby shot glass, she blew out the unnoticeable dust before pouring the clear liquid in. Turning around, she raised the bottle. "Vot-ka?"

It was one of the very few Russian words she'd picked up since arriving in Saint Petersburg a week earlier. A word she quickly associated with one of her favorite drinks. Although here the vodka felt stronger than the one back home, but it still warmed her up.

"No, not while I'm working." Katinka waved her hand in front of her, shaking her head.

Emily took her shot, her head and shoulders shuddering as the pungent liquid traveled down her throat.

Her throat still burning, she rinsed her glass before placing it on the sink. Standing over her mini bar, she steadied herself as the last of the burning sensation subsided.

As she sat behind her desk, she studied Katinka, who was fidgeting. "I don't want to rush you but the invoices I was going to get you to look into next week... Well, there's now an urgency on them."

Katinka pushed the manila folder across the desk. "Here they are. I'm not sure why you need them. I mean, I'm not questioning you, but all this information is available on the server, in our accounting program."

"The screen hurts my eyes. Anyhow, I think better when I have a hard copy in front of me." Emily smiled and proceeded to open the folder.

As Emily thumbed through the pages, Katinka tapped her thumbs on the armrest. Biting her tongue, Emily tried her best to ignore the tapping but the constant noise was beginning to agitate her. She wasn't going to cause any conflict here. Not yet anyway. Not while she was still figuring everyone out.

Emily continued scanning through the papers, occasionally pausing on a page for a few moments more than what may have been deemed necessary. She was not really paying attention to the contents; instead, she was assessing Katinka. Testing her. Trying to develop a picture of who her assistant really was.

Within days of arriving in Russia, Emily had quickly realized the locals were going to be harder to read than she initially thought. Most people she'd come across in her career, she was able to develop a fairly accurate sense of what they were like. But not here. Her tactics had to change if she was going to get any sense of who the staff really were, and who, if any of them, was behind the company funds disappearing.

Emily paused on the last page, the page she really wanted to see—a list documenting the company's creditors.

Katinka's tapping grew louder and faster.

Looking up, Emily saw Katinka's youthful forehead was now riddled with deep lines. Her eyes were focused on the open page on the desk.

"Is there a problem?" Emily asked.

Quickly realizing she'd been caught, Katinka pretended to straighten a crease out of her pants, her face returning to its youthful grace. Katinka shook her head and, smiling politely, she replied, "No, Ms. Lee. Just a... no, it's all good."

Emily relaxed into her chair. "Please. You know you can talk to me. What's wrong?"

"It's nothing. Personal. It won't happen again."

Emily smiled. "I'll have a good read over it later."

Closing the folder, she studied her assistant. Katinka began to fidget again, her frown returning.

"You've got nothing to worry about. I'm just making sure the managers and accounts clerks are processing everything correctly. We do want to make sure the company makes money, don't we?"

"Yes, yes." Katinka smiled, chuckling a little before her cheeks began to blush. "Can I... Can I tell you something, in confidence?"

"Of course you can."

"Your boss, the managing director. Has he mentioned anything about us?"

"Us, as in—"

"Me and the other workers here."

Shaking her head, Emily replied, "No. Was he meant to?"

"You've noticed the other staff members here are weary around you."

Emily nodded.

Katinka continued. "You're not the first accountant that was sent here from head office. No, I've known of at least three before you, all foreigners. Each one of them ripping this place apart within hours of their arrival. Changing our processes to how they wanted to run the company. None of them listening to us, the ones who live and breathe the governance of this country. Were you aware, each time this happened many of the company's good staff, and good friends of mine, left?"

Emily's eyes softened. "I'm not one of them. Give me time and I'll prove it to you and everyone here. I want to ensure this company is going to grow. Provide more jobs for the locals, your family and friends."

Katinka shifted her eyes down to the notebook on her lap. "Is there anything else, Ms. Lee?"

"Please, call me Emily. Ms. Lee is so formal."

"No, no, I can't do that."

"In my office, you can."

Katinka returned a small smile.

"There is one more thing." Emily swung her chair around

to face her computer screen.

"Yes." Katinka sat on the edge of her chair.

Loading her spreadsheet program, Emily clicked on the file pinned to the top of her list of recent files and a workbook full of figures appeared. She clicked on the second tab, labeled *Invoices — Auditor*. About three-quarters of a page of data appeared with columns labeled *Date, Invoice Number* and *Amount*. Emily pressed the shortcut on her keyboard, and the printer beside her monitor sprung to life.

The printer was almost finished when Emily pulled the printout and handed it to Katinka.

"I also need a copy of those documents, also."

Katina's scanned the page. "All of these?"

"Yes, please. There aren't many there. Before you ask, no, I don't know why the auditor wants to see them. He just does."

"Auditor?"

"Yes, he's doing random checks before the company lodges their annual tax return."

"When does the he need these by?"

"Lunchtime."

"Today?"

Emily checked the clock on her computer screen. "Yes. If you need some assistance, please let me know and I can assign one of the accounts clerks to help you."

"I... I should be all right." She stood up. "If there isn't anything else...?"

"Thank you, Katinka. And your English, it's developing

nicely. I'm proud of you."

"I'm trying."

"Your night classes—they're paying off."

"Yes, I look forward to them every week." She smiled before leaving Emily's office.

Emily watched as Katinka walked past her office window. She noticed how Katinka's shoulders were pulled back and head held straight; she looked like a woman on a mission. But there was a problem. Her assistant was heading in the opposite direction to the filing room. There wasn't much on that side of the floor except for more offices and the staff tea room.

Pulling her handbag closer, Emily rummaged through until her fingers located her notebook. She placed it on her desk. The cover and edges were tattered, and along its length were little freshly handmade tabs. Each one was handwritten with the name of either a person or a place. Running her finger along the tabs, she stopped at the one labeled *Katinka*. She flipped through the pages until she located her last entry.

With her favorite black gel pen, she scribbled down: "Split personality. Shy to me, somewhat agitated when shown supplier page (need to follow through). Confident when in presence of peers."

Closing the book, she tucked it back inside her bag, then pulled the bottom drawer open and placed her handbag inside it. Pulling a key out of her pants pocket, she locked the drawers. She stood up, returned the key to her pocket and grabbed her coffee cup on the way out.

Through her office window she noticed the staff appeared

to be socializing, probably catching up on the weekend's events. Over to the far-left side of the open floorspace, she caught sight of Katinka walking into an office alongside the staff room.

"Interesting, very interesting," she pondered.

As she stepped out of her office, whispers and glances in her direction swept through the area. Chairs clanked against desks and heads disappeared behind partition walls.

"Attention, everyone," she yelled.

Heads began to pop up above the walls segregating the individual workstations.

Emily continued. "Some socializing is okay. I'm not a dictator." She smiled as she looked around the room. "Just ensure we still meet our targets."

A young man from a nearby desk stood up and, she suspected, translated what she'd just said. Some minimal noise returned to the floor as everyone smiled and nodded to their neighboring work colleagues.

"Thank you," Emily smiled at the staff member.

"I hope I didn't step over the line. I just know there are quite a few here who only speak the mother tongue."

"Your English is very fluent. What's your name?" She walked over, placing an elbow on his partition wall.

"Russell. I grew up in America but I've been living here for about five years."

"You might make my job easier."

Emily noticed his cheeks blushing.

"I'm more than happy to translate for you," he replied.

"Thank you, I appreciate it."

She walked towards the staff room, her eyes were fixed on the office Katinka had entered. The door had been left ajar and the blinds drawn.

Approaching the corner cubicle, Emily kept her composure and her pace. Schultz winked at her and returned his attention to his computer screen. Emily was fighting hard not to acknowledge him any differently to the others.

As she walked past his workstation, she glanced over at the partly opened office door. She could hear two people talking, but their Russian was too fluent for her to translate any of it. A suited man approached the door. Emily smiled and he returned a wry smile which quickly disappeared as he shut the door.

Emily entered the staff room and everyone scurried out, their eyes on the ground. Shaking her head, she picked up the coffee tins. The labels were all printed in Russian.

Too exhausted by the short wintry days to be bothered with any attempts at translating the labels, she twisted the lid off the first one. Bitter tones wafted out before the lid was fully removed. She quickly closed the lid and proceeded to the next one.

"You're not going to find anything good there," a familiar voice sounded behind her.

She stopped and turned around, then let a big smile emerge. Since arriving they'd barely had a moment alone where she could truly be herself.

Schultz placed a finger on his lips. Emily nodded, trying

9

hard to contain her excitement.

"You need some of this." He pulled his arm out from behind his back and held up a black satchel.

Recognizing the yellow ring in the center of the satchel with 'Humbler' printed inside it, Emily jumped up and down like an excited little child.

Schultz pressed his finger against his lips.

Trying to compose herself, she said more calmly, "It arrived."

"I thought you'd be excited."

"Excited is an understatement. Do you know how long I've been hanging out for a decent coffee?"

"I'd say it would've been since... Melbourne?"

"Pretty much." Emily sealed the jar she'd just opened, watching eagerly as Schultz spooned out their desired quantities of coffee. Two for her, three for him.

"Our first official assignment together. How does it feel?"

"Like a normal day in the office."

"Seriously? Normal day. Wow." He shook his head.

She winked at him. "It'll be good to get a second set of eyes on the place. And your rusty Russian may just come in handy."

"Geez, it's good to feel wanted."

Emily leaned against the counter. Crossing her arms, she asked, "Do you know who works in that office near your workstation?"

"Which one?" He continued preparing their coffees.

"The one directly opposite from you, the other side of that wall." She pointed vaguely in its direction. "The one my *assigned* assistant entered a few minutes ago."

"I sense a hint of frustration. You already running into strife with the locals?"

Emily grumbled.

"That's Ivan Kuzmich. He's a character alright. If you ask me, I think he's a bit full of himself."

"What's his role?"

"Production Manager. Well, that's how he introduced himself to me."

"And he's got an office up here?"

"Yeah, I'm still trying to work that one out. I think he has junior managers working under him who are running the production floor."

"O-kay. It is what it is then."

She smiled as Schultz handed a coffee mug to her. She lifted the cup to her lips, closing her eyes and letting the sweet aromas warm her as she took a sip. It didn't disappoint. After savoring the mouthful, she opened her eyes and asked Schultz, "You didn't happen to hear what they were talking about?"

He smiled and raised an eyebrow. "You sure you want to know?"

Emily raised an eyebrow and stared at him.

"I'll let you know tonight. But, a heads-up. Be careful what you say in front of your assistant, or anyone else here."

Chapter 2

Ivan opened the company's internal messenger application on his desktop computer and clicked on the *To* section. He scrolled through all the staff names until he found the one he was looking for. He clicked on the name Russell Jones, and watched his cursor move to the message area. The cursor blinked while Ivan stared at the blank page.

His shoulders arched over the keyboard, he tapped in a message with his two pointer fingers, backtracking every few words when his fat fingers got in the way.

The final message read:

> *I need to see you urgently.*
>
> *Your upmost discretion is warranted.*

He stared at the screen for a moment, reading what he'd

painfully typed, then hit the send button. A little notification popped up advising Ivan the message had been read.

Looking around his desk he noticed a pile of papers. He stuffed them inside his desk's top drawer then completed one final pass over, ensuring every item was in its correct place, moving them if they were not.

Ivan glanced at the clock positioned above his door. Not long until his meeting at ten. His toes tapped under the desk while he scrolled through his emails, waiting.

He kept checking his clock. Another minute passed and no sign of Russell. Ivan began to feel uneasy.

This was a bad idea. I told them we shouldn't bring outsiders in, he thought as he re-checked the message he'd sent to Russell. Still no reply. Nothing.

There was a light tap at his door.

Ivan shot up in his seat, his knees banging the desk.

The tap sounded again.

Ivan cleared his throat and in a deep, stern voice, he hollered, "Enter."

The door opened. Ivan exhaled in relief when he saw Russell step into his office.

"Close the door and take a seat. Please," he added, his tone mellowing but still directive.

"Have... have I done anything wrong?" Russell's hand shook as he closed the door.

I've made a wrong choice, Ivan thought but instead replied, "No. Not at all."

Ivan let out a little chuckle but Russell still appeared

confused.

"I don't understand. Why have you called me in?"

"Do you enjoy working for this company?" Ivan sat back in his chair and narrowed his eyes at Russell.

Russell pulled his shoulders back. "Of course I am. It's a wonderful company to work for."

"Are you? How do you westerners put it... Happy with your job satisfaction?"

"Excuse my bluntness but how does this affect you? We work in different departments."

Ivan noticed Russell's eyes widen when they dropped to Ivan's collar. Turning his chair around, he looked out the window overlooking the bustling city as he removed his lapel pin, a golden hammer and sickle on a red five-pointed star.

"It's been a while, but I think I've seen that symbol before," said Russell. "Wasn't it popular during Stalin's regime?"

Ivan dropped the badge into his pocket and turned his chair around to face Russell, watching him as his throat moved up and down.

"I like to know the people I work with." Ivan placed his elbows on the table. "You're one of the newest employees I haven't yet had the opportunity to know."

"Me and the Australians."

"Yes, those two as well." Ivan coughed. "Would you like a *votka*?" He walked over to his corner mini bar.

"If you wanted a social chat, we can do it down at the pub after work." Russell stood up. "I have a lot of work to get through."

"Are you happy with your current role?"

"Why wouldn't I be?"

"Sit, sit, sit." Ivan gestured to his seat. "We shall now talk business."

"Business?" Russell remained standing, towering over Ivan.

"Please, sit."

Russell folded his arms in front of him.

"Very well. Stay standing. It doesn't worry me. But do tell me... Where do you see yourself in five years' time, or even two years?"

"Here, in Russia, enjoying these freezing winters."

Ivan erupted in a deep laughter. "With your career. Will you still be sitting in that same cubicle, or do you wish for bigger and grander things?"

"Progression is always good. But if it doesn't happen it's not meant to be, and I'll be happy doing what I'm doing."

"That's a typical response I'd expect between a boss and a worker. Now, what do you truly want? What prospects do you see in your current position?"

"I'm worried about the present time. Now, I really need to return to my workstation."

"You don't need to worry. I'll organize for one of the ladies to help you. How about that young brunette in the cubicle next to yours?" Ivan winked. "I've seen you two darting glances at each other around the office. Yeah?"

Russell blushed but composed himself. "Thank you. What is it with all these questions? If you get to the point, we can both stop dancing."

Maybe we've chosen the right person after all, Ivan thought as he eyed Russell up and down. He was impressed with the youngster's sternness despite addressing someone more senior than him.

"Okay then. I have a proposition. What we're about to discuss must remain inside these walls. Understood?"

Russell nodded.

Ivan continued. "We need someone to join my department. Someone who will shake things up."

Russell sat down. "What do you mean, shake things up?"

"Fresh eyes on the ground. Someone who isn't afraid to do what is best for the organization."

"Why aren't human resources in here with you? Aren't they usually involved in all staff transfer discussions?"

"I've got free rein over my department while I remain under budget. No questions are asked. I'm left alone to do my own thing."

"All right. I'll bite. What would the position entail?"

"It'll be a similar role to what you're currently doing. After a trial period, there'll be opportunities for you to climb the ranks. And one day, when it's my turn to run this company, you could step straight into this chair." He tapped the armrests.

"What about Emily? She still needs a translator."

"Who's Emily?"

"The Australian, the finance person. The one who's assisting with the auditing."

"Oh, her. Hmm. She doesn't understand Russian?"

"No, she doesn't. She's trying to learn it but she's still years away from being close to fluent."

"Hmmm." Ivan rubbed his hand under his chin. "There's no one else here who can do it?"

"No. There's a few that are close but not enough to help Ms. Lee—I mean Emily, properly."

"Okay, continue assisting her. It could come in handy. But, only until someone else is able to step up."

"Is there any incentive for me to take on the new role?"

"I take it you're talking money?"

"Yes. I need a reason if I'm to move positions. Working for Emily has been great. It's been exciting seeing the few changes she's already made."

Ivan clenched his fists, his nails digging into his palm. "Job progression—isn't that enough? We can discuss money when your probation is completed."

Russell stood up, pushing the chair back. "I'll have an answer for you tomorrow. One cannot make an informed decision on the spot."

He bowed and walked towards the office door.

"Your visa. You still work under one. Is that correct?"

Russell stopped.

Ivan stood up and pulled his jacket in front of him. "It would be terrible if your visa became invalid, would it not?"

Russell turned around. "You wouldn't."

"From what I see you only have two options. Be deported from Russia and never allowed back here, or... you could accept my proposal."

"You don't give me much of an option, do you?"

"Wise choice. You'll be well off in my department. And I must say the organization will be all the better with your involvement."

Ivan walked around his desk and extended an open hand. Russell hesitated but exchanged a handshake. "Welcome to my team. Continue in your current role until the appropriate internal transfer papers are completed by human resources."

"And Emily?"

"She'll be advised in due course."

"I look forward to working with you." Russell opened the door.

"Ah, before you go." Ivan placed a finger over his lips. "There is one thing I need you to do right away for the organization."

"Straight away?"

"I'll send through the details after my meeting this morning. But in the meantime, please keep an ear out. In particular, for anything that could affect the performance of my department, or the company."

"You want me to spy on my colleagues?"

"Spy. No, that word is too strong. I like to think of it as keeping ahead of the game."

Chapter 3

Cracking his neck, Schultz peered over his shoulder then looked left and right down the length of workstations. They were all empty. He twisted in his chair.

"Strange," Schultz said, noticing Ivan's office door was open and the room unoccupied.

Standing up a little higher than the partition wall, he looked around the other workstations. Ivan was nowhere to be seen.

"Right." His fists clasped, he stretched them, his knuckles cracking. Shaking his fingers, he tapped into the company's email backup. It wasn't long and he was in.

Thanks, Xander, Schultz thought as he smiled at the little gem Xander had shown him a couple of months prior. They were enjoying a couple of quiet drinks at Xander's place, celebrating the successful closure of an ongoing assignment against a large corporation, when Xander showed him that little hack.

Looking over his shoulder, Schultz quickly inserted a thumb drive into his computer, pulled up the directory listing and clicked on a file labelled firefly.exe.

A DOS window appeared. Tapping his fingers on his desk, Schultz took a moment to recall the code Xander had instructed him to use. He tapped it in and a small DOS command appeared, advising him the files were being copied over to the thumb drive.

Schultz heard a door open up not far from him. Out of the corner of his eye he watched Ivan walk out of the office and towards him. Pressing Alt and Tab together, he shifted through his open programs until he came across the company's accounting software and resumed typing data into the computer. He wasn't typing long when he felt someone standing behind him.

Turning around slowly, Schultz smiled then said, "Morning."

"Busy?" Ivan looked over Schultz's shoulder.

"Always. You know paperwork, it never goes away." Schultz held up a pile of papers he'd been working on earlier.

"You doing anything tonight?"

Schultz thought for a moment, pretending to be visualizing his busy schedule. He shook his head. "No, don't believe I do."

"There's a few of us heading to a local fine bar. You should join us. We'll show you how to have a good time, Russian style." He winked.

Schultz blushed. He knew all too well Ivan was talking about a men's nightclub. On his first day here, he'd overheard Ivan boasting in the staff room about his weekend fun and how each lady either entertained him or not.

"I'll be there."

"Good choice, good choice."

Schultz held his breath as Ivan leaned in, his odor unbearable. Ivan slipped something under Schultz's keyboard.

"See you tonight." Ivan pointed a finger at Schultz. Clicking his finger, he winked as he stepped away.

Schultz gave him the thumbs up and watched as Ivan walked towards the boardroom. When he was out of eyesight, his smile disappeared. He turned and lifted his keyboard. On his desk sat a torn piece of printer paper. Turning it over, he saw in shaky handwriting:

The Fortress Nightclub

Unlocking his Federal Police-issue cell phone, he checked his firewalls were still active before typing in the following private message to Xander:

Ivan Kuzmich and The Fortress Nightclub
See what dirt you can find on them.
Thanks.

He re-read it. He'd seen many messages from his younger colleagues whose communications comprised of a jumble of numbers, symbols and letters, none of which made sense to him. As everything was encrypted and double-encrypted these days, he always wondered why they just didn't use proper words in their messages.

Happy with his message, he hit the send button.

A moment later he received a reply:

Don't you know what holidays are? What assignment's this?

Schultz chuckled and checked the time on his watch. It would be about two in the morning back home. He shook his head and replied:

You obviously don't know what sleep is either.

Xander had learnt the hard way about sending abbreviated messages to Schultz. Schultz had been working on a big assignment when Xander joined the agency. The first message he'd sent Schultz was an incomprehensible text message full of jumbled up words, so he'd ignored it. It wasn't long until Xander was racing down the stairs, yelling at Schultz for still being in his office.

The embarrassment set in for Xander when nearby detectives laughed and guessed Xander had sent an abbreviated message. The detectives enlightened him to the fact that Schultz required all his messages to be typed out fully.

Xander's reply came through:

You know if you learnt shorthand, you'd free up your time. Anyway, what are you working on? I didn't know we had a Russian assignment.

Schultz looked around before he tapped in his reply:

I'll explain later. Just trust me. Please?

There was no reply.

Can you do it? Schultz sent, not liking the feeling of being left to dangle on a branch in the wind. He'd taken a large leap by involving Xander on a case not associated with the agency.

After what felt like a long time, but was only a couple of minutes, Xander's reply finally arrived:

I don't have a good feeling 'bout any of this. I'll be in touch IF I have anything. Until then, try and enjoy your holidays.

Chapter 4

Sitting at the end of the boardroom table, Emily adjusted her earwig. Although there was still interference, she was able to get the gist of what her interpreter was relaying.

Like all the other boardroom meetings, the table was filled with business suited managers. Mainly men, with four women sprinkled between them. From what Emily understood, most were managers from other departments or satellite sites. Many she hadn't seen at any of the previous meetings.

Leaning over, she rubbed her forehead. A pungent odor, a mixture of cheap alcohol and cigar smoke, overwhelmed her. She tried holding on longer between breaths, but that was adding to her nausea. She'd smelled the pungeont odor earlier in one of the offices. Peering through the nook in her arm, she glanced to her side. The businessman sitting next to her had a sense of familiarity.

I'd swear on my father's grave he is the man I caught Katinka talking to earlier, she thought as she returned to her meeting notes.

"If you turn to the next page," her interpreter advised, "you'll see an updated list of our major shareholders. They're still retaining a combined 51% share in the company, the only change being a few major investors moving a couple of percentage points either way."

Emily scanned through the list. The documents they'd been given were in Russian.

"Ms. Lee, before we conclude the meeting, is there anything you'd like to add? Any findings?" her interpreter asked.

All eyes fell on her. She felt the temperature in the room rising. She shook her head and replied, "No."

Everyone seemed to understand, and in the next minute the screeching of chairs being pushed back on the tiled floor pierced the room. Standing, Emily watched as the manager sitting next to her made a quick escape. She scrambled her notes together, glancing towards the exit.

A few of the managers approached her, huddling around, pointing at her, their eyebrows raised as they talked to her. Unable to understand any of them, she made her apologies and pushed her way out of the small group of men. Hurrying out of the room, she saw him—Ivan something, Schultz had said his name but it slipped her memory—as he poked his head out of the office near Schultz's workstation. He was scanning the room, but stopped when he saw Emily. He stared at her for a few seconds before closing his office door and drawing the curtains closed.

"It is him," Emily whispered to herself.

Turning to her assistant's desk, she saw it was empty. Emily walked back to her office slowly, glancing around the workstations. Her assistant wasn't in sight.

Upon entering her office, she pulled her sleeve back enough to see her watch; it was almost eleven. Closer to her desk, a waft of coffee awoke her senses. Following the smell, she saw her coffee mug sitting on a coaster next to her keyboard, the steam still visible. She went to her office door and scanned the open-plan office outside it. There was no one around. Her phone beeped. Walking back into her office, she pulled it out and saw a message from Schultz.

The message read: *It's safe. Enjoy.*

He'd closed the message off with a winking emoji. She looked towards his cubicle but couldn't see him. Shrugging her shoulders, she closed the door behind her. She wasn't going to be sharing her coffee aromas with anyone.

Sitting down at her desk, she took a sip of her coffee while she fired up the employee records on her computer. She typed in *Ivan* in the search box. A list of twenty Ivans appeared.

She clicked on the first record. A photo appeared, along with his personal details. This Ivan was dressed in what looked like overalls. His silver hair and deep wrinkles indicated he should have retired long ago.

Emily clicked through the next few records. The men were either too old or too young. She stopped at the fifth record. The manager's photo stared back at her, his eyes hollow and cold, with no expression. Feeling a cold chill pass over her, she clicked on his employment details.

An error message appeared: *insufficient clearance.*

Clicking on the tab labeled *Employment History* made the same error flash before her.

"Insufficient clearance, my ass." She slammed the mouse down on her desk. "Why?" she whispered. "Why are you blocked?"

Emily unlocked her bottom drawer and pulled her notebook out from her handbag. Running her finger along the tabs, she stopped at the tab labelled *Ivan* and opened the book. Flicking to the next empty page, she scribbled down Ivan Kuzmich—stinky manager. Production Manager – employee record blocked.

Tap-tap.

Looking up she saw a slender outline on the other side of her frosted glass-paned door. Keeping her eye on the door, Emily dropped her book into the bottom drawer.

Tap-tap.

"Come in," she said, nudging the drawer shut with her foot.

The door opened and her assistant poked her head in.

"Excuse me, Ms. Lee, did you receive the requested invoices?"

"Oh yes. Let me just check. Please come in and take a seat."

Emily looked over her desk; it was bare.

"Where are they?"

"I emailed them to you."

"I thought I said hard copies."

"I'm sorry, you said they were urgent and I thought—"

"Please. Don't think."

A few clicks of her mouse and her emails appeared, with Katinka's at the top. Opening the email, she saw it only contained an attachment. Clicking on the file, she made the scanned copies of the invoices appear. She scrolled through the first few pages.

"They're here. Thank you. I'll forward them to the auditor shortly."

Emily stared at her assistant for a moment and noticed her eyes were red and a little watery. "Is everything okay?"

"Yes, Ms. Lee. I couldn't be happier here. If there's nothing else, I must return to my desk."

"Are you still right to work, or do you need to go home?"

"I'll be right." A little smile appeared.

"Okay. If you need to talk to anyone, I'm here. Okay?"

"Thank you."

The door closed and Emily flicked back to Ivan's employment file. She tried the other tabs, but each one flashed the same error message: *insufficient clearance.*

Her eyes darted between her window and her computer. She could hear loud voices approaching. Her heart beat quickening, she escaped out of that area of the system and pulled up the scanned invoices she'd been waiting to see.

Chapter 5

Schultz's cell vibrated on his desk.

His phone to his ear, he popped his head above his cubicle divider. A cluster of female staff were gossiping a few cubicles over. One caught Schultz looking at them and returned a flirty wave and smile at him. Smiling back, he looked around the remainder of the office. It was deserted.

Ducking back down, he crouched over his keyboard and whispered into his cell phone, "Xander, what you got?"

"Yep, I'm well, thanks for asking."

"Sorry. We're not allowed to use our personal cells."

"Seriously? I'm not even going to ask what you're doing. Anyway, the reason I've called is I've done some digging around for you on that Ivan bloke."

"Did you find any ghosts?"

"More than that. The department he manages—get this: it only exists on the books. I couldn't even find any employment records for him. Well, I did but there wasn't anything in there. He's a ghost."

"The question now is... how is he affording his expensive suits and lavish nights out at the nightclubs?"

"I thought you wouldn't ask. Yes, he's earning a salary. But he's not covering all those with his manager's wage. But, wait for it."

"Come on, don't leave me hanging." Schultz poked his head around the office floor; he hadn't been caught.

"Okay, hang on. He's on the books as a director of some shell company who call themselves Prestak. You know who Prestak are, don't you?"

"Aren't they the ones rumored to be causing civil unrest?"

"Yeah. I'm still looking into what they're uprising against. But yes, it's the same organization."

Schultz sat back in his chair and whispered, "Holy smoke."

At that moment one of the gossiping women from nearby leant over his partition wall.

He smiled awkwardly.

"Mom, I need to go. I'll talk to you tonight. Yes... I love you too Mom."

"Seriously, is that the best you've got?"

"Yes, Mom, I'm at work. Okay, okay." He rolled his eyes and the woman smiled. "Mom, I'll talk to you tonight."

He disconnected the call and waved his phone. "Mothers,"

he said chuckling as he turned his phone off.

She looked down at him, somewhat doubtful, waiting to see if he was going to falter. His heart was racing, dreading what was going to happen. He could not afford to get the sack and leave Lee alone.

"Come closer," she whispered, her hand dangling over the partition.

Schultz moved in closer, her perfume flooding his senses.

"You'll need this for tonight."

She held her hand out with her thumb tucked underneath, as if she was holding something. Still wary, Schultz placed his hand under hers. Winking, she pulled her hand away.

Looking down, Schultz saw it was a blank plastic card, about the size of a bank card, but about double the thickness.

"What's this?"

"Ivan said that'll make tonight easier. Oh, and by the way, keep your calls down. That is if you want to keep your job."

"Yes, sorry, I will."

"Don't apologize to me. It's Ms. Lee you should be worried about."

She was already moving away before Schultz could reply. Sitting down, he looked again at the card she'd just given him. Turning it over, he read the back. "VIP."

Chapter 6

Emily pressed the button alongside Katinka's name before placing the call on loud speaker.

"Yes," her quivering voice answered.

"In here, now." Emily disconnected the call.

A moment later her door creaked open and her assistant stepped into her office.

"Where are the missing invoices?" Emily shook a piece of paper in her hand.

"I, I don't understand what you're saying."

"I'm still missing a few invoices. Please tell me there's a second email coming."

"No, there's only the one email."

"Then," Emily slammed the piece of paper down on her

desk and pointed to the few invoice entries that weren't highlighted. "Where are these three?"

"Excuse me, Emily." She placed her hands on her hips. "They were sent. I double-checked them before I sent you the email. They have to be there. Maybe your Russian is a little rusty and you just missed them."

"Right. Show me where they are." Emily pushed her chair back only far enough for Katinka to slide in.

"No worries." Keeping her hand on her hip, she walked over, squeezing in between Emily and the computer.

Emily studied Katinka for a moment. She noticed her shoulder sitting a bit awkward for someone typing. Peering around, she saw Katinka's hand pressed up against the underside of her desk.

"Keep your hands above the table," Emily ordered.

Katinka didn't respond but she moved her palm around so it was on top of the desk as she continued tapping on the mouse.

Glancing over her shoulder, she asked, "Can I please have a look at that list?"

Emily passed it to her while keeping her eyes on Katinka. She could sense her assistant felt uncomfortable but she didn't care, not today anyway. She bit her tongue. The last thing she wanted was to explain to her superiors why she was deported from the country. It wouldn't go down well at all, let alone kissing goodbye any future international assignments.

Moving away from the computer, Katinka apologized. "I don't know why they're not there. I'll get them for you right now."

"Thank you. The auditor is not happy and your sloppiness has been noted."

Her assistant almost ran out of her office. Once Katinka was outside, Emily saw her take a step towards Ivan's office. She hesitated before she turned around. Emily caught her wiping her eyes as she walked back towards her desk, almost knocking another staff member over in the process.

Emily didn't flinch. She couldn't. She had to stay on guard. For all she knew, anyone in here could turn on her at any moment.

She glanced at her computer desk then to her office door and windows. She was alone. For now. Keeping her eye on her office door, she ran her fingers along the underside of her desk. Her fingers touched something.

Pushing her chair back she looked under her desk. She saw the dark outline of something that interrupted the otherwise smooth lines of the cheap office furniture. Grabbing her cell phone, she turned on the torch and knelt down.

The thick beam of light illuminated a black box about five centimeters long by three centimeters across and one centimeter wide. It was smooth all the way around, without any wires coming out of it. Wriggling it achieved nothing; it didn't move but Emily noted it was warm to the touch.

After taking a few photos—close-ups as well as some of its location on the desk—Emily sat back in her chair and stared at it. It was directly underneath her computer, right where Katinka had placed her hand.

There was no reason why that girl should've had her hand underneath the desk. Unless... Emily shook her head.

No, Katinka couldn't have done it. She's my assistant and values her job too much. But if anyone else had been in here Schultz would've let me know, she thought.

Emily decided she would exercise caution until she figured out what the little box was and what it did. She went into her phone's security app and ensured all three firewalls were enabled. Her computer dinged. An email notification popped up with the heading, *Minutes from today's meeting.* Russell.

Clicking on the attachment, Emily scrolled through the document. She was impressed; he'd already sent through the translated version.

She stopped scrolling at the list of shareholders. There was one that caught her attention: Li Global Investments.

Her mouth dropped open. *It can't be him! Can it?*

She punched the shareholder's name into her web browser and scanned through the search results. The top article caught her attention. It was dated November 30.

"Two weeks ago."

She read the article.

Fu Li, Managing Director, advised quarterly profits increased by two million dollars, in part thanks to the steady global property growth.

At the bottom, the article included a photo of the managing director.

"No, no," she said, forgetting the device under her desk. "Why does he have to keep popping up everywhere?"

She opened her phone's messaging app and typed in a message to Schultz.

We need to talk. Now!

Less than a minute later she received a reply.

It's nearly time for lunch. Meet me down in the foyer. Five minutes?

She hurried a response to him, using her phones autocorrect to get the message typed quicker.

Done.

She hit send.

While her printer spat out the translated version of the minutes, she skulled the last of her coffee and seized her handbag. Grabbing both versions of the meeting papers, she shoved them into her handbag as she walked over to her coat.

Her phone dinged.

Act like you do any other day. Don't let it show there's anything wrong. See you shortly.

Thanks, Schultz, I really needed the reminder. She thought, smiling as she put her coat on.

Closing the door behind her, she walked over to Katinka's desk.

"Katinka, I'm going to take an early lunch." Her assistant jumped. "Would you like me to bring anything back for you?"

Patting her chest and laughing her adrenalin rush off, the girl replied, "No, I'll be all right. Thank you."

"I'm still waiting on those invoices."

Katinka nodded. "I've just sent them. You should receive them shortly."

"Thank you." Emily smiled warmly. "Please make sure you do take a break. Please. Get some fresh air, even if it is cold. Okay?"

Her assistant smiled and returned to her work.

As Emily walked towards the elevator, she had a feeling someone was watching her. She pulled her coat in tight around her, holding her handbag close.

Her phone vibrated but she ignored it.

The elevator door opened as she approached. Once inside, she repeatedly pressed the appropriate button to close the elevator doors until they began to move. As the doors shut, she looked towards Katinka's desk. Katinka was staring at her while on the phone.

Chapter 7

Stepping off the last step into the empty lobby, Ivan appreciated its emptiness. His work colleagues' promptness for taking their lunch break was the one thing he could count on.

Taking a couple of steps to his left, he unlocked a door labelled *Cleaning*. As he opened the door, the chime on the elevator sounded. He quickly stepped inside and closed the door behind him. Swallowed in darkness, he ran his hand along the cool brick wall. He depressed the familiar button for the light timer. He descended the narrow, worn stone stairs two at a time.

Halfway down the first flight of stairs he felt his cell vibrate. He ignored it and concentrated on his footing. It vibrated again. He pulled his cell phone out of his pants pocket. The screen illuminated with a notification.

1 new message: Nicholas

Stopping on the landing between the levels, Ivan tapped on the message notification then quickly read the message before sliding his cell back into his pocket.

Maneuvering the landing swiftly, he descended the next set of stairs, taking them two at a time, as well. This flight was shorter than the first, only about a dozen steps before a door greeted him. Alongside the door was his extra security, fingerprint and retina scanner.

Ivan bent his knees a little to line up his eye with the device. A blue light began scanning his eye then disappeared. A couple of seconds later the screen illuminated green. He placed his thumb on the scanner and another blue light began scanning his thumb print. It was halfway down his finger when it beeped and a red flashing light illuminated the area.

"These scanners, there's always a problem."

Clenching his other fist, he took a deep breath before adjusting his thumb's position. The scanner re-commenced. The light reached the bottom of his thumbprint, and a green light confirmed its recognition.

Ivan punched his six-digit pin code into the keypad underneath the scanners, and the thick steel door opened inwards.

A cloud of cigarette smoke greeted him as he stepped through the door. Inside, men dressed in military olive tunic and trousers tucked inside calf-length leather boots were hard at work.

Thud.

The door slammed shut behind him and silence fell over the room, everyone turning to face Ivan. The men stamped their feet together and raised their right fists into the air.

Ivan raised his fist in response.

Lowering his arm, he pulled his shoulders back and walked towards the other end of the room. The men kept their arms raised until he'd walked past them.

Ivan glanced along the wall to where his father's prized collection of Stalin's political posters were hanging. They were an assortment of illustrations and photographs his father had saved from the times when Stalin was in power. On each of the posters the artist had Stalin in different positions, but each one of them had Stalin looking down at the men in the room, watching their every move. Such majesty! Ivan couldn't help but feel a little sentimental.

"My supreme leader," he bowed his head before continuing. "It will not be long and my portrait will be etched into people's memories just like yours was when you were our supreme leader," he whispered.

He paused for a moment of personal reflection. As he finished, he pulled his shoulders back and head straight, then he marched to the far corner where a desk with a line of computer screens across its length sat. The operator's fingers were flying over the keyboard. Along the wall a little farther, another two desks butted against each other, a couple more technicians weaving their magic for him. Approaching the corner desk where the lone technician was working, he tapped the back of the computer chair.

"What's your name? Brian, isn't it?"

A youngish looking man swiveled his chair around.

Ivan looked down at him, his eyebrow raised. Brian turned back to his computer screens.

"Is everything going to plan?" Ivan stood in front of the wall of video surveillance screens.

"Yes. Your message is currently being deployed, on foot."

"Good, good. I cannot have this getting back to the president. No, I want the element of surprise. Just like he did to me when he swiped the candidate vote from under my feet.

"You're still available tonight, yeah? I'll pay double your rate."

Brian paused his typing.

"Tonight? I'm nearly done here."

"I'll be needing your expertise tonight. I'll pay you cash."

"How can I say no?" Brian turned to face Ivan.

"Good. I'll have Nicholas send you the required information. You'll be reporting to him tonight. You need anything, see him."

Brian nodded, his attention drawn past Ivan's shoulder to a broad-shouldered man who was marching over. His head was shaved and his tired eyes had dark circles around them.

Ivan followed Brian's gaze. Turning around, he placed an arm on the man's back.

"Ah, Nicholas. Brian here will be at your disposal."

With his nose up in the air, Nicholas stood beside Brian

and looked him up and down. Snorting, he turned his back and marched back to Ivan.

"That computer geek," he grumbled. "He'll be no good. He won't be able to keep up with us."

"Make it work. You may need his skills tonight."

"Humph," Nicholas said as he marched off.

Ivan turned and looked at the wall alongside him.

"Can I ask you something?" Brian asked.

"It depends."

"What exactly is going on tonight?"

"You'll know in good time. Until then, monitor the chatter. The second you get wind of whispers about the president, or any of his men... No, anyone. I don't care who they are. If anyone shows any hints of retaliating against the Cause, I need to know about it. Understood?"

Brian lowered his head. "Yes, Kuzmich."

"Back to it then." He waved his hand towards Brian's computer screens.

Turning around, Ivan was surprised to see Nicholas was staring at the wall of screens. They streamed images from various strategic locations around Saint Petersburg, inside shops, out in the streets and inside companies.

"Sorry, sir. But you need to see this."

Nicholas clicked his finger. The computer technician closest to him pressed a couple of buttons and the individual feeds were replaced with one image spread across all the screens.

Ivan stepped back, almost falling over his own feet.

"You all right?"

"Yes. A bit surprised, that's all. How long?"

"Not sure. We're backtracking their movements."

"I suspected they were acquainted prior to their arrival."

"Yes. When I approached Schultz... I think that's his name... Anyway, he reckoned he had no idea who the new finance lady was. But looking at those two..." Ivan pointed to Emily and Schultz sitting cozily at a table in a restaurant. "...At how snug they look, I'd have to agree with you. He's known her for a lot longer than the few days he's been here."

"Brian," Ivan yelled.

"Yes."

"I need you to—"

Brian's gaze followed Ivan's to the screens, and his mouth dropped open.

"You know them?" Ivan asked.

Closing his mouth, he replied, "Not exactly."

Ivan crossed his arms. "Not exactly, how?"

Nicholas stepped around from behind Ivan and stared down at him, his arms also crossed over his body.

"There was an incident, and that woman got away."

"She got away?" Nicholas asked.

Taking a step closer, Ivan asked, "Exactly, who is that woman?"

Brian shifted in his seat, avoiding eye contact with either of them before replying, "I believe it's along the lines of a Forensic Accountant or Financial Analyst. I don't know her exact title, but all I know is that she comes into companies, looks over their figures then leaves."

"Okay, so she looks at figures. How did she end up here?" Ivan asked, looking less than impressed.

"I can look into it. But, in the past, I've tried finding a digital trail of her assignments, to see if it feeds back to a company or someone, but there's nothing. Either it's all completed offline or her security is that tight she doesn't leave a digital trace."

"So, she's a better computer technician than you?"

"Not necessarily. I'd hedge a bet that whoever she works for controls her digital security. It's nothing like I've seen before."

"That's not good. I cannot have a woman like that sniffing around this place. What else can you tell me about her?"

"Not much... only that she's kicked some serious butt. My previous client was her uncle."

"Was?"

"Family feud. She disowned him. Anyway, I do know she's done work for the police, both state and federal."

"How do you know that? You said her security was tight."

"Hers is. The government's not so much. And he," Brian pointed to Schultz, "he's a cop."

Ivan returned to the screens and pondered before replying, "Interesting. So, we have a cop and a bean counter on our shores. This will definitely make tonight interesting."

"What are you thinking, boss?" Nicholas asked, also returning his attention to the screens.

"Brian, thank you for the information. It has been valuable

but I now need you to go back to listening out for chatter. And Nicholas," he placed his arm on the man's back and guided him to a long boardroom table positioned to the side of the room. "This afternoon on your way to the Konevets Island you will encounter some unwanted company."

"Right."

"Hunt them down and get the wild beast alive." Ivan nodded towards the screens that were paused on Emily and Schultz huddling.

Nicholas nodded. "How many?"

"Just one. Driver is mine; he's all good."

"And the cop?"

"I'll deal with him. I have a plan for him tonight."

"Are you sure we can trust him?" Nicholas raised his eyebrow towards Brian.

"He's the best money can buy. He came highly recommended by Fu and a few of his... counterparts."

"I don't know, I'm still not sure about him."

"Without him, we'd be years from our cause. He's brought my vision to the forefront, and quicker than I'd imagined."

"I hope you're right. If things go south—"

"If my plans go south, we're all on our own."

Chapter 8

"Any drinks? Beer? Votka?" A waitress asked, standing poised with notepad and paper.

Emily and Schultz looked at each other and chuckled.

"No, no drinks," Schultz replied, trying very hard to keep a straight face.

Emily looked at the waitress. She'd done her best to conceal her identity with semi-tanned makeup. She gave the illusion she was Caucasian but her features indicated otherwise.

"You been in Russia long?" Emily asked in Chinese.

The waitress' eyes widened a little. She looked at Schultz.

"Food won't be long." Her English was now fluent, without her previously heavy Russian accent.

Emily watched the waitress as she walked away before returning her attention to Schultz.

"What was that about?"

"Nothing. Just hate it when people try to portray themselves as someone else."

"What's new?"

Emily looked around, assessing and making mental notes about every patron inside the boutique pub. There were a few couples playing lovey-dovey, quite a few business-suited men eating while they tapped on their tablets, and a few elderly men huddled around a table with the occasional loud celebrational eruption. Content for the moment, she leant towards Schultz and showed him the webpage she'd found earlier.

"He's emerged again."

"Who has?"

He was reading the media release when Emily pulled the papers out of her bag and shoved them on top of her phone, pointing to the heavily circled name. "Look familiar?"

Schultz shook his head before pushing them aside.

"Okay then." Grabbing her cell from Schultz, she shuffled through the printouts. Pulling out the translated minutes. "How about now?"

Emily jumped as the men behind them erupted in loud cheers and banging of beer glasses. Realizing there was no threat, she turned back to Schultz, passing her papers to him.

"I haven't had an opportunity to look into it too much. But at this morning's meeting we were provided with a list of the major shareholders. He's a significant investor."

Schultz read the minutes before passing the papers back. "This has nothing to do with our assignment. You know how important it is to stay focused."

Emily looked around the pub. Happy that no one was watching them, she continued. "Do you know who the director is?"

"Yes, I did just read the article."

"And?"

"Yes, it's huge, and I know my squad are itching to get their hands on Fu and his associates. But we need to remember why we're here and leave the investigations to my squad."

"And how are they going? Have they found out who the beneficiaries of his company are? Do they even know where he's hiding?"

"Oh, good," Schultz smiled as the waitress stood in between them.

"Beef for you, sir." Exchanging smiles, she carefully placed a plate covered in beef, vegetables and some sort of gravy sauce in front of Schultz. "And chicken for you." She nearly threw the plate down in front of Emily, no pleasantries, nothing.

"Wow," said Emily, shocked.

Schultz chuckled.

When the waitress was out of earshot, Schultz leant into Emily while he cut his beef.

"Who translated the notes? Could they have made a

mistake?"

"Russell. And no. He was my savior earlier, and I don't have a reason to doubt him."

"Hmm, I saw him go into Ivan's office this morning. That's not strange in itself. What was, though, was that as he walked in, he was genuinely frightened but when he left, he had an air of confidence about him."

"Interesting. You don't know what they were discussing?" Emily toyed first with her dry chicken, stabbing it in numerous spots, then stabbed her overcooked vegetables.

"No, it was all behind closed doors."

"Okay."

She bit into a dry piece of chicken. It took her a moment to swallow it but she managed it eventually. She was famished and wasn't going to complain.

"There's something else strange that happened this morning." She opened the photos on her phone and showed Schultz. "Have you seen a device like this before?"

"It could be anything. Somewhere to hide a key maybe."

"No, or it wouldn't be warm to the touch. And I couldn't get it to move. All I know is it wasn't there when I arrived for work this morning. You didn't happen to see anyone enter my office while I was in the meeting?"

Schultz thought before replying. "No, not that I've seen."

"Katinka. That bitch."

"You're talking about your assistant there?"

"Yeah. She'd missed sending through copies of some invoices I requested. So I called her into my office, and when

I asked her about it, she got rather defensive." Taking a sip of chilled water, she continued. "I had her double-check the file she sent me, and while she was at my desk, I caught her placing her hand underneath it."

"It's probably a coincidence. You know you can't go accusing someone when you don't have any hard evidence."

"Have you been in contact with Xander since we arrived here?"

"Uh, yeah just the other day. He believes I'm on vacation."

"Well, that's about to end."

"No, we can't drag him into this. No one knows I'm on an assignment with you."

"We need his help. He can creep in and out of networks without leaving a trace. I really need him to tap into my computer and see if that device is transmitting anything to or from my computer."

"Lee, I—I can't. You can't ask me."

"Please."

"No, I can't allow him to get caught. It was a condition of his court case being dropped that the only hacking—intelligence gathering—he was allowed to do was as requested by the bureau."

"I know but I just don't have a good feeling about this assignment. I'm second-guessing everything."

"Neither do I, but dragging Xander into this isn't going to make it any better for any of us."

"What would take me weeks to unearth he can uncover

in a matter of hours, and the sooner we can get out of this country the better."

"It's different this time." Now paranoid, Schultz looked over his shoulder before turning back around and moving in closer to Lee. "This time we're in a country that's not too long ago ceased a cold war with our country's ally. Can you imagine the bureaucracy mess if Xander or either of us are caught? You know there'll be a lot of questions asked."

"Do you want to stick around any longer than needed?"

"No—"

"Good. While he's at it—" Emily flicked through her cell.

"Lee, no. No more."

"I need him to run a trace on these invoices." Emily opened the email and quickly re-read the body of the email. There were a lot of apologies and whatnot. Opening the attachment, she showed Schultz. "These were the three invoices Katinka was all defensive about. I need him to run a trace on the money trail. I want to know who they were actually paying."

"I don't like this one bit." Schultz paused. "Right, is your phone dark?"

"Yes, has been since we left Melbourne. I even double-checked when I found the device."

"Good. Send me the information."

Emily beamed.

"But..." Schultz raised an eyebrow. "I can't make any promises. Right?"

Chapter 9

With his phone to his ear, Schultz looked around the office foyer, puzzled. It was the middle of the lunch break and he was alone. In all of his career he'd never seen an empty foyer at lunch.

"Yeah," a groggy Xander answered on the second ring.

"Oh good, I got you. I need a favor."

"Do you know what the time is? I've only just called it a night."

"I'd help if I were able to, but—"

"What do you have?" Xander grunted at what Schultz assumed was him sitting up.

"In your personal emails..." He looked over his shoulder as he heard voices approaching. Lowering his voice, he spoke quickly. "I've just sent you some files. Can you weave your magic and see what you can find out about them? Especially the payment trail."

"Aren't you meant to be—"

"I'll explain later. Can you help me?"

"How many are there?"

"Just a couple."

"When do you need them by?"

"When you can. Lee had a device of some sort placed under her desk this morning."

"A device?" Xander sounded more awake at the mention of a device. "Lee? What are you up to?"

"I don't know what it is. She said she didn't see any wires or anything."

"Do you have photos?"

"No, but I can soon get you some."

"Send them through to me. I'll see if we can work out what it is. Get Lee to limit what she does at her desk until we know what we're dealing with."

"You know that's a tall order?"

Xander chuckled. "Yeah, but you'll work out a way. I was going to call you in the morning, my time, but now that you've woken me up... 'bout that Nicholas bloke."

"Yeah, what did you find?"

"He belongs to a secret army. This group have been receiving funds from companies all over Russia."

"Okay..."

"They're not sourcing the funds legitimately, of course.

The source of their revenue-raising extends from drugs and bribery to fraudulent invoices."

"What are they planning?"

"Not sure; there's no chatter online. It's like they've gone old school, to the days before internet. There's simply no trail of what they're organizing. I've got alerts set up should they discover the web."

"Good. Any information on the nightclub?" Schultz pulled out his card.

"Not yet."

"They've given me some VIP card to get into the place."

"Is it like a door swipe card?"

Schultz turned it over in his hand. "Quite possibly. It's just got the logo of what I'm assuming is the nightclub and VIP written underneath, and it's a little thicker than an ID card."

"Sounds like it's just a card to get you into the exclusive areas. I've heard the Russians love to drink."

"Enjoy your sleep, Xander."

Hanging up the phone, Schultz became aware of a noise behind the door next to the elevator. It had "cleaner" written on the sign. He looked around. On the other side of the elevator there was a set of stairs.

The door handle began turning. Running towards the stairs, he heard the hinges creaking behind him. He hurtled through the door and took the steps down three at a time. Reaching halfway, he stopped and stood against the wall farthest from the elevator.

His head looking bent over his phone, Schultz kept his eyes on the foyer. A shadow moved into view.

What's he doing in there? Schultz asked himself, his eyes narrowing as Ivan's form became clearer.

Schultz walked slowly down the stairs, his head still bent over his phone.

"Ah, Schultz," Ivan said as he caught up with him. "You ready for tonight?"

Schultz looked up from his phone, an illusion of surprise on his face.

"Ivan. Yes. Not sure what I'm getting myself into, though."

Ivan slapped Schultz's back. "A great night with lots of drinks and maybe some ladies... only if that tickles your fancy."

"A good drink. Count me in then."

"See you tonight. Don't be late." Stepping away, Ivan pointed a finger at him, his face serious.

Chapter 10

Looking out her passenger window, Emily watched as dense forests enveloped them, Saint Petersburg now well behind.

"Russell, how much farther until we arrive at the site?" Emily pulled a manila folder out from under the diary on her lap.

"I'm sorry it's taking longer than you expected. I've been instructed to travel this way. Yes, it's a little longer but they're our smoothest roads, similar to what you're used to back home."

Emily chuckled. "As much as I'm enjoying the scenic drive, I'm not afraid of rough roads. Our roads back home are far from smooth. If your preferred roads are a little rougher, and it's quicker, go for it." Emily looked at her watch. "We don't have much daylight left and one thing I'm not a fan of are the Russian winter nights."

"Very well then. Remember, I warned you."

The hair on Emily's arms stood up. She rubbed her arms. "See what I mean? I'm already freezing and we're only at the start of winter."

Russell kept his eyes on the road, his knuckles turning white as he gripped the steering wheel.

Taking the opportunity to refresh her knowledge of the site and trying to relax her already racing heart, Emily turned her attention to her folder and began reading through the papers, which included loose printouts and handwritten notes.

It was her first field trip to a satellite site, and she had been dreading it from the moment she was advised it was happening.

She'd barely returned form lunch when one of the managing directors marched into her office and, with the aid of Russell, instructed her to accompany Russell on a site visit.

Looking up from the paperwork, she rubbed her eyes. The road had narrowed to one lane and the forest was denser.

"The site we're visiting, how long has it been operating for?"

Russell didn't answer immediately. "We've been there for a few months, maybe three or four." His pure English accent was peppered with hints of Russian now.

"So, still being established?"

He looked at her, his eyebrow raised. "I don't understand."

"I'm having trouble understanding how a natural resources site can be fully operational if you've only been there for a few months."

"Ah. I understand now." He smiled. "When we acquired the site, the infrastructure and equipment were already there."

Emily flipped through her notes.

Russell continued. "The equipment isn't crash-hot, but being a new industry, the directors didn't want to heavily invest in equipment or the site until it started turning money in."

"It doesn't make sense."

"What doesn't?"

"There's nothing in here about it being already established. No record of the infrastructure or equipment." Emily faced Russell.

Russell swerved towards the center of the road and an oncoming truck blared its horn.

Emily's eyes widened as the truck's grill was heading straight for her side of Russell's sedan. Out to the side of the truck she saw smoke developing around the tires. It was braking hard.

"Watch out!" Emily screamed.

She grabbed the door handle and placed her other hand on the dashboard. The truck's rear trailer began to swerve, rubble flicking up as the trailer tires skirted along the side of the road.

With barely centimeters to spare, Russell swerved his sedan out of the way of the truck."

"Sorry, so sorry." Russell patted his heart. "I saw an animal enter our lane."

"An animal? What type?"

"I don't know. It all happened too quickly."

"Do you want me to drive for a while?"

"No, no, no. I'll be all right. It was just a little fright. I'm all good now."

Emily moved her head slightly towards her side mirror. All she could see were truck taillights and a frustrated truck driver standing alongside his truck looking towards them, his fist thumping the air.

"Was it a big one?" she asked.

"What was?"

"The animal. The one you've just tried to avoid." Emily bit her tongue, stopping her comment right there.

"Animal. Uh, yes, it was a big one. I had to avoid it because I don't have insurance and cannot afford a new car. Well, not right now anyway."

"We're alive. That's all that matters." She looked out her window.

The forest was swallowing them, the sky poking through the occasional small gaps in the tree canopy. Even the dense undergrowth was denser.

Her phone rang. Schultz.

Russell glanced at her then her phone. "You going to get it?"

She smiled and took the call. "Hello?"

"Are you able to talk?" Schultz asked.

"Oh, Dad, it's great to hear from you. I was going to call earlier but I've been busy."

She smiled and mouthed 'sorry' to Russell.

He smiled and returned his attention to the road.

"Russia is great," she continued. "It's a little cold but the people here are very friendly."

Schultz contained his laughter. "Now I know you're talking hogwash. I take it you have company. Russell?"

"Yes, I'm eating properly."

Her hand over the microphone, she whispered, "Dads," as she rolled her eyes.

She received a small smile from Russell but it disappeared quicker than it appeared.

"Where are you?" Schultz asked.

"No, I haven't been doing any sightseeing. It's all been business so far."

"I'll get Xander to track your phone."

"Why? Is she going to be all right?"

"The invoices you requested. Xander has found—"

The sedan turned sharply. Her body was slammed against her door. Emily screamed, fearing another truck or something coming head-on for her. She used her hands to brace herself, dropping her phone in the process.

"Are you okay? What's happening?" she heard Schultz yelling out.

With shaking hands, she retrieved her phone as Russell noted, "Your father sounds young."

Emily ignored him. She bounced around as Russell's

sedan traversed the many holes in the one-lane road.

"Sorry about turning sharply, I almost missed the corner. I didn't mean to scare you," Russell said tonelessly.

"Just get us there in one piece," she said, turning the phone so that Schultz could hear the conversation as well as possible.

"I hope you don't mind this route. You said you were fine with bumps." Russell's focus was still ahead, on swerving around the bigger holes.

"No, bumps are good, but maybe a little slower. Please."

"We don't have time. We're running out of daylight."

"Dad, I'm going to have to call you back later," she said into her phone.

"Stay alert and safe. Keep your phone on you." Schultz ended the call.

"Where exactly are we?" Emily looked around as she tucked her phone into her coat pocket.

Forest vegetation scraped against the sedan, the ear-piercing scratches sending shivers down her spine. Ahead a deer stepped out from the brush and stopped in the middle of the road.

"Stop," Emily screamed.

Russell travelled a few more meters, his focus straight ahead.

"Russell, stop!"

He showed no signs of slowing down. The deer was within throwing distance. Emily unbuckled herself and opened her door. Preparing to jump out, she looked at Russell then the deer. Both were staring at each other. Looking back at her opened door, she took a deep breath.

Thump.

A thick tree trunk stood its ground and her door was slammed shut.

"Hold on," Russell said with no emotion in his voice.

He slammed on the brakes. As Emily flew forward, she put her hands out in front. Her arms stretched out, her hands pressed to the dashboard, while her head continued to travel forward.

Her braced arms stopped her from smashing into the dash. A little shaken, she looked out the front window. The deer stood there, inches away from their bonnet, looking at them both before moving around to her side. Shuffling towards the rear end of their car, the deer glanced at her for a moment, sniffed, then disappeared into the forest. Moving back in her seat, Emily pressed her hands to her chest as she caught her breath.

"That was close," she said, her hands shaking.

Russell shifted his sedan into gear and moved on, travelling a little slower than earlier.

Emily kept her eyes ahead, sweeping the sides of the road, expecting an animal to walk out in front of them at any moment. The forest canopy enveloped them, blocking out what daylight was left, and just as she was beginning to wonder what game her driver was playing, Russell flicked on his headlights.

"You travel these roads often?" Emily asked while keeping

her attention on the road ahead.

"We'll be on smoother roads soon, and then we won't be far away from our destination."

They slowed as they neared the next intersection. Russell seemed to be undecided about which way to go. Emily looked around. Ahead and out her window the forest was dense. Out his window, she noticed the road widened, allowing some light in.

"That way," Emily pointed out his window.

He looked out his window, then to the other roads. "No. That heads us away from the site. No, we need to go that way," he pointed out her window.

"Right now, I don't give a damn about the site. I want to get back to the office."

A set of headlights appeared in her side mirror.

"The bastards, why aren't they dipping their lights?"

She tried shielding her eyes, but it proved useless. The lights from the vehicle behind were too bright. Her eyes dazed, Emily buried her head in her lap.

Emily felt their car turn in the opposite direction to the one she'd requested.

"Why are we heading deeper into the forest? Are we lost? We're lost, aren't we?"

"Zip it."

"You need to take me back to the office. Now."

"Okay. I'll stop right here. You can find your own way back, that is if these clowns behind us don't get to you first."

She felt their car slowing while the vehicle behind them

began blaring their horn.

Russell continued, "Do you want to risk yourself out there? Night is only a couple of hours away."

"No, keep moving." She wasn't about to admit he was right about her options.

She tried blocking her side mirror with her arm, but the headlights still flooded their car.

Crash.

Their car jolted forward.

Thud.

Another thump to their rear. This time their car veered towards the trees.

Russell put his foot down on the accelerator and, fighting against the car, he steered it back onto the road.

"What aren't you telling me?" Emily asked in a shrill voice.

"Nothing at all."

"It just seems strange you slowed down just before they appeared, then they were gunning for us. What aren't you telling me? Do you know them, because I have a feeling they know you... or at least this car?"

"I have no idea who they are," Russell replied through gritted teeth.

They were able to gain a little ground as they maneuvered around the next bend. Emily breathed a little easier as Russell continued to gain distance from the vehicle behind them.

"Don't get too comfortable." Russell glanced at his rear-view mirror.

Emily looked in her side mirror and noticed a set of headlights bouncing off the trees. As they rounded the corner, she quickly realized their lights were brighter. Squinting at the reflection in her mirror, Emily saw what appeared to be a set of lights on the vehicle's rooftop and movement to the side, like someone was hanging out their window.

Emily turned back to the road in front. Their measly lights failed to illuminate their way.

"Whoever it is... They mean business."

Chapter 11

Deep inside a snow-capped mountain, two old men whose appearances indicated they should've retired years earlier leaned back in their lounge chairs as they puffed on cigars. They were focused on a wall filled with screens. Every camera showed a different person. They were either under attack, hiding, or going about their normal daily life.

"Hold on a minute." The older of the two stood up and hobbled over to one of the lower screens. He clicked his fingers towards the corner of the room where a computer technician was working. "Pull up camera thirty-two."

The technician acknowledged his request, and a moment later camera thirty-two was displayed as one image across all the screens.

"What's wrong with that feed?" He pointed to the screen.

"Leo, it's okay. That agent is in dense forest. She'll be back online the moment she clears the trees."

"I don't like this one bit," he said as he braced his back and limped back to his chair. A wisp of silver hair fell over his eyes. "Bert. You know I don't like her being out there. We shouldn't have sent her on that assignment. We need to get her out of there, now. Charlie wouldn't want to see his daughter in this situation."

"There's a lot that Charlie won't like. If he knew just how tightly we managed his agents and knew what we know, he'd have her here in a heartbeat." His attention never wavered from the screens.

"Isn't that confirming we should be pulling the pin on her assignments. Bringing her home to where she should be?"

"No. She needs to prove to us what she's made of and that she's the rightful leader for the next generation. Not only to herself and us, but to everyone she'll oversee, including all future agents."

Chapter 12

Schultz checked his watch. It was nearly mid-afternoon. The pile of papers on his desk was growing.

"Excuse me," he heard a faint voice.

Looking up, he was greeted by the woman who'd handed him the VIP card earlier. Her face was distraught.

"What's wrong?" Schultz asked.

"The Australian, Ms. Lee. Have you spoken to her this afternoon?"

"Why do you ask?"

"We've just received a phone call from the manager of our new site up north. The site Ms. Lee and Russell were visiting today."

"Continue." He stood up.

The woman looked down.

"What's wrong?" Schultz asked.

The woman shuffled from foot to foot.

"What's happened?"

"We're not sure. They haven't arrived at the site yet."

"What's the travel time there?"

The woman gave him a blank stare.

"How long does it take," he pulled on his jacket, "to get there?"

"Oh, sorry. They should've been there about half an hour ago."

Schultz looked at his watch again. It was a good hour to an hour and a half trip.

"Has anyone tried calling their phones?"

"Yes. There was no answer."

"The authorities?"

"They won't do anything for at least twenty-four hours."

"Damn. I'm meant to be meeting Ivan after work."

"The nights can get quite cold out there. Here," she dangled her keys, "take my car. It's the hatchback just out front."

Schultz looked at them then back to her. "You sure?"

"If you go now you should be back in time to still meet up with Ivan."

He grabbed the keys from her and shoved them into his pants pocket.

"You don't have to."

"I know." She pressed a piece of paper into his hand. "My

number. Ms. Lee is a good woman and those roads can get cold and dangerous at night."

"Keep trying their phones, yeah?"

The woman nodded.

"I'll call the office when I hear something."

Buttoning up his jacket, Schultz ran towards the elevators.

"Thank you," he yelled out over his shoulder.

He didn't look twice at the elevator, he went directly to the stairs next to it and descended them. Halfway down the first flight he pulled up Xander's number and dialed it.

Xander answered on the first ring.

"Hey, Schultz. You freezing there yet?"

"I might be by the end of all this. I need you to do me a favor."

"Again? You're not going away again. Since you've left this office you've created far more work for me than ever before."

"Settle down. Lee's missing."

"Missing?"

"She was performing a site visit today and neither she nor her driver have arrived there yet."

"Maybe she grabbed a coffee before leaving the city?"

"No, she took one with her. Xander, she's not answering her phone."

"You're worried about her, aren't you? Don't answer that. Give me a moment and I'll see if I can locate her cell phone."

"Thank you." Schultz cleared the last few steps and landed in the foyer.

"She's got quite a few firewalls up. It might take me a little bit to punch through them all."

"Do what you need to do. We need to find her."

"Do you think she's in danger?"

"There's a lot of things I'm not sure about right now, and one of them is not knowing who I can trust around here."

There was silence while Xander busily tapped away at his keyboard. Schultz received a few disgruntled looks from a group of staff members as he stepped into the foyer. He pointed to his phone and rolled his eyes. They shook their heads as they stepped outside the building.

"That was interesting," Schultz said as he made a last-moment decision to step up the stairwell, away from prying ears and eyes.

"What was?"

"A group of staff were leaving the building, looking at me strangely. One of them made a call the moment she saw me."

"They probably haven't seen anyone like you before. You're not wearing your Hawaiian top, are you?"

"It's too cold for that here. While you're trying to find Lee, have you got any news on that device?"

"Yeah, it's been used as a gateway to access her computer."

"Any files in particular?"

"I haven't found any traces yet. But it's too early. Still working on that."

"How about those invoices Lee was querying? Did the money go where it was meant to?"

"Ah, not exactly."

Schultz heard a set of footsteps approaching.

"Hold on a moment," he whispered as he stepped farther up the stairwell.

Hidden by the darkness, he leant down just enough to notice Ivan walk past. Schultz stepped down lightly, moving to the other side of the stairs to peer around the corner without being noticed.

He watched Ivan open the cleaner's door, and as Ivan slipped away, he caught a glimpse of a badge on his jacket, a red star with intricate gold work inside it.

"They're not being re-directed to Ivan Kuzmich, are they?"

"How did you know?"

"It's either that or he has a cleaning habit and a love for Stalinism."

"Okay, what's happening? Talk to me, Schultz."

"That's the second time today he's walked into the cleaners' room."

"I'll see if I can pull up some blueprints on the building. But yes, the funds are being directed to his organization."

"Organization or political party?"

"The sedan she's been travelling in has been slowly making its way towards a large body of water—a lake. There is a small island a few kilometers offshore."

"How small?"

"Small enough to fit a couple of monasteries and a few buildings."

"Okay, that small. Is that lake going to be frozen?"

"Anything is possible out there."

"Shit, that doesn't give me time." Schultz rubbed his hand

across his forehead.

"We have bigger problems than that."

"What have you got?"

"I detect quite a few Russian and Chinese registered devices in Lee's close proximity."

"How far away is her current location?"

"You're not going to get there and back and be at the club on time."

"Stuff the club. Lee's more important."

"Look, I could be wrong here but we don't want Ivan to be wary of you. I'll keep an eye on Lee while you get what information you can out of Ivan. Who knows what he'll spill after a few drinks?"

"I don't like this." Schultz looked around. He was still alone. "I need to be out there getting her back."

"I know. You two do make a great team, that is when your heads aren't banging against each other's. But right now, you need to stay in Saint Petersburg. Are you still in the office?"

"No, I'm near the foyer."

"Right. So they know you've left. You can't return to the office. I suggest you go for a drive so it appears you're out looking for Lee then go to the club tonight as planned. Then I'll get you to Lee."

"I still don't like this. What if we get there too late?"

"For once, will you do as you're told?"

Chapter 13

"Son of a—" Emily glanced in her side mirror as their car swerved. "We've got to get out of here. Now."

Bang.

"Shit. What was that?"

Emily spun around to the sound of glass smashing only to see a hole in their rear window.

Bang. Bang.

Another two holes appeared, and a fracture line was forming between the holes.

"You may need a new car."

"The bastards! Did they just shoot at us?"

"You sure you don't know them? Are you in some sort of trouble?"

She looked out the back in time to see the window disintegrate into lots of tiny shards of glass.

"You'll definitely need a new back window."

Their sedan slowed as Russell navigated a bend. Coming out of the bend, Emily glanced in her side mirror and caught sight of the vehicle as it rounded. A light truck with a tray, with someone hanging outside the cabin.

"Get us out of here, NOW," Emily yelled.

BANG.

Emily ducked, covering her head with her hands. They were still moving. Sitting up, she kept her body aligned with her seat. A glance over told her Russell was unharmed. Slowly turning towards the front, she saw a hole in the middle of the windscreen.

"If I was back home..." She checked her rear-view mirror. The distance between them and their pursuers had grown. "...These bastards would've been dealt with by now."

"You've run into trouble before?"

"Only with those who had it coming."

"You hiding any dark secrets?"

"Dark secrets?" She swallowed the large lump in her throat.

"Yeah, like why are these people chasing us?"

"We're back to this, are we? No one knows I'm in this country."

"Someone does."

"Why couldn't it be someone after you?" Emily stared at Russell.

His eyes darted between her and the road. "I'm just an

office worker. I work. I go home. That's my life."

Emily studied him in the glow of the headlights behind them, his face not flinching. "Well, that's boring."

"Let's hope we live to tell the tale so I could be a cool grandpa one day, not just a boring office worker."

As they passed under a break in the tree canopy, Emily's phone vibrated. Checking her notifications, she saw one missed call.

"We have signal! Quick, what's the number for the police?"

In between the bumps and knocks, she unlocked her phone and pulled up her phone keypad.

"Police? No good."

"Why?"

"We're on our own out here. By the time help arrives, if it does, we'll either be at their mercy, or worse—dead."

"Isn't there a town near here?"

"Have you seen one lately? If you haven't already noticed, we're alone, with them for company."

She pulled up Schultz's number and pressed the dial button.

"This phone call cannot be connected," an automated response on the other end advised.

The signal strength flickered between one bar and none.

"Damn it."

"Told you. We're alone."

Emily tried Schultz again. Nothing.

"Duck," Russell yelled.

Their car swerved. Emily held her head in her lap, her

hands protecting the back of her head. She heard glass shattering, a few small shards hitting her hands, but she could still feel the momentum of their car moving forward.

"You can get up." Russell grabbed the back of her coat and pulled her up. "You all right?"

Most of their windscreen was missing. Checking herself over, she replied, "Only a couple of tiny scratches. Nothing too bad. What the hell is going on? Come clean, Russell. Now."

"What do you mean?"

"Only two people knew I was leaving the office today. You and the managing director."

"What are you implying?" Russell removed his foot from the accelerator pedal. "For all I know, your father could've tracked your phone. He could've sent them after us."

"Even if he were alive, he wouldn't even know where to start. He had a major phobia of technology."

They rounded another bend in the track. The trees made way to open skies. There wasn't much daylight left. Emily checked her phone again. Still no signal.

"Great," she whispered.

A ding came from the dashboard.

"What was that?" Emily tried to peer over to the dials in front of Russell.

"We're low on fuel."

"We're what? How much have we got?"

"Out here, not enough."

Bullets were ricocheting off their car.

The forest around them was thinning and the undergrowth was disappearing. Emily checked her cell phone again—still no signal. She activated her data—nothing.

Feeling the car climbing, she looked out her window.

"Where on Earth are, we?"

"Russia. Where else would we be?"

"Oh, I don't know. Maybe we crossed into Finland."

Russell chuckled. "Not quite. What you're looking at is Lake Ladoga."

"And how far away from the site are we?"

"Not sure. I can stop and check the map."

Emily shook her head and looked at the vast water beside them. Movement in her rear-view mirror caught her attention. Behind them the shooters came into sight.

Their car lurched.

"What's going on?" Emily looked around. Her eyes widened as the light truck behind them came closer.

Their car crawled to a complete stop.

"Come on, move," she screamed.

Russell turned the key in the ignition. Nothing. He tried again. Still nothing. Emily leant over and looked at the dashboard. A yellow fuel light came on.

"Are we empty?"

"There might still be something in there." He turned the ignition. Nothing.

Collecting her papers, she swung her bag over her shoulder. Hopping out of the car, she noticed the truck that'd been chasing them had stopped on the rise behind them. She slid her phone inside her boot.

"Hope you're ready for a run." Emily leant back into Russell's car.

Russell wasn't moving. His eyes were focused ahead of him.

"Come on," she yelled.

"I can't run. Bad hip. I'll only slow you down." His eyes turned glassy. "Go. Get out. Leave."

Taken aback by his sudden change in attitude, she looked around. Water on one side and forest on the other.

Behind her, she was outnumbered. Four broad-shouldered armed men in a beast of a truck against her, on foot, and her bare hands. Dust stirred around their rear tires as their vehicle was revved, the rear end sliding from side to side.

Emily yelled at Russell, "Get out. Now."

Russell placed his sedan in neutral. His arms firmly on the steering wheel, he pushed his shoulders into his seat. He glanced into his rear-view mirror. Closing his eyes, he made the sign of the cross on his chest.

Looking up, Emily saw the light truck drift before straightening and heading straight for Russell's sedan. The men in the back tray banged on the cabin's roof and cried out what she assumed were meant to be their war cries.

Clutching her bag, she ran down the sandy track, her feet tripping on the uneven surface.

Bang.

Glancing over her shoulder, she saw Russell's sedan being pushed along.

"No," she screamed.

As she ran down the track, Emily looked around for any opportunity to disappear, to get some distance between her and them. Up ahead she spotted a boat heading towards her.

"Help," she yelled, waving her hands in the air.

The boat was about fifty meters from shore before suddenly turning and speeding away.

Behind her she heard the truck chase her down. Her ankle twisted on the uneven ground but she pushed through the pain. She was in the wrong shoes and attire for a cross-country run in the wilderness. Her coat was weighing her down, but with night fall not far away she didn't dare get rid of it.

The truck stopped chasing her. Instead, heavy footsteps pounded the dirt behind her.

Emily dug deep and pushed her legs faster. Her muscles were screaming for her to stop. She blocked out the pain, focusing on the coffee Schultz had imported for them, its warm aromas warming her.

In the distance, she heard another boat engine nearing her.

If I could only hold out long enough, she thought.

It wasn't to be.

Her feet flew out from underneath her. Emily landed on the sand with a loud thump.

Coughing, she got up on all fours. She was pushed back into the sand. Wriggling, she glanced over her shoulder and caught a glimpse of a camo sleeve. She felt a hand around her head before it was turned back around and slammed into the dirt.

Through her dizziness, she heard men talking. A moment later her hair was pulled back and a piece of material was placed over her nose and mouth. A peculiar odor percolated her senses and in a moment Emily's world went black.

Chapter 14

Ivan lounged in a high-backed booth seat as two barely dressed ladies danced to the beats of the night club music, their movements highly suggestive. Around his VIP booth, belly laughs were erupting from many of his six guests as the club's best girls joked with them. In the corner next to him, there was a small gap in the seats, enough room to fit through. Behind his sofa, heavy draped curtains partitioned off the wall and hid a door used by the club's wait staff to bring him his refreshments, bypassing the lineups at the bar.

He looked towards the front of his booth and nodded at his two broad-shouldered security guards positioned on the other side of the roped-off entrance when he saw his guest arrive. He signaled to his two security guards, who allowed

Schultz into his VIP area.

"Ah, good, you're here. Here. This is for you." Ivan handed a shot of vodka to Schultz.

Schultz accepted the shot. "Bit early to drink, isn't it?"

"In Russia, it's never too early. If we're not working, we party. Drink, drink up." Ivan upturned his shot of vodka.

He watched Schultz's body contort as he skulled the shot.

"Well done. Here, here. Take a seat. Oy, Franco, move over. Let our Australian friend in."

"Australian, you say?" Franco asked as he shuffled down the sofa. "You're a long way from home. What did you do there before you came to this glorious place?" His hand waved around the nightclub.

"White-collar worker."

"A what?"

Schultz chuckled. "Sorry, office worker."

"What type of office work did you do?" Ivan asked.

"Just a public servant working for the government."

"Council? Defense? Law?" Ivan poured more shots.

"Forestry."

"Land Management. Do you have a problem with everyone telling you how you should be running things?"

Schultz chuckled and nodded. "Yes. Sounds like it might be a global problem."

Ivan stared at Schultz, who pulled his gaze away.

"You like what you see?" Ivan swept his arm around his VIP area.

"It's different."

"Don't you government folk have men's nights out like this?"

A woman dressed in a studded mesh garter set walked over to Ivan, her hips swaying as she approached.

"Not like this." Schultz leant forward to grab a small handful of bar nuts.

Ivan noticed Schultz turn his eyes away from a woman who was approaching him.

"You don't like what you see?" Ivan placed his hand around one of the women's waist.

Schultz looked towards them, and the woman pouted and dropped a frown. He quickly blinked and gazed away.

"Don't tell me, you're a committed husband?" Ivan elbowed him in the arm, chuckling.

"No, no wife. Not yet anyway."

"Here, have another one." Ivan handed a shot glass to Schultz then passed the rest out to his remaining guests. "Here's to what happens here stays here."

Glasses clunked and Ivan swallowed the shot of vodka. Empty glasses banged against the table and masculine roars erupted around the area.

"You don't need to be shy around here. This is all courtesy of the company."

"The company?" Schultz asked as he pushed away one of the women who was trying to sit on his lap.

"Yeah, the one we work for." Ivan forced a laugh and Schultz followed suit.

"Love, give him a little space." Ivan waved her away.

The woman nodded and walked over to the opposite side, glancing over her shoulder and blowing kisses to Ivan and Schultz. Ivan winked at her and she continued walking around the group of men until one of them showed her a hint of attention.

"You enjoying Russia?" Ivan asked Schultz.

"It's a lot cooler than back home. But I'm liking it."

"Is the company apartment up to your standard?"

"Couldn't complain at all. It's warm and dry."

"Very good. I'd love to meet your significant other. We should organize a dinner. I'll bring my wife along, as well."

Schultz looked away.

"Oh, I'm sorry. How bad for me to assume. Did you bring your significant other over? Your girlfriend? Or is she back home? If you get what I mean?" His eyes moving towards one of the entertainers.

Schultz appeared to be stumbling over his words.

"It's all good. I'm sorry for being so rude. Just trying to get to know who I'm working with. No bad feelings. Yeah?"

Schultz waved it off. "It's all good."

"Tell me, how long have you worked for the government?"

"It must be around fifteen years now."

"Hmmm, I see." Ivan sipped his drink, keeping his eye on Schultz.

Franco leaned over, almost lying on Schultz's lap, and in a drunken slur said, "Don't worry, boss. Back home he's probably a cop. He smells like a cop. You a cop?"

"Yes. Are you a cop?"

Ivan studied Schultz as he pushed Franco off his lap.

"No. I'm not a cop. I keep busy managing my local national park, including dealing with the drunken brawls every weekend." He raised his glass to his lips, taking his shot. "Give me the quiet forests any day over the pubs."

"Boss, phone," a suited younger man approached, handing a cell to Ivan.

Ivan looked at Schultz then to his cell phone screen. It read: Russell incoming.

"Excuse me, ladies, gentlemen, Schultz." He pointed to his phone. "I won't be long. Business call." He whispered into Schultz's ear, "And I've got my eye on you, forest boy."

Ivan slipped behind the sofa and through the curtains, stepping into a red-lit corridor. The music here was reduced to a low thump.

"Yes," Ivan said into the cell.

"Ivan, it's Russell. The wild beast has been captured."

Ivan looked around him, up and down both ends of the corridor. "Captured, you say?" he said in a lowered voice.

"Yes, and my car was shot at. I was rear-ended and pushed off the road by a bunch of crazy mavericks. Of which—"

"You were meant to have already killed and dumped her."

Russell's restrained laugh rang out. "I hadn't had a chance. I'd barely entered the forest when we were set upon. My car is destroyed. How am I meant to get home?"

"Not my problem. There's a cost in all wars." Ivan ended the call before stepping back into his VIP area.

Chapter 15

Emily's eyes weighed too much for her to keep them open. She swept her hand along the floor as far she could reach. Concrete flooring, its coolness sending shivers through her body.

Tucking her arm under her body, she used what strength she could muster and lifted her head up. Her head spun, her upper body swayed under its own crushing weight. With enormous effort, Emily pushed herself up until she was sitting upright.

The groggy feeling began to dissipate. She cracked an eye open. Dark. Nothing distinguishable. Not even an outline was visible.

Patting her sides then up to her shoulder revealed only her

coat. Her bag wasn't there.

Shifting onto her hands and knees, she swept her hand around, moving a little farther afield and feeling around for her bag. Still nothing.

"Shit, shit, shit. My passport."

Sitting back on her knees she felt her phone press into her ankle. Thanking her instinctual habit of shoving her cell into her boot, she pulled it out and tapped the home button.

"Damn it. Bugger all service."

She watched as her phone shifted between no reception and one bar. Pulling up her recent messages with Schultz, she typed:

Don't call. In trouble. I've been drugged.

Then she hit send.

A red exclamation mark appeared, advising her the message hadn't been sent. She tapped resend and moved her phone around until she had one bar. *Message sent.*

Relieved, she swiped through the icons on her phone until she located her torch application. She activated it and the area around her feet lit up. Still a little lightheaded, she staggered to her feet and tripped over something, landing on the floor with a loud thump.

Behind her, in the distance, she heard the sound of metal clunking. Then silence. She turned towards the sound. More metal being dragged on metal. Closing her application, she slid her phone into her boot.

The creak of a door opening caused Emily to crawl backwards. Light spilled into the room and someone stood in the doorway, their face hidden by a cape. They stepped into the room and a hand emerged. They clicked their fingers.

A second later a white light filled the room. Her eyes stinging, Emily covered her eyes with her coat and huddled into a ball. The door closed and the only noise remaining was the dull hum from the light. They'd left her alone? Emily tried to open her eyes but the light was still too intense.

To her side, she heard a couple of sets of footsteps scuffing along the floor. They were heavy-sounding, like men walking in steel-capped work boots.

She felt someone grab her arms and pulled her along, her feet dragging behind her. Squinting, she noticed shapes began emerging. The outline of a chair appeared in front of her. They tossed her into it and pulled her arms behind her. Wriggling her hands, she tried to break free but the grip around her wrists tightened as cold metal enclosed around her wrists, its grip tightening.

Handcuffs, seriously? How original, she thought.

Emily was still trying to break her hands free, the metal from the handcuffs clunking against her chair, when a man moved around from behind her and knelt down at her feet. His arms and shoulders moved as he was tightening something around each foot. As he tightened her last restraint he looked up and grinned. His tanned face wore deep lines, a scar stretching down the side of his face.

"You." Her eyes widened with fear.

She tried to jump her chair back, but the chair wouldn't move.

Leaning in close, he whispered, "Isn't Fu going to love hearing about this?"

She wriggled, hissing at him.

He laughed as he stepped away. "She's all yours, Nicholas."

"We've got a real little fighter here." A male voice with a deep Slavic accent chuckled behind her.

She continued wriggling her shoulders but she had to concede she was thoroughly locked in.

"It's Ms. Lee, isn't it?" He sounded closer.

Emily felt the hairs on her neck rise.

"Or do you prefer Miss Lee?"

She felt him breathing down her neck. Hoping she'd gauged his chin right, she put all her strength into shoving her shoulder upwards. Nothing. She tried again. Still nothing. Her hands were locked in place.

He walked around to stand in front of her. He appeared shorter, less stocky than his scarred counterpart.

"Over here, please," he directed.

Emily glanced over to see two men walk in, carrying a table between them. They positioned the table in front of her, unnecessarily just out of arm's reach.

"Thank you." He nodded, slamming a manila folder on the table.

The men left the room.

"What brings you to Russia?" He sat down on the edge of the table closest to her. "Love?" he asked, raising an eyebrow.

She refused to show him any acknowledgement.

"Sightseeing?"

Her eye twitched.

"Did you enjoy your drive around our grand forests and lake? They're quite magnificent, aren't they? There's nothing like it elsewhere on the planet."

Emily narrowed her eyes as she stared at him.

"The lake. That's where you were found, wasn't it?" He looked behind her for a brief moment before returning his attention to her. "My men here found you out cold on the side of the lane."

Unconscious, my ass, she thought. *More like drugged with who knows what substance.*

He continued. "This folder was found in your bag. Will I find my answers inside it?" He watched her as he pulled it towards him. "Or will this only scratch the surface?"

Chapter 16

Emily watched on as he opened the folder.

"You won't find anything in there," she snarled.

"Won't I?" He turned over the next page.

"They're just my notes and some financials for a site we were supposed to be visiting."

"We?" His attention returned to Emily.

"I." Her eyes narrowed as she stared at him. "You found me alone, did you not?"

He shifted his gaze. "Yes... alone, out cold."

"What aren't you telling me?"

He stood up and, collecting the folder, left the room. His scarred companion followed and closed the door behind them.

Emily scanned her surroundings. This time she really was

alone.

Her fingers fiddled with her watchband. She slowly pulled out a pin and closed her hand around it. Turning the pin around in her fingers, she dragged the pin along her handcuffs until she felt it fall into a keyhole.

She twisted and turned the pin until her cuff clicked, then wriggled her wrist until it dropped free. She turned her ear towards the door, listening. Everything was silent. Quickly, she unlocked the other one.

Emily took a moment to rub her wrists and look around the room, from roof to floor. Bare walls. Nothing out of the ordinary. Either there weren't any cameras in here and there was a stronghold of men outside the door, or the cameras were well concealed.

After a moment's hesitation she decided to take her chances. She tucked the handcuff under her bottom and unlocked the restraints around her ankles, leaving them dangling from her ankles in the hope that would be enough to give the illusion she was still secure, then quickly replaced her pin back in her watch strap.

The door hinges creaked as the door opened. Grabbing her handcuffs, she placed her hands behind her, holding each cuff in her hand, her coat sleeves hiding her hands. The same two men entered, their steps deliberate and rigid. Another four broad-shouldered men followed them.

The additional four men wore camouflage pants, short-sleeve shirts, and calf-length laced boots. Balaclavas concealed their faces, only exposing their eyes. All of them had tattoos on their biceps.

One of the men positioned himself beside the door while the other three stood behind Scarred-Shooter and Shorty.

Emily's eyes darted between the open door and her captors.

Why was the door still left open? she thought before returning her attention to the shorter man.

Sitting on the edge of the table, he extended his feet until they were almost touching hers.

"Where am I?" Emily asked.

"Don't worry, you're still in Russia. Just."

The other men in the room smirked.

Standing up, he crossed his arms, looking down at her as he circled her. She clenched her hands tighter around her handcuffs.

"Your Australian friend, Schultz."

Emily stared ahead, biting the inside of her cheek. She held her breath as his stale cigar breath lingered.

"Hmmm, I sense something there. You two lovers?"

She fought the temptation to swing her fists, putting him on the ground. She'd be quickly outnumbered.

"Your friend." He swept her hair away and placed the side of his face against hers before continuing. "He's been doing some digging around." He grabbed a clump of her hair and pulled on it. "He's been poking his nose in other people's business."

She gritted her teeth. "He doesn't know how to operate a computer, let alone how to poke around in others' affairs."

He let her hair go and stood in front of her, his arms

crossed and face expressionless. "So. You do know him."

"Yeah, we shared the same flight over here."

"Hmmm. Let's say your friend is computer illiterate, like you say. Then there must be someone helping him. Is it you?"

She stared at him. "I am not a spy. I am assisting our head office with the company's financial reporting until they find a suitable replacement."

"The funny thing is... I don't believe you."

"Believe what you want. It's the truth."

"I've had a colleague do some digging around. His name is Brian. I believe you've met him before."

Emily felt her heart rate increase, growing louder.

"Yes. I believe you two had a run-in in Melbourne."

The only way he'll have Brian is if Fu lets him. Brian's been exclusive to Fu for the last few years, Emily thought.

Shorty continued. "Now are you going to start talking?"

"Bite me," she snarled.

Emily wriggled her shoulders, being careful not to let go of the cuffs.

"Fu warned me you'd be feisty. That's why I have my best men with me."

Looking around, she saw each one stand to attention, crossing their arms across their bulging chests, all staring down at her.

"Now, tell me if I'm wrong," he continued. "Your friend, Schultz... he's been digging around some employee files. I want to know why."

"No idea."

He leaned in and she felt his open palm slap the side of her cheek. Despite her cheek throbbing, she kept her focus on her hands. It would be suicide to fight back right now.

"My men keep this side of the country in order. You pay your dues and your life will be all good, for now. You miss your dues, your life will be... how shall I put it? Miserable. You'll be looking over your shoulder. Wary of shadows. Wondering when and where one of my men will appear. Is that how you want to live your life?"

"You'll need more than this handful of clowns."

The men moved closer. Shorty raised his hand. The men moved back to their original positions.

"Now that you seem to have found your tongue maybe you'll start talking." Turning towards the door, he called out, "Brian, show her the video."

Chapter 17

Schultz raised his shot glass, joining the others in Ivan's VIP booth.

"To new friends." Ivan looked squarely at Schultz.

"To new friends," Schultz replied.

The others in the group chorused something in Russian. Then everyone leaned in, clunking their shot glasses together before leaning back and taking their shot. Schultz leaned back on the couch, holding his shot glass so that when he tipped it up the liquid from his glass would fly over his shoulder. He slammed his glass down on the table with the other men. A roar erupted as the vodka cleared their throats, and Schultz followed their lead.

A few of the men tucked into the assortment of finger food

on the table, while Schultz and the others sat back in their chairs.

"Another one, Aussie?" Ivan yelled.

Schultz snapped around and saw Ivan was pouring another round of drinks. Waving his hand in front of him, Schultz shook his head, but Ivan still thrust a shot glass into his hand.

The man sitting alongside Ivan made a toast in Russian, then everyone swallowed their shots. Schultz drank this shot, keeping his body taut as the burning sensation travelled down his throat.

Placing his glass down, he felt his cell vibrate against his chest. It vibrated again. He stood up.

"Going so soon?" Ivan asked, standing up and looking confused.

"No. Nature calls. You know..."

Ivan erupted in a belly laugh. "You Australians, you're all the same. You all have trouble holding in our top-notch Russian liquor."

Schultz chuckled with Ivan before excusing himself.

"Restrooms?" Schultz asked security as he stepped over the red rope that cordoned their area from the public.

The first security guard looked at him like a twat, returning his attention to some barely clad girl groping a fellow patron in public.

"That way," the second one replied in perfect English, pointing down the wall to their right. "Down at the end. It's all signed, you won't get lost." He winked at Schultz.

"Thank you. Do I know you?"

"Just helping a fellow tourist."

"Thanks."

Schultz walked in the direction he was indicated, glancing back at the guard as he walked away. The man had already resumed his stare ahead. Schultz noted he was middle-aged, clean shaven and, although of a similar build as his Russian counterpart, his appearance looked a lot healthier. Something didn't seem right but he couldn't put his finger on it.

Confused, he turned around and weaved in between a few drunken patrons as they staggered out of their booths, tripping over their feet, the men relying on the support of the women who had their arms swung around their waists. He was impressed by the way most of them were managing to keep their glasses or bottles upright. A few of them yelled out drunken slurs, raising their glasses at Schultz as he walked past.

Moving in between the nightclubbers, he took in his surroundings a bit more. Over on the far side of the club, he found the bar behind a five-deep line as patrons waited to be refueled. Bar staff were turning out the drinks one after the other, snatching notes from the patrons and handing back change—that was if the patrons waited for it. In the center of the club was a large throbbing dancefloor, strobe lights and smoke machines filling the area. Along the back wall of the club were booths, some manned with security guards, others just clubbers enjoying the night.

Finally reaching the door, Schultz took one last look behind him. No one was watching him. As the door closed behind him, the loud beats died down to a throb. Ahead was a barely lit corridor. As he made his way along it, a few ladies walked out of the first door. They looked him up and down before chuckling and making their way to the club. Schultz shrugged it off.

His cell vibrated again. Pulling it out, he read: four missed calls.

Looking behind him and then again in front, he saw he was alone. He opened the notifications. They were all from Xander.

He slipped into what he hoped was the men's room. Once he was inside, he was relieved to see it resembled a recognizable men's restroom. After checking all the cubicles to ensure he was alone, he called Xander.

"Sounds like you're working hard," Xander answered on the first ring tone.

"Always." Schultz poked his head out of the restroom door. He was still alone.

"I didn't know you were the clubbing type."

"I'm not. I'm analyzing Kuzmich."

"How's it going?"

"No expenses have been spared tonight. Your kind of night, ladies and alcohol."

"Maybe twenty years ago. With my well-sculptured physique, I'm sure the booze mixed with the girls would now give me one mighty heart attach."

Schultz chuckled. "Don't be so unsure of yourself. When I return home, you and I are going down to the local pub." He poked his head out again. Two men entered the corridor. Schultz instantly recognized them as belonging to Ivan's VIP group. Closing the door, he locked himself in one of the cubicles.

"I don't have long," he whispered.

"Company? Right, you two have hit the motherload. There's going to be some really pissed off people over there. I'm talking half of Russia will be after your heads. If they aren't already."

"What do you mean?"

Schultz heard the restroom door close. The two men were boisterous, without a care in the world.

"I have no idea what you're really doing over there and I don't want to know. But you two have got to get out of Russia. Now."

"What's—"

His phone beeped in his ear. Looking at his phone, he saw Xander had disconnected the call.

Schultz's heart was racing. There was no escape with those two keeping him company. He slid back the latch a little at a time, being careful not to make any sharp sounds. The door hinges creaked as the latch was freed from the lock. Schultz froze, listening. The two men were still carrying on, their conversation becoming more of a slur.

Peering through the gap between the frame and the door, he saw the two men standing at the urinals, their backs to Schultz. The one on the left was a good foot taller and bulkier than the other one. Both of their postures looked off a little, too straight. Schultz shrugged it off, putting it down to their being drunk and probably forgetting to unzip their pants first.

The men seemed to be in no hurry to leave so Schultz pushed the door against its hinges and slowly pulled the door open until it rested against the partition wall. Looking over at them, he saw they were still absorbed in their drunken slur.

It's now or never, he thought.

Not looking twice at the men, he began taking large steps towards the door. His hand on the door handle, his cell vibrated, silencing the drunken men.

Schultz didn't have a good feeling. Drunken men don't fall silent suddenly. Ignoring his phone, he quickly pulled the door open and took a step.

Thump.

A boot connected with the back of his head. Stunned, he felt his forehead smash into the narrow edge of the door. He staggered backwards on his feet and felt another boot sink into his stomach. Clenching his stomach, he looked around, turning in a small circle. The two apparently drunk men looked perfectly sober now.

"Had a bit too much to drink, have we, Aussie?" the man behind him asked, a hint of Russian in his English accent.

"Shit," Schultz muttered.

Chapter 18

Emily had lost count of how many blows she'd received to her face but she was enjoying a few moments' reprieve as the video finished playing. She was still surprised that Brian was there.

Brian turned the laptop around.

"At the time this video was recorded, our servers were accessed. Where is the hard drive?" Nicholas said.

"That video doesn't prove squat. Timestamps can be easily changed. And our servers? I've never seen you before tonight, so how should I know anything about your or anyone else's servers? Who are you?"

"Yes, maybe the timestamp could've been changed but the clock in your office matches our records. And the shirt you are wearing matches the video."

"You're going to need to do better than that if you're going to try and pin this one on me." Emily leant back in her chair.

Nicholas circled around her. Emily braced her arms, and before she knew it, she received a blow to the back of her head.

"I know nothing about your stupid hard drive."

"There is no denying it. That was definitely you in that video. When you finally accept you've been caught out, we can all move on."

"How about you release me now and find the real woman who has the damn hard drive you're chasing. Because I'm not confessing to something I didn't do."

Nicholas leant in and whispered into her ear, "Where is the hard drive?"

"What makes you so certain that was me in that damn video?"

Brian looked up from the laptop. "It's a spitting image of you, right down to what you're wearing today and how you walk. I'm one hundred percent certain that is definitely you in the video."

"Check the video again. Go back to when that woman walked into my office."

Brian looked at Nicholas, who nodded. "We'll entertain Ms. Lee."

Swinging the laptop around, he hit play.

Soon after the video started Emily pointed to the screen. "Stop there. Now, look at her. What do you see?"

"I see you." Nicholas was becoming frustrated.

"Brian?" Emily asked.

"I'm agreeing with Nicholas. It is you."

"Have a look at her shoes."

They both moved closer to the screen. They then looked at the pair of boots she was wearing.

"You've probably kept that pair," Nicholas pointed at the screen, "in your office."

"Nope." Emily shook her heard. "I can't stand heels. They hurt my back. Let alone wearing low-hanging tops. Brian, hit play."

The video continued playing for another fifteen seconds, during which time the woman kept her face hidden from the cameras.

"Pause..." She studied the screen, waiting for the right frame to appear. "Right there," she snapped.

Brian's shoulders flinched before pausing the video.

"Do either of you see anything or do I need to point it out to you?"

They both shook their heads.

"Seriously?" Emily shook her head in disbelief at their inability to catch sight of the obvious difference. Even she could easily see it from where she was.

"Look at her hair. There's a strand of blonde on her right side. Last time I checked the mirror I was a brunette. That woman is wearing a wig."

Nicholas shook his head in disbelief.

"If that's not you, then who is she?"

"Any number of people. I'd be looking at everyone on

payroll."

Nicholas returned his attention to the screen, staring at the woman.

Emily continued. "Brian, on that laptop, can you work your magic? There's a reflection on my computer screen."

Brian nodded slowly as he studied the paused image.

"See if you can tidy it up. If you can, you'll have your woman."

Brian turned to Nicholas, waiting for approval. As soon as he got it, he began.

"I'm still not convinced. Of course you'd say it wasn't you."

"I've been trying to tell you since you cuffed me to this chair it wasn't me. And that woman has done a shocking job on trying to frame me for this. I'm fairly certain I know who that woman is. What servers are you referring to?"

"That's confidential. And you don't get to ask the questions around here. What difference does it make anyway?"

"Because that woman wouldn't use my computer to access the corporate server. She can do that from her own desk. We've both been played here. Let me go and I'll be able to help you. I have contacts."

Nicholas turned to Brian, who slowly shook his head.

"Your old friend here," Nicholas pointed his thumb in Brian's direction, "doesn't believe so."

"What would he know?" Emily taunted them. "He doesn't know squat about me."

Brian turned around and crossed him arms. "Okay, you asked for it. You're here with a close Australian friend. Does he know about Tom?"

Emily glared at him, biting her lip.

Brian turned to Nicholas. "Her friend, the other Australian in the office, is a cop."

Nicholas stood up and stared down at Emily.

Brian continued. "She's often assisting him with cases that relate to finances. She's probably on another one right now."

"Who do you work for?" Nicholas demanded.

"You got an identification on that woman yet?" Emily asked Brian. He ignored her, and she continued. "That woman is my personal assistant, Katinka. She's set me up."

"I don't give a damn about that right now. Who do you work for?"

"I'm employed by REA International Energy until they find a suitable local to step into my position. What I want to know is who you and my assistant work for."

"Boss." Brian looked up, his face white.

"What?" Nicholas snapped.

Brian turned the laptop around until everyone could see the screen. "Emily's right. It is her assistant."

Chapter 19

Leaning on his side, Schultz looked up to see the two men towering over him.

In between shallow breaths, he asked, "Who have I pissed off this time?"

Wiping the corner of his nose, he flinched at the discomfort he'd just caused himself. On lowering his hand, he discovered it was smeared in blood. "You prick."

"That's the least of your worries," Pipsqueak said in a girly voice.

"I don't understand." Schultz staggered as he stood up. "How is it not my worry? One of you broke my fricken' nose."

"I'll straighten it up," the taller one offered.

As Schultz turned, he saw a foot swinging around.

Grabbing the leg, he twisted it. The attacker landed on the floor. Schultz gave the leg another sharp twist and dropped it. The man lay there holding his leg, cursing.

"Think you're a hot shot?" Pipsqueak shoved Schultz's back.

"You want to try that again?" Shultz said, turning around and walking up to him. There was barely enough room to slide a hand between the two men. Schultz looked down at the man, his eye level a good couple of inches higher. Pipsqueak stepped back. Schultz stepped forward. "Who sent you? Ivan?"

"What's it to you?"

"So I know whose ass to kick after I've kicked yours."

"I'd love to see that."

"Who sent you?"

His attacker raised his eyebrow and smirked.

Schultz raised his closed fist and swung. Halfway around his hand stopped. He slowly turned towards his hand. He'd forgotten to keep the door in sight. His new attacker stepped away as Schultz felt his arm being twisted all the way up to his shoulder.

"Hey, Franco. I didn't hear you come in. Don't you have more vodka to drink and ladies to enjoy?"

"Pleasure later. Business first." Franco pulled Schultz's arm farther down his back.

"You're making a big mistake."

"No, no, no. You're deeply mistaken." Franco's English was a lot clearer, Schultz noticed.

"What happened to your Russian accent? You lose that,

too? It won't be the only thing you'll lose tonight." Schultz grimaced as his arm was pulled farther around. "Maybe you should quietly leave now and return to those ladies. I'm sure they'll be getting lonely without you men there to keep them occupied. Isn't that more interesting than hanging out here in the toilet block?"

A kick from Franco cut him across the stomach. Schultz tried to bend over, but Franco pulled his arm back, his right shoulder exposed.

Right, you son of a bitches, he thought.

His eyes narrowed. Without moving his head, he glanced around, assessing where everyone was positioned.

Franco was breathing down his neck, sounding almost like a snarling coyote. Pipsqueak was barely two steps away and appeared to be weighing Schultz up. His first casualty was still on the floor, clutching his leg and moaning.

"You guys don't have much fight in you," Schultz taunted.

Franco pulled Schultz's arm around farther and Schultz clenched his teeth.

"Plus, you seriously need to work on your stamina, and what you're pushing. Maybe double the weights, because there's nothing behind any of your kicks."

He still wasn't getting any action from them—maybe a snarl but nothing more.

He tried again. "I swear my sister's punch has a lot more bite than yours."

Hook, line and sinker.

Pipsqueak's eyes fired up, his cheeks puffing out as he

clenched his fists. Schultz waited and watched him exchange stares with Franco, behind him, unflinching. Then he felt Franco's grip loosen.

Keeping perfectly still, Schultz puckered his lips and blew a kiss to Pipsqueak, then bent down and threw Franco over his shoulder, watching on as Franco's wildly kicking legs bowled Pipsqueak over. A sickening thud echoed through the room as Pipsqueak's head connected with the floor.

Schultz stood over them, clenching his fist.

"No, no. Please don't." Franco waved his hand, a look of terror in his eyes. He tried to crawl backwards but his hand slipped on the wet floor. "I'll do anything for you."

Schultz sniggered. Seeing how close they were to the urinals, Franco was probably slipping in piss.

"You sold out pretty quickly."

"I have a young family. Two little girls. And a wife."

"What does your wife think about your VIP nights?"

Franco looked away.

Schultz leant down, grabbed Franco by the front of his shirt and pulled him up.

"Thank you, thank you."

Schultz walked over and snibbed the restroom door locked before approaching the first attacker, who was still moaning in a heap on the floor. Grabbing the man's head, he twisted and let go. The attacker slumped, limp, to the floor.

"You... you just killed him with your bare hands?" Franco stammered.

"What do you think, Franco?"

Schultz rummaged through the guy's pockets and pulled out a handgun and some loose bullets.

"Why didn't he just use these? It would've been so much easier," Schultz asked, not expecting a response from anyone.

He loaded the gun and tucked it inside his pants' waistband before slipping the ammunition pants pockets.

"They were instructed not to," Franco quivered.

"Was I asking you? No, I didn't think so."

Schultz investigated Pipsqueak's pockets, retrieving his firearm and ammunition, too. He stopped at the hip pocket and pulled out a wallet. Flipping through it, he found a driver's license and one hundred US dollars in crisp notes.

"Why's he got US dollars when in Russia? This currency isn't any good here." Schultz turned to Franco, who had inched towards the only exit.

Franco shrugged. "No idea. Sorry."

Schultz pulled the notes out and felt a hard object in between them. A red swipe card, blank on one side and on the other side was a gold-printed logo, very similar to what he'd seen on Ivan's shirt earlier. A symbol that had been rampant during the soviet days.

He waved the card in the air. "What's this?"

Franco looked down and inched closer to the door.

Schultz stepped in between Franco and the door.

"Don't even think about it."

"I... I don't know what you're talking about." Franco changed direction and shuffled towards the cubicles.

"You don't sound like someone who doesn't know what's

going on. What. Is. This card. For?"

"I... I don't know. I've never seen it before." Franco shifted his eyes to the left then back to Schultz.

"Do you want to try again? And this time don't piss me around."

Schultz took a step closer. Franco's back was now pressed up against the toilet door. He tried stepping to the left but Schultz slammed his hand against the door. Franco flinched.

"I'll tell you but you need to offer me protection."

"Protection? What makes you think I can offer something like that?"

"You're a cop."

"No, I'm a government worker."

"Yes, and a cop is a government worker."

"Why do you need protection? You're just an office worker like I am, aren't you?"

"Yes. Kind of." Franco glanced sideways. "But we're both hiding secrets, aren't we?"

Pulling one of his newly acquired guns out, Schultz ensured it was ready to fire before he stepped between Franco and the door.

"Don't piss me around. What's the card for?"

"Before I say anything, I need protection."

Schultz pressed the gun barrel against Franco's throat.

"I'll ask you one more time. What does the card gain access to?"

"Why don't you just kill me and get it over with? You know you want to. If you don't, one of Ivan's men will."

Schultz pushed the gun deeper into Franco's throat. Franco grimaced but refused to talk. Schultz moved his finger over the trigger.

"Okay, okay, I'll tell you. Just move the gun away from my throat."

Schultz studied him for a moment before moving the gun from Franco's throat to his temple.

"Talk," Schultz said.

"That card... it'll get you into the basement below our office."

"What do you mean, basement? I've seen the plans; there isn't anything underneath the building."

"Officially, it doesn't exist."

"Keep going."

"Can you put that gun away? I'm not going to harm you. I'm here to help you." Franco placed his hands behind his back.

"You had a funny way of showing that earlier. Move your hands back out to the front where I can see them."

Franco slowly moved his hands around in front of him, his open palms facing Schultz.

"Now, this basement you claim exists. Why does it have carded access?"

"I've said too much already. If it's so important to you why don't you go down there and have a look for yourself?"

Schultz thought for a moment. "That's a good idea."

Franco looked down to his feet.

"That's why you are going to come with me. You're going

to show me what I need to know."

Shaking his head, Franco replied, "No, I'm not taking you in there. If you want to have a look, you'll have to go in by yourself. I won't be seen dead in there."

"What's going on in that so-called basement?" Schultz pressed the gun against Franco's temple. "This emblem." He held the card up in front of Franco's face so he couldn't not see it. "I haven't seen this logo used since Russia's Soviet days. What does this emblem represent to you, to Ivan?"

"You're a dead man. If I'm not back out there in the next two minutes, Ivan will send more of his men in here."

"Well, you'd better start talking then." Schultz thumped the butt of the gun handle against the side of Franco's head. "Because you'll be a dead man before I am."

"Fuck you."

Schultz right-hooked Franco in the stomach, not caring about the gun still held tight in his fist. Franco winced and Schultz punched him again.

"Talk. What does the emblem represent?"

"I'm not talking unless I get protection."

"How's this for protection?" Schultz lowered the gun and fired a round.

"Gahh! You shot my foot!" Franco hobbled on his other foot, his face contorted in pain.

"Talk or it'll be the middle one next time."

"Alright, alright. There's a revolution brewing. The rightful Vozhd, our supreme leader, will be our guide."

Schultz turned towards the sound of drunken voices on the

other side of the men's restroom door. The door rattled.

Schultz shouted over his shoulder in Russian, "Closed for cleaning. We'll be finished in a few minutes."

The door stopped rattling and the drunken voices faded. Schultz kept his gun pointed at Franco's chest.

"Where's the money coming from?"

"I've told you enough. I'm already a dead man."

"Then keep talking."

"I owe you nothing. You're just a government worker."

Raising an eyebrow, Schultz lowered his gun, aiming it between Franco's legs.

"Alright, alright. Don't shoot them. I still need them."

"Not if you're a dead man. Now talk. Where's the money coming from?"

Franco shifted his gaze towards the door. Schultz punched him in the stomach.

"Alright." Franco clutched his stomach. "Most of the funds are coming from the company we work for. But there are other companies from all over Russia who are also providing funds."

"Willingly?"

"If they don't double-check their invoices before paying them then that's no one's fault but their own." Franco glanced at his watch. "With any luck, your little Australian girlfriend should be dead about now, and you'll be joining her shortly."

The crash of splintering wood made Schultz turn around. Gunfire sounded behind him. Turning around, he used Franco for shelter and opened fire towards the door. Three men tried to make it through the doorway and fell to the floor with each bullet Schultz fired.

Two more men emerged from either side of the door. Franco was now a dead weight. Schultz dug deep and held Franco's limp body up in front of him while opening fire at the two men.

As the two attackers dropped to the floor, Schultz threw Franco's body down. He pulled his cell out and called Xander.

"What's up?" Xander answered on the first ring.

"Have you got a copy of the blueprint for this club? I've got about eight down so far. I need an exit now."

"Certainly have."

Schultz peered outside the door. The corridor was empty. The night club music was still churning out its beats.

"Xander, I need that exit. Now."

Chapter 20

Sirens sounded outside the room Emily was being held captive in. She looked over towards the open door. A brick wall was visible through the opening, and a red light above the door flashed on and off. A group of men in fatigues ran past, their guns drawn.

"What's going on?" she asked, looking around at everyone.

No one answered. Instead, their guns pointed at the door. She noticed Scar Face press something against his ear. He issued a hand signal. Guns drawn, they all ran out, leaving the door open, and followed another group of armed men who ran past.

The siren continued to sound when her cell beeped.

Dropping her handcuffs, Emily pulled her cell out of her

boot. It was still ringing.

"Follow my instructions precisely if you want to live tonight," Xander ordered as soon as she answered the call, his tone serious.

"O-kay. But first I need to know what is going on."

"Get out of that room. Now."

Fatigue now the furthest thing from her mind, Emily ran to the open door.

"Go left. Now."

Emily pulled her coat in around her as she looked to her right, in the direction the men were heading.

"Run. NOW."

Taking one last look around, she began running down the long passage. She noticed it was quite wide, reminding her of older buildings. Solid brick walls surrounded her. She could see no escape if she was ambushed. Ahead of her the corridor ended into another, perpendicular to the one she'd been in.

"Stop and lean against the left side wall. Now."

Emily did as she was instructed but poked her head around the corner just enough to notice two armed men having a quick smoke. She ducked her head back behind the wall and waited.

"Be quiet. Schultz will fill you in on everything when you see him next.

Emily bit her lip.

He's been digging around again. That's why I insist on working alone, she thought.

Xander continued. "Now, take the corridor to your right."

Emily peered down the corridor. The guards had gone.

Her heart pounding, she stepped away from the wall.

"Now," Xander yelled into the phone. "Run to the end then turn left."

"You two have a lot to answer for."

"I think we all do. But first we need to get you out of here. Preferably alive." Xander paused for a moment before continuing. "Two men are about to round the corner at the opposite end. You'd better run faster."

Already feeling battered and bruised, Emily dug deep and pushed her legs faster, focusing only on putting one foot in front of the other and picking up speed. She hurtled around the next corner and leant against the wall, catching her breath.

Her breathing under control, she peered around the corner. Two men turned into the corridor she'd just left. Pulling her head back behind the wall, she whispered into her phone, "Where to now?"

"Run to the end and turn right. Now."

Emily didn't wait for a second invitation. Gritting her teeth, she bolted for the other end of the corridor. It felt like her heart was throbbing in her ears as she pushed through the pain.

As she neared the next corner, she brought the phone back to her ear. "Okay. What—"

The question died on her lips as she skidded to a stop. Standing there, staring at her, were two Russian soldiers in combat fatigues.

Emily heard Xander yell into her cell, "Pull back. Now."

But she couldn't move.

The men raised their guns and yelled something to her in Russian.

"Ah, I'll be a little tied up for a moment. I'll be right back." She slipped her cell into her back pocket.

Raising her hands above her head, she positioned her legs a little wider apart, one foot slightly in front of the other.

The men continued to yell at her in Russian. They stepped closer, their guns still pointing at her.

Unable to understand them, she stood there, arms raised, waiting for the best time to strike. A glance over her shoulder confirmed the corridor behind her was still empty. But it would only be a matter of time before more soldiers arrived from behind.

Taking deep breaths, she remained on guard. Waiting. Their guns were now just out of arm's reach.

The men fell silent, their dark hollow eyes staring at her. They positioned their fingers around their triggers.

Emily stared them in the eye. First, the one on the right. His stare was empty. He meant business. Then she turned to the one on the left. His right eye twitched then his trigger finger began shaking. His gun slipped.

He shifted his focus. Emily swung her left leg up and around, knocking his gun from his hands and grabbing it as it traveled through the air.

The other man pointed his gun at her, yelling. This time she heard a quiver in his voice. Keeping her eyes on him, she leant down fast and grabbed the weaponless man's head.

Jerking his head down, she connected it with her knee. She let the body fall to the ground, out cold. The soldier didn't have time to raise his hands in defense.

The remaining soldier took a couple of steps back, his gun still pointed at her.

Emily swung around and fired a shot at the quivering man. She heard a thud as he fell to the ground. She grabbed his handgun and looked up and down the corridor. She was alone, for now. It wasn't going to be long until all the soldiers were onto her position.

Emily pulled her cell out of her pocket. "Xander, you still there?"

Silence.

"Xander?" she repeated, checking her cell for reception.

"Sorry..."

"Are you okay? Talk to me."

"I, I thought I heard something outside. It's stopped now. Right, I see you made easy work of those two."

Emily heard his computer chair clunk against the table and his knuckles cracking.

"Let's get you out of there," Xander said.

"That'll be great."

"You need to get moving."

"Which way?"

"Straight ahead. Run."

Without looking back, she ran. Approaching the next intersection, she looked down the left side of the corridor. Darkness and coolness wafting towards her sent shivers up her back. Either a ventilation shaft or a door to the outside.

Down the right side, the corridor was lit similarly to the ones she'd just ventured through. Dim red flashing lights speckled the walls down its length giving just enough lighting to see to the next light.

"Go left. Now."

"It's dark."

"They're on your tail."

She looked down the pitch-black corridor. The hairs on her arms standing up, she rubbed her arms and turned her head. Voices. Heavy footsteps. Taking a deep breath, she extended her arms out, stepping sideways until she felt the rough bricks of the wall.

"You're going to have to move a little quicker than that."

"Shit! You fricken' scared me."

"They're about to turn the corner and see those men you knocked out."

"Knocked out?"

"I know you wouldn't have killed them unless it was warranted."

Emily smiled nervously as she continued inching deeper into the dark corridor.

"Lee, I need you to run."

"In the dark?"

"NOW."

Chapter 21

Adrenaline raging through her body, Emily stumbled on the uneven floor. Still travelling deeper into the pitch-dark corridor, she kept her arm on the wall.

Beyond her thumping heartbeat, she heard men yelling "poluchit' yeye." From the little she understood, they were yelling "get her."

"Xander, how much farther?"

"Twenty meters in front of you."

"Twenty? I don't have that long."

Her phone beeped in her ear. She looked at the window that popped up. *Low battery. Less than 20% battery remaining.*

"Shit," she whispered.

"No, you don't. You'd better be wearing something dark."

"Yeah, my coat. Why?"

"That wall you are next to. Crouch against it with your back to them and your head tucked in. Now."

This had better work, she thought as she crouched into position and pulled her coat collar up. Placing her hand in her coat pocket, her hand fell on some wires. Her earphones. Pulling them out, she glanced over her shoulder. Still clear. She placed one of her ear pieces in her ear and inserted the headphone jack into her cell.

"Stop moving," Xander whispered.

Ducking her head back down, she tucked her phone into her coat's inside pocket and folded her arms inside her coat. All visible skin was now hidden.

Everything fell silent. Emily's breathing quickened. She closed her eyes and her mind drifted away.

She drifted to their extended stopover in Abu Dhabi. To her and Schultz lounging under the shade of the palm trees, soaking in the last of the warm weather.

They were free there, with not a care in the world. No one except for her manager knew where they were. For the first time in a while, they were unreachable.

A smile emerged on her face. As night fell, the lagoon came alive with lights. The water was still warm from the desert sun. She swam lengths of the lagoon, Schultz trying to keep up.

Emily heard a faint voice in the distance.

"Lee, move now," the voice said again.

She opened her eyes.

"Lee you still with me?" Xander asked.

"Yeah," she whispered, sounding dazed. "I'm still here."

"Good. You're doing well. They're gone, for now. Next time you may not be so lucky."

"Thanks for reminding me."

"We're almost there. I need you to get up."

Emily stretched her neck from one side to the other, then back and forward before standing up.

"I know this is hard but you need to get to the next corner."

Closing her eyes, she took two deep breaths in before placing her hand against the wall and proceeding farther into the blackened corridor.

"Be strong, be strong," Emily whispered.

"You're doing well."

"Ouch." Emily rubbed her head.

"What's wrong?" Xander sounded worried.

"Trust you? There's a fricken' wall here."

"Hang on a minute."

Emily heard Xander tapping away at his keyboard, then silence.

"I don't know why. There shouldn't be anything there. You're still about five meters away from the next split in the corridor."

Emily ran her hand around, along the wall. She ran her hand up and down, the brick wall continuing in either direction.

"It's definitely a wall."

Emily slid sideways, her hand following the wall. She

stopped as her hand tapped against an object. Carefully moving her hand around it, she discovered it was rounded and cold. She grasped it and turned it; it moved. She turned it a little more.

"Hang on. There's a door here."

"A door?"

"Yeah, hang on a moment."

She turned the handle farther. The door clicked and cracked open a little.

"What have you got?" Xander asked.

Emily didn't reply.

"Don't do anything yet. Let me just see if I can dig deeper and find out what it is."

"Xander, it's just a door," she whispered, "I don't have time. I'm going in."

"You're just like your partner."

Emily stopped. "What do you mean?"

"Jumping in before we've fully assessed the situation."

Emily turned around and cocked her ear. In the distance she heard the familiar yelling of angry Russian men.

"Xander, I know you mean well—"

"But, they're on your tail."

"Exactly. You'll still be with me."

Torch lights bounced off the wall where she'd just travelled. Taking a deep breath, she stepped inside the room and closed the door behind her.

"You still there?"

The line was silent.

"Xander?"

She checked her phone screen; it showed a couple of bars.

"Xander?"

Xander's mock-evil laugh sounded through her phone. "Got you."

"No, you didn't," Emily replied, on the defense.

"Oh, my goodness. Wish I could've seen your face."

"Focus. Mind back on the job."

"Yes, boss. I've got some of the guys tapping into a couple of servers."

"Guys?"

"Don't move until we can find out where you are, exactly."

"Not sure..." Emily covered her nose and mouth, "How long I can last in here."

"Why's that?"

"Something's rotting in here."

"Shit. I don't like you doing this, but do you have enough battery to run the torch on your phone?"

Emily checked her battery levels. "It's getting low. Just hang on while I turn it on."

Emily turned her torch on and a light from the back of her phone flicked on. Her stomach was churning, but she fought back the feeling.

"Just putting you on speaker," Emily said. "You there?"

"Yeah. What do you see?"

Emily swung her phone around starting at the roof then along the wall opposite her.

"Not much. What appears to be a modern-day brick wall

opposite me." Emily scanned around a little more, the light bouncing off more bricks no more than a couple of arm's lengths away. "Holy shit." Emily stepped back, her head tapping the door.

"Lee. Talk to me. What's happening? What do you see?"

Chapter 22

Bobbing his head around the women who were straddling him, Ivan noticed a few empty seats. The remaining couple of men were behaving like boys in a candy store. He looked to where Schultz had been sitting. His seat was empty. So was Franco's. He looked up to his guards. One of them nodded towards the restrooms.

One security guard approached Ivan and leaned in. "I've taken a few of your men off their posts and sent them in to sort the foreigner out."

Ivan nodded and returned his attention to his party, the liquor finally having a relaxing effect. Out of the corner of his eye, he saw one of his guards talking into his sleeve. A moment later his guard unhooked the red rope and a slender-built woman entered his private booth.

I didn't request any more girls, Ivan thought as the woman stopped just inside the booth, her youthful face illuminated by a screen she was tapping on—a tablet, he suspected. He quickly refocused when he realized she was from his club's video surveillance team.

"Boss, you need to see this." She tapped the screen before handing it to Ivan.

"This had better be good," Ivan mumbled.

"The alarms on the island have been set off."

"How?"

"Still looking into it. There's no answer on the main lines. And your so-called computer geek? He's not answering his phone either. Nor can I ping it. He's gone dark. I told you he couldn't be trusted."

"Enough. Pull up all of the video feeds." He handed back the tablet.

She tapped on the screen before handing it back.

"Which room is she meant to be in?"

"The top left one."

Ivan tapped on the image. An empty room with the door wide open stared back at him. He took a deep breath before handing the tablet back.

"Thank you. Keep looking into who set the alarms off. I'll deal with the rest."

She nodded and his guard let her out.

"Excuse me, ladies," Ivan said, rising. "Business."

Mandatory disappointment flashed on their faces before

they split and moved onto the remaining men who weren't currently entertained.

Ivan walked to the corner and slipped through the small gap in the seats. Looking around, he ensured everyone was busy, content. He pushed the curtain aside, opened a door and slipped through into a darkened corridor.

He dialed one of his recent call contacts.

"Ivan, how are you?"

"How is she settling in?" Ivan winked at a waitress as she passed by with a tray of drinks.

"She hasn't been too much of a hassle."

Ivan heard fingers clicking on Nicholas' end.

"Is everything okay, Nicholas? You sound... busy."

"Just one of the men checking in. Everything is going to plan."

"Going to plan? Do you mind telling me..." Ivan thought for a moment before raising his voice. "Why are the damn alarms going off?"

Nicholas tried to answer but Ivan kept yelling. "The alarms have been going for ten minutes and you haven't notified me. What on earth is going on there?"

"It appears to be a system malfunction."

"Keep someone with her all the time."

"Okay," he said, his voice a little shaky.

"Problem?" Ivan snapped.

"No, no. All good."

"Someone will meet you at the rendezvous point to collect her. Your life depends on you not stuffing this one up."

Chapter 23

Fighting the nausea, Emily sent the last photo.

"Check your phone."

"Bloody hell. There's got to be—"

Emily scanned the floor. "At least a dozen bodies, if not more. It's too hard to tell."

"I can see that. They're all either butchered or in various stages of decomposition."

"How far are they from me?" Emily took the call off the phone speakers.

"They're closing in on your location. Hang on a moment."

"Yep." Emily swung the light on her phone up the other end. The light disappeared into the dark.

"Anyone got anything?" Emily heard Xander yell in the

background. She chuckled. He always tried to project authority in his voice but his voice still sounded very young.

Not waiting a moment later, she stepped back to the door. She pressed her ear against the door. Nothing.

"Lee?"

She stepped away from the door, her stomach churning, saliva building up.

"Lee?"

"Sorry, Xander." She swallowed. "What on earth is going on in this building? Who are these people?"

"We've pinged your location. We'll deal with the bodies later. Right now, you need to move before you're added to the pile."

"Some of them appear to have been tortured."

"There's a dead end to your left. Keep moving to your right."

Her cell beeped. Emily looked at the screen.

"Crap. Xander, we're critically low now."

"How critical?"

"Very. Nine percent."

"If you haven't already, turn the torch off."

"But it'll be dark. The bodies... Some of these piles are within inches of me."

"Lee, listen to me." His voice sounded unusually stern. "I know you're scared but I'm here, guiding you. You'll be safe. You trust me, don't you?"

"Of course I do."

"Turn your torch off or I will."

"You can't—"

Darkness enveloped Emily.

"You—" She stopped herself. She knew he meant well, but the hairs on her arms said otherwise.

"Continue heading down. About fifteen stride lengths."

Emily dragged one foot along the floor, then the other one until her feet were together. Her heart was racing and beads of sweat were dripping down her face.

"You're doing well," Xander reassured her.

Emily closed her eyes and slid her foot along. Her leg knocked into something. She squealed and jumped back.

"Lee. What's going on?"

"I—I... I just felt something."

"It's okay. Probably just another body."

"Thanks."

"You're not going to like this."

"What do you need me to do?"

She heard Xander breathing deeply into the phone.

"You're going to have to use your feet as your eyes."

"As my eyes?"

"You'll need to run your foot around the body. Outlining it with your foot so you can navigate your way around it."

"You want me to—"

"Yes, touch a dead body."

"Seriously? Can't I turn my light back on?"

"Then within minutes you'll be navigating the corridors alone without any guidance."

"Why do you always need to be right?"

"Not right. Just another set of eyes."

"I'm going to need a stiff drink when I'm out of here."

"Your shout?" Xander chuckled.

"Definitely, and I'll buy myself a lottery ticket as well."

"Don't let that humor slide away."

One arm firmly against the wall, she wiggled her foot until her shoe touched the body. Her leg shaking, she shimmied her foot farther along the body, her other leg following. Her arm trembling, she moved her hand along the wall until it was parallel with her body. She continued taking each step slowly when her cell beeped.

"Shit."

"Lee, you're doing great."

"No, it's my cell reminding me it's getting low."

"Okay." Emily heard him tapping his keyboard before he returned. "You're almost there. A few more steps, then to your left is a door."

"Thank goodness."

Her focus on the exit, Emily quickened her pace.

"Lee, you're at the door."

Keeping her feet pivoted, she moved her hand away from the wall and swung it around until it connected with the wall on the other side. She ran her hand along the wall.

"I think I've found it," Emily said as her hand swept across a smooth surface.

"Good. You're all clear."

"Please, let this be the end," she whispered.

She slowly turned the handle and pulled on the door.

"Xander, we've got a problem. The door won't budge."

"Is there anything blocking the door?"

"How am I to know? It's kind of dark in here."

"Don't I know about it! Remember, I've been with you every step of the way. Can you see any light under the door?"

Emily didn't need to look. "It's still pitch dark in here."

"You're not going to like this."

"Like... what?"

"I need you to feel around, see if there's any bodies blocking the doorway."

"Isn't there another way?"

"There are a few more options—"

"What are they?"

"You can stay where you are and hope we get to you before they do."

Emily huffed.

"Or you could backtrack and go out the door you came in."

"Option three?"

"Move the bodies."

There was a moment's silence on both ends before Xander continued, "I'm your eyes to get you out of there. We don't have much time. If your cell dies, you're on your own."

"Thanks for the reminder but my cell is doing its fair share of reminding me it's desperate for a power source all on its own."

"Sometimes your stubbornness gets in your way and you just need to be told."

"Thanks." Emily strained as she used her foot to slide the

bodies away from the door. "Think I'll be needing more than the one drink when I'm out of here."

"You can have as many as you want. When you're safe."

"Trying again."

Locating the handle, she slowly turned it. Pulling on the door, a stream of light bounced off the wall behind her.

"Thank goodness. We have light."

"Good-o." Xander tapped at his keyboard. "There's nothing in sight. You're good to go."

Not looking back, she opened the door a little farther, just enough to slide through. A bright white light filtered through. She shielded her eyes with her hand while pulling the door shut with her other.

"Lee, we're nearly there. At the end of this corridor you're free."

"I'll move when I can see."

"I'm your eyes."

Emily widened the gap between her fingers. White light filtered in. Squinting, she looked around. White polished walls, fluorescent lights and polished concrete flooring. Looking ahead, she saw an outside door. Halfway down she saw a gap in the wall on either side—more corridors.

"There's another intersection ahead?"

"Yes."

"Right, here goes." Emily walked towards the door, her pace quickening with each step, her eyes on the exit.

"Xander, thank you for helping me today."

"Thank me when you're out of there."

"What do you mean? We're almost there."

"I know. But we have—"

Entering the two corridors' intersection, Emily froze.

Nicholas stepped towards her. "You thought you could get out of here?"

Chapter 24

"You don't want me. I'm just an office worker."

"No," Nicholas took another step closer. "You are more than that. Aren't you?"

Emily took a step around, her back almost to the exit.

"I have no idea what you're talking about. I've already told you, I'm here for a working holiday."

"Hmmm, then why do you keep moving away from me? What are you afraid of?"

"You're armed." Her eyes glanced down to his gun holstered at his hip. "And I'm unarmed." She pulled her coat back.

"Twirl." Nicholas circled his finger around.

Emily pulled her coat back in around her.

"Don't tease a bloke. Now twirl." Sounding more forceful, he reached for his holster.

"You can put your hand back where it was."

He thought for a moment. "Very well."

Emily waited until he'd moved his hand away before she slowly turned around, turning her head to keep him in sight.

"Remove the coat."

"It's cold. It's staying on."

He moved his hand back towards his gun.

"Okay, okay." Keeping her eye on him, she removed her coat and threw it behind her, towards her exit.

"Nice. Twirl. Now."

She slowly turned around.

"Raise your arms."

No worries, she thought.

A smile emerged as she raised her arms above her head. Her smile disappeared when she felt him pressed up against her back, heavy-breathing on her neck. She wriggled but he had a firm grip of her arms.

"Oh, isn't Ivan going to love you?" he whispered into her ear. "He loves feisty ladies. Even more so after I break you in."

He pushed his body harder against hers.

Emily closed her eyes. "You sure about that?"

"Huh?" He nuzzled into her neck.

"How feisty does he like his women?"

"Oh, very."

"Good."

She pulled her elbows down and shoved them into his ribs.

"You bitch." He staggered, releasing her.

She turned around to find him bent over, one arm across his front. Grabbing him around his neck, she tightened her grip. He tried to reach her arm but she pushed her elbow into his shoulder. It wasn't long until he became unresponsive. Placing him down, she checked his pulse; there was still one.

"Not very tough, now, are we?"

She bent over, trying to control her breathing. The countless months of noodle boxes were still taking their toll on her health despite resuming martial arts training the previous week.

"Lee. Lee," she heard someone calling out.

Still catching her breath, she placed her earbud back in.

"Thanks for the heads-up."

"I tried. He didn't appear on the radar until the last moment."

"He'll have a small headache for a while."

"I'm not going to ask."

"Nope, need-to-know basis only. Just need a minute."

Checking Nicholas' pockets, Emily found his cell and a portable charging device connected to it. Unplugging the charger, she checked the connection.

"Alright."

She plugged her cell in. It beeped, then the charging symbol appeared.

"Not sure for how long, but we have some power thanks to Nicholas."

"Great. You need to get out of there. Now."

Emily checked his other pockets; only ammunition. She pocketed some and grabbed his gun.

"You won't be needing this." She tucked his gun into her pants' waistband.

"Lee, you need to move, now."

Chapter 25

Emily turned the handle. The door clicked. Pulling the door open, she was greeted with darkness and an ice-cold breeze slap to the face.

She put her coat back on and stepped outside when another gust of wind almost knocked the breath out of her. Darkness enveloped her as the door closed behind her. Ahead, she could see a reflective surface expanding to the horizon.

"Ocean?" Emily whispered.

"No, it's a lake. The largest in North-West Russia."

"Holy smokes. You serious? It expands as far as I can see."

"You need to head towards it. On the shoreline there's a boat ramp. A boat and our American contact are waiting for you nearby."

"A boat?"

"Get moving. NOW."

The line went quiet.

"Xander? You there?"

There was no reply. She tried again. Nothing. Pulling out her phone, she checked the screen.

"He hung up on me." Shaking her head, she took her earphones out and tucked them, her phone and her newly acquired charger into her hip pocket.

She pulled her coat collar up and wrapped the sides tight against her body. On the horizon, she thought she caught a glimpse of a set of headlights but they instantly disappeared.

Hungry dogs barking in the distance brought her back to reality. Although they were still far away, she didn't hang around the exit.

Venturing towards the lake, she began maneuvering the uneven terrain towards the shoreline as fast as the darkness allowed. It would normally be a quick dash for someone a lot fitter, but her heavy coat and work shoes were not favoring her running style, or the lack of.

As she stumbled on the rocks, the dogs' barks began to sound closer. Her heart thumped loudly, like it was going to jump right out of her chest and onto the ground. Up ahead, the sandy shoreline appeared. She hopped over the last line of rocks and her feet sank into the sand.

"Now, where is this damn boat?"

She located the boat ramp not far away. Past it she could just make out the slightly darker outline of land and shrubbery jutting out into the water. A slopping wet noise brought her gaze closer. Against the ramp, something bobbed in the water.

Emily turned around. The shoreline was empty; nothing for as far as she could see. She ran towards the boat ramp.

The dogs' barks were fading, the emerging silence making Emily feel on edge.

"That's not good," she whispered.

An aluminum boat appeared ahead, bobbing in the water. As she neared it, she saw it was a little bigger than what they called a tinny back home. A dark outline of something at the front end drew her eye for a moment.

No matter how she tried to dress up this boat, it still didn't look very safe considering she was heading into open waters. There was no cabin, no ladder to climb up. All Emily saw was a poor fisherman's boat. She looked up the shoreline then out to the open water. This was the only boat around.

"Hello," she whispered. "Anybody there?"

The only reply she got was from the water lapping at the shore. The sound urged her to pee, but there wasn't time to hide behind a bush. Trying to push back the thought, she continued approaching the boat.

The heap on the front of the boat began to move.

"Hello," she whispered again, now a couple of steps away.

A man jumped, his arms flapping. The boat rocked as he held on, trying to steady it.

"Hello," she repeated.

He turned towards her.

"Who are you? What do you want?" he said, a hint of

Russian in his American accent.

"Are you waiting for a passenger?"

"Who's asking?"

Emily took another step closer and saw a small light turn on, a torch. The man pointed the light towards her.

"Don't come any closer. I don't need your type causing me any trouble."

"My type?"

"Have you looked at yourself? All bloodied and bruised. No, I'm too old for that caper. You best keep moving on."

"My contact told me there'll be an American and a boat waiting for me."

He studied her for a moment before replying, "Your contact, hey? Who may that be?"

Emily risked a glance over her shoulder. The dogs began barking again. This time it sounded like there were twice as many.

"They after you?" the man asked as he sat down in front of the boat's motor and turned the torch off.

"I'd say so."

"Who's your contact?"

Emily struggled with the decision. She didn't want to answer him, but the barks were growing louder. She looked at the water then back at the fisherman.

"Xander."

Sirens pierced the stillness of the night.

"Hmm... you the one who escaped?"

Emily took a step back towards the boat ramp, towards the

exposed shoreline.

The man chuckled. "Well, you best be hopping in, then. Come on. Xander told me to expect you." He gestured for her to hop in.

Her heart racing, she flashed back to the last time she was in a similar boat with her family. She was only about ten. They were caught in a violent storm. White-peaked waves crashed against their boat to the point of almost capsizing it. She'd never hopped in a small boat since.

"Maybe you're not who I thought you were after all. I'd best be leaving, then."

Turning his back on her, he pulled the cord on the engine. It coughed and spattered. Nothing. He pulled the cord again, this time a bit farther and with more strength. The engine came to life.

"I'm not waiting around for them to join us. I suggest if you're coming you better hop in. Now."

A couple of lights bounced around on the trees nearest the shore.

"I'm coming."

She walked to the edge of the lake, the water lapping at her boots.

"Well, you coming or you just going to watch me?"

The water depth slowly rose up her boot as she reached his boat. Holding his hand out, he helped lift her in.

As she sat down, she glanced over her shoulder again. The men's yells and dogs' barks were growing louder and fiercer. The boat edged away from the shoreline.

"Get down and put the tarp over you."

"What about you?"

"Don't you worry about me. It's you we need to worry about," he whispered as he cast a line out into the water. "If you want to get out of here alive, do as you're told."

Chapter 26

Driving over a small rise, Schultz dimmed his headlights. The dense forest gave way to a large body of water.

Pulling his messages up on his phone, he checked the co-ordinates Xander had sent him against the hatchback's GPS system. The track continued ahead. Driving along the water's edge, trying to dodge the large potholes, he watched the numbers on the GPS as they closed in on Xander's co-ordinates.

The two sets of numbers finally matching, Schultz stopped the car. He was in the middle of an intersection. The current track continued along the water's edge and the other veered right back into the forest.

Winding his window down, he heard sirens piercing the

night's stillness. He scanned the water, looking for any sign of anything. Nothing. Flat.

He re-positioned himself in his seat and looked farther over the water. In the distance, high above the water level, a faint red light flashed.

Preparing for a quick escape, he returned to the GPS and selected a saved favorite. The new route would be taking him back into the forest. He looked to his right. The road he would be taking was edged by shrubs on one side. One last glance at the water assured him it was still flat.

Restarting his engine, he steered his car right, towards the forest and maneuvered behind the shrubs. Content he was hidden, he killed the ignition and hopped out. He checked the signal strength on his cell phone; barely one bar.

Wouldn't want to be in an emergency out here, he thought.

Pulling his jacket tight around his body, he tucked his hands under his armpits and approached the lake. At the lake's edge, something in the water caught his attention. A small boat was approaching. He crouched behind a boulder. He peered around the boulder as the boat stopped just off the shoreline. He saw movement under a tarp.

He glanced back towards the hatchback. It was concealed but he'd be spotted if he made a run for it now. Looking back towards the boat, he saw someone hopping out.

"Lee?"

The fisherman pulled his boat around and steered it eastward.

"You going to stand there all night, or are you going to

lend me a hand?"

"I take it those sirens and lights are for you." He asked as he grabbed her arm, hoisting her up the bank.

"The one and only."

"Car's just up there. Well, it's a hatchback." Schultz pointed up the road as he helped Lee find her land legs.

"Great. I'm looking forward to getting back to civilization. Relaxing in nature is a little overrated tonight."

"Don't blame you."

"You smell like a pub. You been out drinking?"

"Not exactly. You've heard Ivan boasting around the office about his lavish party nights?"

"The one with the ladies or the pokies?"

"The ladies."

Lee laughed. "Yeah. How did that go?"

Reaching the hatchback, Schultz leaned against the roof. "Put it this way... the suits and the ladies? He cannot afford half of it on a manager's salary."

"What do you mean?" Lee asked as she also hopped in the hatchback.

"They're quite lavish. The alcohol and the entertainment. He doesn't hold back on any of the costs."

"And you've got a pearler of a black eye."

Schultz felt his face warming as his cheeks blushed. He quickly closed his door and darkness shrouded them before Lee noticed.

He looked up and down the road running along the lake. As far as he could see, they were alone. He fired up the hatchback and followed the road that led into the forest.

"How did that happen?" Lee asked.

"What?" Schultz kept his eyes on the road as he applied more pressure to the accelerator pedal.

"Your face." She turned to face him.

"He's got a private area at the club, which included his own personal security guards and waitresses. I ducked into the restroom to take a call from Xander and two of his men followed soon after. A scuttle broke out between us."

"Do you know who these men were? Were they from the office?"

He shook his head. "No. I haven't seen them before tonight. The only ones who really talked to me were Ivan, Franco, and one of his security guards who sounded like he might be British."

"You don't recognize them from anywhere? Previous assignments? Anything?"

"No. I've been scratching my head. I've got Xander and the team running their photos through the systems right now. Still waiting." He checked his watch. "I would've thought he'd have something by now."

"He could be under the pump. He's got his own cases, and we've relied on him heavily today."

"Maybe, but he usually touches base periodically."

"That's not good, then."

"No. I'll give him a call when we get enough distance between us and your captors."

"There's no service until we get back to the main roads."

"Seriously?"

"What happens if Xander misses the next scheduled call?"

"We can worry about that then. Right now, we need to get out of here."

Chapter 27

Schultz was relieved when he turned onto the bitumen road. He glanced over at Lee. Her eyes stayed closed longer each time she closed them.

He checked his cell. It danced between one and two bars of phone reception. He flicked through his contacts and called Xander. The cell rang through the car's speakers.

"Damn Bluetooth." Schultz swiped through his phone's settings.

Lee stretched as the call continued to ring.

"Watch out," Lee yelled.

Their wheel hit rubble on the side of the road. Schultz looked up and swung the hatchback back onto the road. The call diverted to Xander's message bank.

"Where did you find this old thing?" Lee said as she stretched her back and neck.

"Work."

"Seriously? With their profits this is what they gave you?"

"It's what was offered by one of the ladies in the office. She'd taken a phone call from the manager of the site you were meant to have visted this afternoon rang. He was asking her for your whereabouts."

"Who answered the phone?"

"Not sure but the call was answered at your assistants' desk. The woman who passed the message on to me said the phone had been ringing solidly for ten minutes so she thought she'd better answer it."

"Where was Katinka? Why didn't she answer her phone?"

"No one knows. She didn't return from lunch."

"Seriously? She'd better have a good explanation in the morning. I have deadlines to meet this week, and she was adding the final touches to my presentation."

"I don't think there'll be a tomorrow."

"Why? We've been given an assignment. It needs to be completed. I've never left an assignment unfinished."

"This might be a first then. While those guys are on the loose neither of us are safe. They know I'm a cop."

"Great." Lee sat up and leant closer to her side mirror.

"What is it?" Schultz asked.

"Do you see those headlights behind us?"

Schultz looked in his rear-view mirror and nodded. "Yeah."

"How long have they been following us?"

"Soon after we turned back onto the bitumen."

"How far away are we from home?"

"Not far, about ten minutes."

Chapter 28

Ivan sat back in his chair, puffing cigar smoke as he stared up at the wall full of screens. One the girls from the club sat on the arm rest, caressing him, his double-breasted coat draped over her bare shoulders.

"Oy." He clicked his fingers. "Get Nicholas on the phone."

A computer operator nodded and walked over with a cordless phone already ringing. The call was answered on the third ring tone but the receiver didn't say anything.

"Nicholas?" Ivan sat up in his chair.

"Yes."

"She's not being too much trouble, is she?"

"No, boss."

Ivan looked up at one of the screens. A hatchback was

moving along, heading in the general direction of Saint Petersburg. He'd been watching the hatchback since it left the lake.

"That's funny. I'm looking at her right now."

"We're... we're on her tail. I've got backup assembling around the city. They'll be cornered as soon as they hit the outskirts. I'll get them both."

"Then why do I see her on the camera, in a car with that Australian cop, Schultz?"

"We're right behind them."

"No. Pull back. I know where they're going. You still got Russell and his sedan?"

"Yes, in a nearby town."

"Good. Finish him off, good and proper. No evidence of him, his car or any other property he may own. At least get something right tonight. Understand?"

Chapter 29

Emily and Schultz were a couple of blocks away from their apartment building when a fire truck sped past them, its blue and red lights flashing and its siren echoing through the street. Emily looked around but the high apartment buildings blocked her view.

"Poor people and this close to Christmas," Emily whispered.

"It doesn't look good," Schultz replied.

As Schultz turned into their street, blue flashing lights greeted them.

"Holy smokes. That's our apartment building."

Halfway down the block she saw the lower levels of their apartment building were engulfed in flames. A police car was positioned in the middle of the road, with a policeman directing traffic.

"Holy smokes."

"Well, that changes our plans a little."

"Where do we go now?"

"Let's get through here first."

Their hatchback was the next to pass the chaos. The policeman stood in front of their car and raised his hand. Schultz pulled to a stop. The uniformed man walked around and tapped on Schultz's window. Schultz wound the window down about a quarter of the way. The policeman said something in Russian, which neither of them understood.

"Sorry, English?" Schultz asked.

"Business here?"

"Home." Schultz pointed up the street beyond the fire.

The officer studied Schultz for a moment before he leant down and peered inside their car. Emily smiled and she swore she saw a flash of recognition appear on his face.

"Very well." He waved them through.

They slowly drove past the fire. Fire fighters were on ladders, spraying water from above. Others were fighting the fire from the street level. Emily peered over her shoulder and saw the officer looking at their hatchback as he talked on his hand-held radio.

"Did you get the same uneasy feeling about him?" She nodded back towards the officer.

Schultz looked in his rear-view mirror. "I don't like any of this. Let alone our apartment up in flames on the same night everything else went down."

"Someone is desperate. They're pulling the big guns now."

Another officer frantically waved them on.

Emily looked in her side mirror. The officer had stopped a black SUV behind them. He slid something into his pocket and quickly let them through.

"That was a bit too quick," Emily said.

"What was?"

"That black SUV behind us. It was as if the officer did a deal with them. The officer slid his hand in and out of his pocket before waving them through. You didn't see it?"

"No, sorry. It's probably just a local. You know, everyone knows everyone."

"Only we're not in the country."

"Don't know, then."

"Have you seen that SUV around here before?"

Schultz peered into his side mirror then his rear-view mirror. He shook his head. "Too hard to tell. It's probably no one. We've been here two seconds. We still don't know how this city or its people tick."

"Watch out," Emily screamed.

Schultz slammed on the brakes.

A man leaning on his cane waved his free hand in the air at Schultz. Schultz tapped his fingers on the steering wheel. The man walked slowly, pausing every time his feet met. Schultz honked the horn but the man ignored him and continued at his own pace.

He stopped in front of Emily. Their eyes locked. His stare

was hollow, and darkened circles encircled his eyes. The hair on her arms stood up. She narrowed her eyes, and a crooked smile appeared on his face. She watched as the man raised his hand up to his chin. His sleeve slid down exposing a tattoo on his hand—five black dots. He then began moving again, a little faster than before.

"Lunatic," Schultz yelled at the man as he drove off.

"I've seen him somewhere before."

"Here in Russia?"

Emily shook her head. "No. I don't think so." She was trying to recall everyone she'd met since they'd arrived. There weren't many as they really hadn't been there long.

"And that tattoo on his hand... I've seen that somewhere before, too."

"You're starting to worry me and so's that SUV behind us. We're the only two cars travelling down this street."

"Yeah," Emily replied but she wasn't really listening. She was on her cell, digging deep into her cloud storage, retrieving files from her last assignment in Australia.

"What are you thinking?" Emily felt Schultz leaning over, trying to see what she was doing.

"Not sure yet. I could be wrong."

"When are you wrong?"

Emily smiled but she was still focused on her cell. She was scrolling through the images Harry and Sharon had sent her that helped seal her last assignment—mug shots and brief biographies for all of Fu's known associates and investors. A few pages in, she stopped.

Chapter 30

Emily looked up from her cell. "I... don't believe it."

"What is it?" Schultz asked as he navigated the street corner. He glanced at her quickly. "You look like you've seen a ghost."

"I have. There's going to be no stopping Fu, is there?" Emily showed Schultz her cell.

"What are you doing with those files? Weren't you meant to have handed over everything you had on that case?"

A small smile appeared on her face. "It is him, isn't it?"

"You're unbelievable." He shook his head and looked at her screen again. His smile disappeared. "It can't be Lewis... Lewis—"

"Lewis Robinson."

"Yes. I remember that case. I personally saw him in the morgue. What? It would have to be a couple of years back now."

"Either he has a spitting image of himself getting around, or—"

"He's pretty good at playing dead." Schultz rubbed his chin, thinking.

"On the body you saw in the morgue..." Emily scrolled down the page and showed Schultz another photo of five dots close to each other. "Do you remember seeing this tattoo?

"No, I don't believe so. I'd need to get Xander to pull up the coroner's report to confirm if the body had the same tattoo. I'd hate to think there may be a family still waiting for answers on their loved one's disappearance."

"Xander sounded tired earlier. I wouldn't hassle him with this. Anyway, that old man was probably in shock. More than likely, he doesn't know me and it's all a coincidence."

"A coincidence? Halfway across the globe, we run into a spitting image of one of Fu's known associates. Not to mention the stare he gave you. There was pure evil in those eyes. No, I'm confident he knows exactly who you are. I'll see if Xander can pull up surveillance on the area and find out who destroyed our place."

Schultz navigated another turn, this street was darker. Emily saw a set of headlights follow them around the corner. Schultz made another turn, and it wasn't long until they had company again.

"Fluke?"

"This will soon tell us." Schultz made another couple of turns, going back towards the way they'd just come. As soon as he'd straightened their car, he put his foot down on the accelerator pedal and Emily was pushed into her seat. Tyres screeched behind them and headlights came into view. Schultz applied the brakes until their brake lights just appeared. The SUV behind them stopped. Schultz removed his foot off the pedal.

"They've started moving again," Emily said.

"Right, let's see if they want to dance."

Chapter 31

"All done, Lewis?" Ivan asked as he answered his cell.

"Yes. They won't be returning to their apartment."

"Good. Now I need you and the SUV here. We need to be on the road soon."

"Understood."

Disconnecting the call, Ivan walked over to his boardroom table. Huddled around the table, six of his finest men were looking at his map.

"Soldiers, you're all aware of what's expected tonight?"

Ivan looked around the table; all the men were nodding. That was until he stopped at the one standing opposite him. He was a lot younger and bonier than the other men who towered over him.

"And you? What are you to do?"

"I... uh..."

"Do I need to make your second in charge step up and take your place?"

"No, sir." He stamped his feet together and pulled his shoulders back. "I'll be leading my convoy south of the city before travelling east towards the Kremlin. My convoy will wait on the outskirts of Moscow for further instructions from you."

Nodding, Ivan looked the young man up and down. "Very well. We'll all be driving through the night as I need to ensure we get most, if not all, of the driving done before sunrise."

The men nodded.

"We will be rolling out of here on time tonight. You all need to ensure we're loaded and ready to go." He started rolling up his map. "Dismissed."

Chapter 32

After the next corner, the streets widened but traffic was still scarce. Emily leant forward, looking at her side mirror.

"It's been a little while. Looks like we may have finally lost them."

Schultz looked in both side mirrors then his rear-view mirror. "Maybe. We'll pull up here." Schultz pointed to a lit coffee shop, its lights illuminating the dark street. "We'll grab a coffee, regroup, and work out what we're going to do next."

Schultz pulled up a couple of car spaces back from the entrance. As Emily stepped out of their car, she pulled her coat in tight around her and looked around. Across the street she saw a darkened space—a park perhaps.

The coffee shop was positioned on the ground floor, about half way down the multi-story complex. What appeared to be a closed-in verandah jutted out onto the footpath.

Stepping inside the quaint shop, they were greeted by a waitress who placed them at a table alongside the front window.

"Thank you." Emily smiled at the waitress.

The waitress looked her up and down, clearly disapproving of her disheveled appearance. Emily brushed it off. The only things on her mind right now were food and staying alive.

"Sorry we're so late," Schultz said.

"It's no problem, sir. We open late. You're English. British? Australian?" the waitress asked.

"Why not American?" Schultz winked at the waitress.

"Your accent. Totally different. Now food, drink?"

Schultz tried to read the menu but quickly closed it. "I can't read this. You have coffee?"

"Yes, we also do tea."

"I'll have a tea," Emily said.

"Flavor? Type?"

"Surprise me. Maybe something with a bit of a kick. We have a long night ahead of us."

The waitress raised an eyebrow at Schultz and smiled. "You'll need all the energy you can get. She looks like she's a rough one."

Schultz blushed and shook his head. "No, no, no. It's not like that. We're working."

"It's all right. You call it what you want. I'm not here to judge. I bring you tea, and coffee."

She shuffled off towards the back of the restaurant.

Emily chuckled and looked around the quaint shop. A few late-night diners, mainly couples canoodling over shared desserts, and all she could think of was food.

"Are your assignments usually this... eventful?" Schultz asked.

"Only when I'm treading on toes." She looked out the window to the parkland, then down the street. It was quiet. No one was around.

"O-kay. How many toes have you stood on so far?"

Emily shrugged her shoulders. "I lost count after the first five. Now, all I worry about is cleaning up companies' bad accounting and record keeping. That's if I don't end up in a gun- or fist-fight first."

"And I take it you've been through this more than the two times I know of?"

"Tea. Coffee." The waitress placed a teapot, milk, coffee plunger and cups on their table.

"Thank you." Emily smiled at the waitress.

"Food? You both look famished."

"Yes, food will be good. Do you have meat pies here?" Schultz asked.

The waitress looked down at him, confused.

"It's an Australian favorite. It fits snugly in your hand." He cupped his hand to show her the size. "Beef and gravy enclosed inside a buttery, flaky pastry, with a good dollop of tomato sauce on top. I could really have one right now."

Emily buried her head in her hands, shaking her head.

The waitress shook her head. "No, not here. We cook proper food. Food that gives you energy."

"What do you recommend?" he asked.

"I surprise you. Yes?"

Emily and Schultz exchanged looks. Emily shrugged.

Turning back to the waitress, smiling, Schultz replied, "Thank you."

"Won't be long." The waitress bustled back to the kitchen, tending to tables on her way past.

When the waitress was out of earshot, Schultz asked, "Melbourne and tonight aren't the only times, are they? You've been in similar situations before, haven't you?"

Emily looked around at everyone. All the other diners were absorbed in their own conversations. She leant over the table and replied, "No, it's not, and tonight won't be the last either."

"Why won't it be the last? We've talked about protection."

"Yes, we have. My answer hasn't changed. I'm not afraid of a couple of bullets and a little bit of roughing up."

"Next time you may not be so lucky."

"I'll worry about that then. Currently my main concern is completing each assignment as it's handed to me. No questions asked. My father..." She sat back in her chair, her eyes sad. "My adoptive father... he always told me never to knock back anything. Grab it with both hands and run with it, as you never know where it'll take you. But I need to do the hard yards now, and I believe the day will come when I'll reap the rewards and I won't be out in the field as often."

"What if something happens to you before that day?"

"Then it wasn't meant to be."

"Don't you worry? Aren't there any things you want to do before that time comes?"

"You're assuming I'm going to be killed on assignment."

"Well, yeah. Or left too crippled to live your life the way you want to."

"Schultz, I'm already living an exceptional life. I was fortunate a good family took me in and brought me up as one of them. They provided me with an exceptional education and taught me how to focus on my future."

"Your father... He was a good man."

"Yes, he was."

"You ever thought of trying to find your biological family?"

"Excuse me," the waitress said as she placed a wooden board in the middle of the table.

"That was quick." Emily smiled at the waitress, relieved for the timely interruption.

"The chef cooked up too much. He said it's on the house."

"You don't have to. We can pay," Emily said.

"Now, eat up. Enjoy."

The aromas made Emily's mouth water.

"Ahh, chicken kebabs." Schultz touched a metal skewer but quickly withdrew his fingers.

"Yes, hot," the waitress scolded.

Emily jumped as she felt her phone vibrate in her hip pocket. A moment later Schultz's and the waitress' phones buzzed. She looked around; everyone else were all looking at their phones.

"Something's going on?" Emily returned her attention to Schultz and the waitress.

The waitress squinted her eyes at her then back to her phone.

"What's going on?" Emily asked Schultz.

"This is what." He showed his phone to Emily. "We've just hit the most wanted list."

She read his screen.

EMERGENCY ALERT
WANTED
Emily Lee, 35-year-old Caucasian female. She is armed and dangerous. Do not approach. Call 1-1-2.

Below the message was a mug shot of her, a recent one. Her face was bruised and battered, and her hair was all messed up. She studied the background. It was brick, like the one where she'd been held hostage earlier.

The waitress stepped back from them, her finger hovering over her cell's keypad.

Emily waved her hands in front of her. "I'm not dangerous. I'm innocent. That photo—it was taken earlier today when I was held hostage." She looked around. Everyone had returned to their lives. Turning back to the waitress, she continued. "That's why I look like this. I was tortured, held against my will. Do you understand?"

The waitress studied Emily then Schultz and put her phone away. "I see nothing. But best be quick. This way." The waitress walked towards a door not too far from their table.

Emily and Schultz exchanged surprised looks before following her. The waitress held the door open. Schultz stepped through. Emily stepped past the waitress.

The waitress grabbed Emily by the arm and whispered, "My poor child. Whoever it is... God speed you get out of this. Alive." She made the sign of the cross and smiled at her.

Emily placed her hand around the waitress's hand. "Thank you."

"Go now." The waitress ushered her out.

Emily had barely stepped outside when the door was shut behind them and the locks turned on the inside.

"Hope we can trust her," Schultz said as he glanced back at the door.

"I'm not hanging around to find out."

Emily quickly looked around her. In front of them was a parking lot with a few parked cars; she suspected they were staff cars. To her left a dead end, and to her right a high arch greeted their exit.

"This way," Emily said as she walked towards the arch.

"We need to find some warmth. It's starting to get cold, fast," Schultz said as he pulled his jacket collar around his neck.

"If we keep moving, we'll be fine. You know that."

Reaching the arch, she peered around the corner. A brick wall extended from her position to the main road. Across the dual-lane road, she recognized the dark parkland. The street was still deserted. Staying close to the building, Emily headed towards the street and their hatchback.

She was almost there when she stopped and held up her hand. She cocked her ear. In the distance, the sound of a vehicle accelerating was getting louder.

"Quick, back." Emily turned around and pushed Schultz ahead of her.

They reached the arch and ducked behind a nearby van as the car approached. It began slowing down as it neared their position. Emily closed her eyes and listened. The streets were quiet again.

She placed her finger against her lip. Schultz nodded. They edged out onto the street, towards the front of the building, to where their car was parked.

Chapter 33

"They should be right about here." Nicholas looked up from his cell.

Touching the back of his head, he grimaced. His eyes took a moment to adjust. Ahead of him the long stretch of road was deserted except for two cars parked outside a restaurant.

"Stop. There. That's the company car. Ivan's hatchback. We've got them now."

"Ivan," Nicholas spoke into his handheld radio. "You can pull your men back. I've got them cornered."

"I told you to stand down," a crackled response came from Ivan.

"You're breaking up. Sorry. Uh. Sorry. I can't hear you."

He turned the dial until the radio was off. Stepping out of

the passenger's side, he walked straight to the suspected car and placed his hand on the hood.

"It's still warm. They've got to be in there." He nodded towards the restaurant. It was the only shopfront with its lights still on.

Checking his gun was loaded, he tucked it back under his jacket.

"Time for some action. That bitch is mine. You hear me?"

Chapter 34

Emily peered around the corner of the building and saw two men standing at the front of their hatchback. She recognized one of the men as Nicholas, but not the other one. Pulling her phone out of her pocket, she snapped a couple of photos of the men and the cars.

She pulled her head back behind the building. "It's them."

"Who?" Schultz leant forward but Emily stopped him.

"One of the men is Nicholas. He was the one holding me hostage, questioning me."

"Right, let me get—"

"Settle," she hushed him.

Schultz pushed his body against her hand, but she pushed back against his body. Finally backing away, he lent against the brick wall. Emily peered back around the corner and saw the men entering the restaurant.

"Your car has to be hot. There's no way they could've just found it."

"I have no idea. I was about to leave when one of the office ladies handed me a set of keys and told me to take her car."

"I'm going to take a closer look."

Emily stepped around the corner but Schultz grabbed her arm and pulled her back in.

"Look around us. This is the only cover we've got. And those cars out the front are too close to Ivan's men."

"Why do you have to always be right?"

Emily peered around the corner. Through the window she saw the two men talking to the waitress. They were showing her something on a cell phone. She shook her head. The men were getting agitated, waving their arms about. Nicholas took a step towards the waitress and she stepped back, shaking her head and waving her arms in front of her as she looked at the cell phone for a second time. The other man raised his arm and the waitress fell. Emily gasped and pulled her head back around the corner. She took in a couple of deep breaths.

"Savages. They killed her because she protected us."

Emily turned to Schultz but he was gone.

"Schultz," she whispered.

She looked around the nearby garden. It was dark and she couldn't see anything. The laneway that stood between her and the garden was empty, too.

"Schultz," she called in a whisper again.

She peered around the corner and saw him crouching at the rear of the shooter's black SUV.

"Psst!" She waved him back.

Schultz crouched down as he moved around to the other side of the SUV. Emily looked in the restaurant window. The shooter pulled the waitress' limp body towards the back. Nicholas followed, keeping his gun poised at the patrons, who were now huddled in the far corner.

The moment Nicholas was out of sight, she yelled out to Schultz, "Quick, before they come back."

Schultz poked his head above the door before he moved around to her side of the SUV. There was no protection between him and the restaurant.

Emily moved out onto the street. She could no longer see the shooter. Crouching, Schultz ran towards her. He looked in the restaurant window as he ran past, his pace quickening.

"They're on their way out." He grabbed Emily's arm as he approached her. "Don't look back. Run like you've never run before."

Chapter 35

An icy breeze greeted Nicholas as he stepped out of the restaurant. Usually the winter nights didn't affect him, but this one was blowing from the north and sent a shiver through him. He pulled his collar up and was barely two steps out of the restaurant when he stopped. His driver walked into the back of him.

"Son of a bitch." He unclipped his holster and placed his hand over his gun. Walking around to the other side of their SUV, he continued. "You see what they've done? They've slashed them all."

"Yes," the shooter replied.

"They can't be too far away."

They both looked up and down the street. It was just them

and the two cars. Not even a hint of a headlight or taillight in the distance.

"No, boss. They've vanished."

"No one just vanishes." Nicholas looked up and down the street again. "They couldn't have gone far. Their car's still here, which means they've got to be on foot."

Nicholas listened, his ears cocked, trying to catch any hints of disturbances. Not even a barking dog or a roaming cat.

"Two can play this game."

He pulled his swiss army knife out of his pants pocket. Moving around to the front tire of the Australians' hatchback, he leant over and stabbed the tire.

Pulling his knife out, he turned to his driver. "Release the drone."

Chapter 36

"Do you hear that?" Schultz stopped, listening.

"Where's that buzzing coming from?" Lee asked.

"That's what I'm trying to work out."

A sound like a swarm of buzzing bees grew louder. They looked towards the sky.

"There it is." Lee pointed to a set of red lights floating in the night. "It's a drone. About a block away now."

"Clever bastard."

Schultz looked around. All he could see were walls of communism era apartments. He spotted a gap in the buildings.

"Quick, this way." He pulled Lee into a narrow side street, running past a few cars parked along it.

"It's a dead end," she said.

"Yeah, I know. Here, behind this van."

About half a block down, they crouched behind a small transporter van. The buzz from the drone grew louder. Schultz pulled out his cell phone and quickly dialed Xander.

"Xander," Schultz whispered as the call was answered.

"At your service. How can I help you on this fine evening?"

"We need the closest safe house."

"Onto it." Xander tapped away at his keyboard. "You do know you have two hot targets behind you?"

"Really? Thanks for the heads-up. Anything would be great now. Lee's kung fu—"

"Muay Thai," Lee interjected.

"Same thing. She's already pissed off these guys tonight. They're out for her blood."

"Yes, she kicked some serious butt out there."

"Both of our blood," Emily corrected him. "I could just shoot them but you don't want me doing that."

"No."

"And you're armed, too," Emily spotted his gun tucked into his pants' waistband.

"Illegally, just like you are." He covered the gun over before returning to his call. "X, have you pulled some magic for us?"

"Not sure. You're meant to be on long-service leave and not working, let alone on a case in a foreign country. I don't believe this case has been passed through the relevant government channels. If the Russian president finds out there is an Australian agent working on his soil, he's going to be pissed."

Schultz peered around the corner of the van. He spotted movement about half a dozen cars away.

"Xander. We're under fire. We need that safe house. Now."

Chapter 37

The buzzing subsided. Emily peered around the corner of the van. The dead-end street was empty. Looking along each of the parked cars, a few cars down, she saw a head poke out.

"I spy you up there," she whispered, pulling back behind the van.

Another shot was fired, this one hitting the side mirror of the van they were hiding behind.

"Right, it's just come through." Schultz loaded the co-ordinates into one of his map apps.

"Thank you, Xander. I owe you," he whispered.

"How far away is it?"

"About two blocks away."

"Seriously? And our only exit is blocked."

"Apparently."

"Right, time for some action." She pulled out the gun she'd borrowed from her kidnappers, and ensured it was loaded. "Time to sink one of these bad boys into them."

"Hang on a second." Schultz pulled out his cell to make a call.

The gunfire ceased and the drone moved away.

"Psst." Emily pointed towards the drone.

"What are they up to?" Schultz asked, his eyes on the disappearing drone.

"Not sure. But let's get moving while we can." Emily stood up, brushing her pants.

Schultz's phone beeped. Emily glanced over Schultz's shoulder as he tapped on the notification.

"That explains it."

"Explains what?" Emily asked.

"It's not going to take them long to realize they've just been sent on a wild goose chase."

"I'm not going to ask."

"Xander's up to his tricks again. He sent them a new mission. Take out a supposed armed SUV that's meant to be in hot pursuit of their location."

"And the armed SUV doesn't exist?"

"No."

"We need to get moving. It's not going to take them long to realize they've been misguided."

His phone beeped again.

Schultz looked at his phone screen then at Emily. "We've

been given the all clear to get moving. Now."

Emily edged out from behind the van, following Schultz out of the dead-end street. They were alone, for now.

"This way." Schultz waved his hand over his shoulder as he crossed the street, then again before walking past a small garden area giving some reprieve from the bleak buildings.

"I don't have a good feeling about this." The hair on Emily's neck rose, the cool breeze sending chills down her back as the communism era apartment blocks closed in around her.

"Quit being paranoid."

Crack.

Emily froze, looking over her shoulder.

"Seriously, Lee." Schultz grabbed her arm. "It's probably an animal. We need to keep moving."

"There. It's there." She pointed into the night.

Looking where she was pointing, he shook his head. "There's nothing there."

"No, I saw someone crouched as they ran towards those bushes."

Pulling her arm from Schultz's grip, she took a couple of steps towards the garden they'd just passed.

"Lee, we need to keep moving."

"No, there's someone there. We're being followed."

Crack.

"Tell me you heard that," she whispered, her eyes glued to a small shrub near the outskirts of the garden.

Nothing.

Out of the corner of her eye Emily saw three dark figures run across the street. She stepped backwards, her eyes on their movements.

"Schultz. I'm coming," she whispered.

No answer.

"Schultz?"

Nothing.

Turning around, she started running in the direction she'd seen Schultz leave.

"Schultz, where are you?"

She scanned the street from one side to the other, but the area was empty. She was quickly approaching the next intersection. Glancing over her shoulder, she couldn't see anyone following her. As she turned back around, she felt someone grabbing her shoulders. Clenching her fists, she swung her arms around, her hand connecting with her attacker.

Her attacker bent over, and Emily took a couple of steps backwards and brought her closed fists up in front of her face. One leg in front of the other, she lowered her body in a defensive stance, watching, waiting for her attacker to move.

"Boo," he whimpered, holding his hand up.

"Schultz?" She lowered her fists.

"Yeah. Why... did you do that?"

"Why the hell did you scare me, then?"

"Because you were being so damn paranoid."

She caught another glimpse of movement in the gardens.

"Me, paranoid? Look out there."

His arm supporting his ribs, he looked out towards the garden. "Shit. How many?"

"You saw them?"

"I saw something."

"Maybe three or four. They're keeping back."

"Nicholas and his companion?" Schultz asked.

"It's too dark to tell."

"Shit. Okay." Schultz rubbed his ribs.

"You right to get out of here?"

"I'll have to be."

Taking one last look over her shoulder, Emily saw they were alone, for the time being.

Chapter 38

"This is it," Schultz said as he checked the location against his cell. A red dot flashed on the location Xander had sent him.

Emily looked around. An old building, just like all the others, greeted them. No doors, just windows and brick walls.

"You sure?"

Schultz showed at his screen. "It's what Xander's organized."

"O-kay."

"Come on. The entrance must be around the back."

Walking around to the back of the building, Emily saw the outline of a path leading to a central lawn area with trees from one end to the other. Shadowing the little park were a number of apartment buildings, all about five levels high.

As she walked alongside one of the buildings, she saw little gardens separating the road from the buildings. Some patches were bare, some were alive with vegetation.

"Which one is it?" Emily asked as they walked past little walkways that led to doors.

"This one here." Schultz turned into what looked like the last entrance.

Emily followed, peering over her shoulder, trying to see into the shadows. Leaves rustled. The hair on the back of her neck stood up. She quickly followed Schultz, who was already inside, shutting the door behind her.

A dim yellow globe halfway up the stairwell was their only light as they navigated the narrow steps. Travelling in silence, they arrived at the next floor.

"What number?" Emily asked, stepping into the corridor.

She saw Schultz was already looking for the apartment.

"202. This one."

Schultz knocked on the door; two quick knocks, pause, then another knock.

Emily heard rustling inside before chains rattled on the other side of the door. Silence. Then the door opened ajar and part of a stubbly older man greeted them. His eyes were sunken and deep wrinkles cascaded across his forehead.

"You're expecting us?" Schultz asked.

The man looked at them, his expression unchanged.

Schultz pointed to himself. "I'm Schultz, and this is Lee." He pointed to Emily.

The man nodded before closing the door. Another chain

rattled against the door before it creaked ajar and he poked his head out the door. Looking up and down the passage, he motioned for them to come in.

"Quick, quick. Inside, now." His English was barely understandable behind his thick Russian accent.

He grabbed Schultz by his elbow as he stepped inside, trying to usher him through the doorway quicker. He reached out for Emily's arm but she glared at him. He pulled his arm away and nodded his head towards the inside of his apartment.

The door closed abruptly behind Emily. She turned around to confront their contact but the man snuck past her. By the time she turned around he was already half-way down his small passage.

Following him, she stepped from the passage into his living area. Looking around, she felt like she'd been transported back to Soviet Russia.

The wall was covered by a wall-length cupboard. Three coats were hanging from hooks on its edge and three shelves had dinner plates and cups on display. Alongside the display were two closed doors.

Along another wall was a simple two-seater couch that looked like it'd been here for as long as the building had been. Walking past the glass-topped coffee table in the center of the room, she glanced at the three books sprawled over its surface. She did a double take at the book poking out from the bottom of the pile. On its cover was a symbol she hadn't seen for a while. It was red and gold. She leant in to move the top book.

"Over here. We don't have much time."

Emily flinched. Leaving the book where it was, she looked up in time to see the man disappear into an adjoining room. Schultz followed without hesitation. Emily followed a few steps behind but stopped at the end of the sofa, her attention drawn back to the coffee table. Turning around, she drifted back to the books.

"In here. Please."

Emily jumped. The man's head was poking around the open door.

"Now. We don't have all night." His English was a lot clearer.

Standing in the doorway, Emily looked on as Schultz and the man stood looking at a backlit wall filled with a range of guns and ammunition. The other two walls were lined with closed and chained doors.

"You like?" The man's thick accent had returned.

Schultz ejected a magazine and clicked it back in, repeating the action once more.

Emily approached, standing alongside Schultz. Sprawled out on a table were four pistols and three different types of submachine guns. Some had duplicates alongside them. They looked almost like the ones she'd seen back home. She assumed these were the Russian equivalent. There were three AK-74s positioned at the end closest to Schultz's contact. Emily picked up one the submachine guns and weighed it in her hands.

"You know your way around a gun?" He sounded surprised as she checked out the gun, holding it in position.

She stared at him as she loaded the spare cartridge.

"So... Schultz, was it? You like?"

"You got laser pointers we can attach to these?" She placed the gun down on the table.

"Yes, I do."

"Good." She walked over to the display of larger weapons just visible through the gap between two open doors.

Hurrying over, the man closed the doors. "You won't be needing those."

As he was locking the doors his sleeve moved up his arm, exposing a small weathered tattoo on the inside of his arm. Five black dots. Emily's heart skipped a beat. She turned back to the table to hide her expression.

"We need to be prepared. Don't we? The locals haven't been exactly friendly," Emily said.

Schultz was about to give her a quizzical look but stopped when she moved her eyes towards their contact, tapping the inside of her hand. He nodded.

She returned her attention to their contact. "Are you going to help us or should we go elsewhere?"

"You won't get help anywhere else in the city. Anyhow, those guns will be enough to quieten a couple of rogue employees."

"Rogue employees?" she asked as she checked another gun. "Who said they were employees? We don't know who they are, but they're sure as hell pissed." Staring at him, she loaded the magazine. The man stayed quiet, watching her. "We'll take these."

"Very wise choice." Their contact patted Schultz on the back, his eyes narrowing as he looked over at Emily.

"Cash?" Emily asked as she tucked a pistol in her pants' back waistband.

"You already have gun?" He nodded towards the one she had tucked in her front waistband.

She pulled it out. "You can have it; it's too small for me."

"Is it legal?"

"What do you think?"

"Okay, I'll dispose of it. Now, cash? You want American? Ruble? Australia? British Pound?" He removed a painting from an empty wall and grabbed a nearby backpack.

"Bit of every one." She placed the gun she'd acquired earlier on the table.

Schultz grabbed the backpack from the man and placed the extra ammunition inside it, on top of the currency.

"We've been here too long. We need to get moving." Emily made her way out of the room.

Schultz looked at his watch. "Yes, too long."

"You need to make your way to the port. How you get there is up to you. When you get there, ask for this man." The contact shook hands with Schultz, his hand sliding away and leaving in its wake a crumpled piece of paper. "Memorize the details then burn the paper."

Schultz opened it as they walked back into the living room. Emily made a bee line for the passage leading to the door.

"Would you like a votka? Warm you up before you go back outside?" their contact asked.

Schultz went to reply but Emily interrupted with a forced apologetic smile. "Thank you but we really need to get moving."

"Just one." The man picked up two repurposed jam jars and blew into them.

"Thank you for everything." Schultz extended his hand. "We really must get moving. We need to get to that port before daylight."

Their contact appeared to be studying Schultz before taking his hand in his and shaking it.

"Very well." He turned to Emily before continuing, "Be safe. It's dangerous out there."

Emily shuffled before turning and walking straight to the passage, her exit out of the dated apartment.

"Excuse me, excuse me."

Emily ignored their contact and kept moving towards her exit. It was now two steps away.

"If I were you, I wouldn't be going out that door."

Her hand on the door handle, she turned around. "And why not?"

"You don't know who could be waiting out there. You do want to get out of this country... alive, don't you?"

Emily took a deep breath and with a raised eyebrow, she replied, "Is this is the only door out of here?"

"Yes, it's the only door, but I do have a small courtyard garden you can get through."

"Where does it lead to?" Schultz asked.

"Straight out onto a main street."

"That's not going to work, not when we're carrying all this. What are the chances there are men out there in the passage or in your courtyard waiting for us?"

"This will work," their contact advised as he walked out of view.

Unimpressed, Emily crossed her arms and walked back into the living room, where she watched him open two doors on the wall unit. Behind it were four screens with four smaller windows on each screen. Stepping closer, Emily and Schultz took a closer look. Each frame showed video surveillance of different areas from the apartment's front door, the passage and the common area outside the apartment building.

"What was that?" Schultz pointed to the lower right screen.

"Which one?" their contact asked.

"The far right, second one from the bottom."

Emily focused on the footage. It showed the driveway alongside the apartment building. The footage played back until Schultz pointed to the screen. "Right there."

The video replay started.

"Right there." Schultz pointed at the screen again.

The video footage paused and a blurred face stared back at them.

"Can you slow down the frame replay?"

"Huh?"

"When playing the footage, can you slow down the playback speed?" Emily asked.

Their contact's eyes lit up. "Ah, yes. Of course I can." He looked over his shoulder at Emily. "Why didn't you just say that?"

She ignored his backhanded comment and concentrated on the paused video footage.

Turning around, their contact played the footage, this time a couple of frames per second.

"Pause right there," Emily snapped.

"What do you see?" Schultz leant in closer.

"No time to explain. We need to get out of here. Now." Emily pulled her weapons over her shoulder.

"This way." Their contact waved over his shoulder.

Emily and Schultz followed the old man as he scurried through the adjoining dining room to the rear of the apartment. Windows were positioned on either side of the steel door.

"In the right-hand corner there's a small gap between the hedges." Their contact glanced between her and Schultz. "When you're on the other side, turn right and head down that street. I'm sure you kids will be able to find your way from there."

"We'll be able to protect ourselves now that we've got these." Schultz tapped his submachine gun, "and an exit point. Thank you."

The man opened the steel door and unlocked the security door. Schultz stepped through and walked directly to the corner of the small yard. Emily stepped towards the door but stopped suddenly and looked down at her hand. He'd cupped his hand in hers, the tattoo on his hand exposed again. Her heat skipped a beat. She tried to pull away but he held her hand tighter and leant in.

"Be careful out there. You don't know what's hiding in the shadows."

Emily pulled her arm back but his grip tightened. His sunken eyes stared at her for what felt like ages. Emily tried once more to pull free.

"Come on," Schultz hissed.

The man let go. Without looking back, Emily walked straight to Schultz. Behind her, she heard the door being shut. With one foot in the hedge, she took one quick glance towards the apartment.

A foot back from the window, their contact was on his phone. Emily pulled out her phone and snapped a couple of photos of him. His focused look turned to shock when he spotted Emily looking back at him, her camera still pointed at him.

Chapter 39

The echo of the rear personal access door being slammed shut caused Ivan to turn around. Brian was already halfway between the door and his workstation, his fist and jaw clenched. He walked straight to his computer and threw the tablet down on his workstation. Ivan looked over at Brian's workstation and saw a red rectangle flashing in the middle of his main computer screen. He slowly approached, as Brian began tapping on his keyboard. Windows were appearing and disappearing as his fingers flew over the keyboard, then Brian stopped, his head moving left to right.

Ivan leaned over Brian's shoulder, looking at the computer screen not understanding what he was seeing. He asked, "Is there a problem?"

"There's been another breach to your servers."

"What do you mean, another?"

"It's, uh..."

"Spit it out. We don't have all night."

Ivan snatched the tablet off the desk. In bright red, the word 'BREACH' blinked before him. He clenched his fists and bit the inside of his cheek.

"The hacker has just been in the system again."

"What did they access? Did they take anything?"

"He, I mean they... were sloppy this time. They only accessed your financial records."

Ivan leaned on the desk and looked between the tablet and the computer screen. He couldn't comprehend the different windows that Brian was flicking between.

Taking a deep breath, he looked over his shoulder. His men were quietly packing the contents of the room. It was beginning to look bare. The ceiling-to-floor posters that reminded them of their cause were now packed away. His men were bringing crates in to pack all the guns and ammunition.

Ivan returned to their conversation. "They? There's more than one?"

"I can't tell from here."

"But you have an idea of who hacked into my system?"

Brian's eyes were on the screens when he replied. "It could be anyone from anywhere in the world, especially when they start bouncing their location between continents."

"What aren't you telling me?"

Brian held his hand out for the tablet.

As Ivan handed it back, he asked, "Who was snooping in my system?"

"He's an old partner."

"Is he smarter than you?"

"We're on par with each other."

"So, he is smarter than you. He got into a system you protected."

"He's not necessarily smart, but he's definitely cunning."

"Bit of bad blood there?"

"You could say that."

"How bad?"

"It happened in the past, and it stays there."

"Is he going to cause a problem for the cause?"

"All I know is if he's digging around, it's because he'll be looking for something in particular. And he'll be doing it for someone else."

"Why are you so sure?"

"It was early on in our careers when the federal police caught us. I almost landed in jail, but was able to pull a few favors and my charges disappeared overnight... and so did I. The last I heard from my partner was that he was given a choice to either join the federal police or be sent straight to jail."

"And you believe he's still working for the police department? Which country?"

"I do believe so. I haven't seen him hanging out in the usual cyber spots. Last I knew, he was in Australia."

Ivan swore. Australians again! "And you're certain the one

in my system was your ex-partner in crime?"

"I'm certain. Part of his deal was that the only place he was freely permitted to do any hacking—I mean, intel searching—was while he was at work. If I was a betting man, I'd say the feds are behind it."

"Interesting. Does he have a name?"

"His name doesn't matter. I'll put further security up."

"I'll determine what's necessary and what's not. What is the name of this hacker?"

"He goes by the name..." Brian lowered his head and muttered, "...X."

"X? Is that it? Never mind. I need you to keep your focus on the cause. We're at the crucial point now, the final twenty-four years. Nothing is to interfere with our plan, including your past. Understood?"

Brian lowered his head and nodded before turning away. Ivan watched as Brian returned to his workstation, and when he saw him back at the computer, which he was readying for relocation, he pulled out his phone and made a call.

The call was answered on the second ring. "I need you to contain a situation over there. At any cost. We're close to victory. We cannot allow anything or anyone derail us. Understood?"

"Mmmhmm," the reply came from the other end.

"Good. The details are on their way."

Chapter 40

Schultz was walking a few steps ahead of Lee, glancing between his phone and his surroundings. As they rounded the corner from their contact's apartment, Lee spoke.

"We need to ditch all of these. The guns. Backpack. Everything. That agent wasn't who he said he was."

"What do you mean?" Frustrated, hungry and tired, Schultz turned around to see she'd stopped a few steps back.

"That person in there wasn't our contact. He was one of *them*. You saw the tattoo on his hand."

"Maybe he was, maybe he wasn't."

"Okay. Why did you have to introduce us? And that last image we saw on the video surveillance... Did he look familiar to you? No? The scar under the eye?"

Schultz shook his head.

"He was one of the shooters from the Melbourne attack."

"You're positive it's one of Fu's men? All of his men went into hiding after the Melbourne attack and they haven't been seen since."

"Brian's made an appearance. That means Fu's other men could be emerging."

"We're still at least half an hour's jogging pace away from the docks." He showed her his phone screen. "We need to keep moving and stay focused." He grabbed her arm.

"Okay, okay. You're hurting my arm. Let go."

"Only if you promise to keep moving. You want to get out of here alive, don't you?"

Lee didn't reply. Instead, she pulled out her cell.

"What are you doing now?" Schultz asked as they approached an intersection.

The street was deserted. Crossing the road, he glanced over at Lee. She was still tapping on her phone.

"Just sent Xander a message."

"How do you have his number?"

"How do you think I got off that island?"

"You don't take no for an answer, do you?"

Lee froze in the middle of the street. She held her hand up. Schultz stopped and drew his gun. Lee slowly pulled one of her guns around. Poised, she scanned the area.

A twig snapped behind them. They dropped to a crouch. Shots sounded behind them. Blindly shooting in the direction of the gunfire, Schultz and Lee ran to cover behind a corner building.

"What a place to get caught. There's no cover at all, just sheer walls of apartment blocks."

In the distance, Schultz heard hinges creaking and people in the neighboring apartments yelling out in Russian at whoever was causing the disturbance.

"Yeah, we didn't instigate this," Schultz muttered as he stepped around the corner and let out a few more rounds of gun fire before stepping behind the protection of the building once again.

"How many?" Lee asked as she checked her gun over.

"At least three. Two across the street in the parkland and one around the corner, down half a block."

Schultz looked around their exposed area. Apartment buildings lined the streets. The footpaths were empty. Looking back the way they'd arrived, he noticed a street off to the side with trees in the center. Street lights dotted one side of the roads and down center of the parkland.

"I'll keep them distracted. You make your way over there." He nodded to the tree-lined intersection. "Take cover in there. I'll be right behind you."

"No, you go. They're after me."

"When I step out, you make a run for it. Right?"

"I don't have a good feeling about any of this."

"You'll cover me when I follow you."

Lee leant in and whispered in his ear, "Be safe."

He felt her lips brush against his ear, and a shiver ran down his back. He turned around to face her but she was already moving towards their new location.

A shot narrowly missing him brought him back to reality. Turning back towards the shooters, he opened fire. In the moonlight, he saw one of the shooters fall to the ground.

Lining up the second shooter a little farther down the street, he hit his mark. He moved his gun around until he located the third target and returned fire.

Lee's phone rang. She answered it straight away and the call on her phone's speakers. "X, what have you got?"

"I got the photos, thank you. Did he give you any weapons?" Xander asked.

"Yeah, he did. We've already had to use them."

"Use them?"

"Yeah, three down. Why, what's wrong?"

"That agent isn't one of ours."

"Shit. He's one of them, isn't he?"

"Possibly. I'm still running his face through our systems. It may take a little while to pick anything up."

"He had a tattoo that looked like the one Nicholas had on his wrist."

"Right... you need to ditch those weapons."

Schultz snatched the phone off Lee. "X, it's Schultz. We need a new location, and now."

"Working on it right now." Schultz heard him tapping away.

"We're too exposed out here, and did I tell you it's fricken' freezing?"

"Right. Details are on the way, including a current photo

of your contact. You need to search out Barry's workshop. He's a close friend of mine, and he'll look after you and give you whatever you need. If he doesn't have what you're after, no one in Saint Petersburg will."

"X."

"Yeah?"

"If I don't get a chance later... thank you."

"No, it's talk soon. Be safe out there."

Chapter 41

Arriving at the co-ordinates Xander had sent her, Emily looked around. She wrinkled her nose.

"This can't be the location of the workshop, can it? It's some sort of old deserted warehouse."

Schultz checked his phone. "Apparently so. It should be on the left side of the complex. Barry was going to leave a light on."

Emily froze. Ahead of her, two multi-level beige-bricked buildings guarded a narrow driveway. A gangway between the two buildings was positioned above the driveway entrance, with enough room beneath for a small truck to fit through. Trees and shrubs shrouded the driveway.

Stepping underneath the gangway Emily looked around.

The complex was dark except for a lone yellow light to her left that dangled above a steel door.

She quickly ran up to Schultz as he knocked on the steel door, the knock echoing through the stillness of the chilly night. The brick wall didn't lend itself to a workshop but she wasn't going to stand out there in the dark, alone. To the right of the door she saw a sign that read *Barry's Workshop*.

Emily heard metal being pulled along metal and chains rattling, then the old hinges creaked. A woman with hot purple hair poked her head through the gap. "Yeah." She looked between them both and her eyes settled on Schultz.

"Sorry, we must have the wrong place." Emily turned around.

"Lee? Schultz?"

"You're not Barry," Schultz replied.

"Barry's my father."

Emily turned around, her arms crossed. "Is he around?"

"Yeah, asleep upstairs. Come inside. You must be freezing." She opened the door enough for them to slide through.

Emily took a step back. "Schultz, we need to get out of here."

The woman raised an eyebrow and waved Emily in. "Quick. Inside before someone sees you. You two have now made it to Russia's most wanted list. I've heard there's a big cash incentive if you're delivered. Dead or alive."

Emily felt her stomach twist and turn. The rules of the game had just changed. They were now playing for their lives.

Her phone vibrated with a message from Xander. Tapping

on the notification, she saw an image pop up. It was of the woman standing in front of her. Another message came through.

She's Barry's daughter, Lydia. It's okay, go inside.

Emily shook her head as she tucked her phone into her coat pocket and entered the workshop.

"I check out, I take it?" Lydia asked as she locked the door behind Emily.

"Sorry. It's just been one of those nights," Emily replied as she pulled her coat off.

Emily looked around and didn't see anything that resembled a workshop. Instead there was a fireplace halfway along the wall to her right. Positioned a couple of meters back from the fireplace were three lounge chairs that formed a u-shape around a coffee table. On either end of the coffee table were piles of magazines. Opposite her was a door she suspected must lead to the actual workshop area. On the left side of the room she saw a bench with a waist-height ledge.

"Don't say any more. Warm up over there near the fire. Do you guys want a warm cuppa?"

"Coffee would be great," Schultz piped up, having already positioned himself on the lounge chair in front of the fireplace.

"You American?" Emily asked as she stood in front of the fire.

She glanced down at the roughly stacked pile of magazines to her left. The cover on the top was a performance car magazine, written in English. Halfway down, she spotted a piece of paper jutting out. A golden hammer and sickle were printed in the top corner.

What is the soviet symbol doing in this workshop? In a place Xander assured us was safe, she thought.

Emily bit her lip as she looked at Lydia then back to the pile then back at Lydia. She was behind the bench, her back to them, pouring the cups of coffee. Realizing she didn't have much time; Emily quickly pulled her phone out of her coat pocket and snapped a photo.

"What is it?" Schultz whispered.

"Later," she whispered back, sliding her phone into her coat pocket.

"Yes. I've been over here since my father became ill. My mother is American," Lydia replied as she turned around, a cup in each hand.

"Your father, Barry—that isn't a typical Russian name."

"His parents were American. They came here for work. My father was born and spent his childhood and teens here in Saint Petersburg before returning to America as a young adult."

"He got homesick, did he?"

"After my parents divorced, he had nothing keeping him in America, so he returned here to be amongst his friends. Anyhow, I don't want to bore you with our personal life. How long have you two been together?"

Emily blushed and saw Schultz stumbling over his words. She quickly laughed it off. "No, no." She shook her head. "We're not dating. We work together on the occasional assignment, that's it."

Lydia raised her eyebrow again as she handed a warm cup to Emily. "Ah-ha."

"Thanks." Emily smiled and took a couple of sips. She closed her eyes and let the warmth travel through her body.

"What brings you to Russia?" Lydia asked.

"Work," Schultz replied as he accepted the cup from Lydia.

"Here in Saint Petersburg?" Lydia plonked herself on one of the lounge chairs surrounding the fireplace.

Schultz nodded as he sipped on his coffee. Emily stood in front of the fire, studying Lydia, trying to find anything doubtful about her, but the girl was coming across sincere and genuine.

"I just got off the phone to Xander a few minutes before you guys arrived. He's filled me in on a few things. Once you've warmed up, I'll show you out the back. I think you'll love what we've got lined up for you. They have X's seal of approval."

Schultz chuckled, shaking his head. "Good ol' Xander."

"I'll leave you two to warm up. I'll be just out the back. Come out when you're ready."

Emily nodded and watched Lydia as she exited through a door at the back of the room. After the door closed, she sat down next to Schultz and lent back until her head was resting on the back of the lounge chair.

"Don't get too comfortable. We've still got a long night ahead of us."

"Night's are for recharging the batteries."

"True. But we've got a fight on our hands."

"What do you mean?"

"I got attacked at the nightclub by some of Ivan's VIP guests."

"Serious?" Emily sat up straight and turned to face Schultz. Schultz's phone echoed through the room.

"X, have you got an update for us?" Schultz asked as he answered his phone.

He put the call on his phone's speakers. Emily could hear Xander typing.

"Right." The tapping stopped. "The IP address you sent through to me earlier today. I've finally finished going through the information on the server."

"Anything interesting?" Emily asked.

"Hi Lee. Yes, I did. Ivan has some big plans in the pipeline for tomorrow night. It could have its origins going back a lot earlier but the information I have here only goes back five years. Anyway, in that time he's been collecting funds mainly from his employer, but also from smaller companies throughout western Russia."

"Where was the money deposited?" Emily asked.

"In a personal off-shore account."

"How much are we talking?" Schultz asked.

"We're talking millions. Multiple, millions."

"That explains how he can afford his lifestyle."

"He's been spending up, and in a big way."

"On what?" Emily asked.

"An army."

"A what?" Schultz interrupted.

"After doing a little more digging, I've located details of their plans. Lee."

"Yeah."

"Do you know Brian is over there?"

"Yeah, I do. I saw him earlier with Nicholas."

"Well, he's helping Ivan with a takeover."

"What sort of takeover are we talking about?" Emily asked.

"A political revolution."

Emily forced a chuckle. "What, you mean they're planning on overturning the Kremlin? Kick the president out? That's a brazen move."

"Midnight tomorrow night is when they're planning on taking possession of... of..." His voice shaky, he whispered, "...of the Russian Gov—"

Emily's heart skipped a beat. She leant in closer to the phone and yelled out, "X? You there, X?"

There was silence. She looked at Schultz. Her eyes widened, her bottom lip trembling.

"How did you—?" they heard Xander yell out.

"X, you okay?" Emily asked.

Emily clasped her hand over her mouth as she heard a commotion on Xander's end, what she assumed was a chair being thrown against a computer. Then a single gunshot echoed through the room. Emily collapsed into her chair, a tear rolling down her cheek.

"Back away now," a deep male's voice came through on Xander's end. Emily couldn't place it. It may have had an East

European, perhaps maybe even a Russian accent. She wasn't sure. The caller repeated his warning. "Back away before it's too late, or you'll face the same fate as your friend."

Another gunshot sounded before the call was disconnected.

Schultz shook his head and stood up. "They're going to pay." He stormed off, thumping the back door open as he walked through.

Emily sat back staring at Schultz's phone, X's name at the top of the recent calls list.

Chapter 42

All Emily wanted to do was to crawl into a ball in the corner of the room and hide from the world. Finally conjuring the energy to leave the comfort of the fireplace, stunned, Emily pushed open the back door. In front of her a room spanned for as far as she could see. Polished concrete and an assortment of vehicles, from small four-cylinders through to SUVs and army vehicles, were lined up on either side of the room.

Approaching, she saw Lydia pull away from Schultz, wiping her tears. Emily and Lydia both exchanged grim smiles. Lydia's eyes were red and swollen.

"What is this place?" Emily asked, looking around.

"My playground," Lydia said, sounding a little more upbeat. "You like?"

"That's an understatement. It's insane. You've got everything in here." Emily walked over to a nearby work bay fully equipped with a full workshop, including drive-over hoists in the center, toolboxes along the wall, and various chromed parts lining the wall above the toolboxes. "Enough to keep your clients happy."

"Right." Wiping her eyes, Lydia forced a chuckle. "Now, for you, guys. Up the far end."

Following behind, Emily took in the workshop. All the bays were set up identically.

"What's over there?" She pointed to wall opposite them where a section was caged off, with boxes stacked behind wire mesh.

Lydia waved it off and kept walking. "That? That's nothing. Just stock."

About halfway down, a couple of the bays were filled with heavily tinted imported Japanese cars, all with their number plates removed.

"When these are done, these bad boys will be heading to the street races." Lydia tapped the hood of one of the imports. "They're getting kitted out with top of the line nitrous oxide systems and a couple of other little tricks. You know..." She looked at Emily with a dead-straight face before continuing. "If I ever tell you what we're doing I'd have to kill you."

Emily didn't know how to take it until she saw Lydia with the biggest grin.

"Loosen up, girl. We're not all bad."

Waving it off, Emily joined Schultz at the next bay. Lydia

began lowering a black SUV from the hoist. It's badges were removed.

"Now this, boys and girls, will be your mode of transport for tonight."

Emily walked around one side of it, inspecting it as she went around. Apart from the wider tires she couldn't see anything different about it. It appeared to be a standard SUV.

"You don't like?" A little Russian accent poked through Lydia's question. "This isn't any ordinary SUV. Wait till you see what she's hiding." Opening the door, she said, "Hop in."

Lydia gestured for Emily to hop in the passenger's front seat and Emily obeyed. Her eyes widened as she leant onto the center console. Switches and dials lined the entire dash.

"Where's the radio?" Emily asked.

"You'll be too busy kicking ass to worry about music. In there, you do have a hand-held radio and a scanner."

"You didn't just have this lying around. Who was this built for?" Schultz asked.

"We've been liaising with the Americans on a prototype for a tactical response vehicle for them."

Emily had more questions than answers but right now there wasn't time for that, nor did any of it have anything to do with her, besides being nosey.

Lydia opened the glove box and pulled out a laminated sheet. "Here's a detailed diagram." She held it in front of Emily. "This will tell you what all the switches and dials are for. Most of them you won't need tonight. That switch above the radio, that's for the rocket launcher. It'll get a little chilly if you have to use that one."

Emily followed Lydia's eyes up to the sun roof and nodded.

"The switch alongside the rocket launcher switch, that's for the two side rockets. Above those switches is this button." She lightly tapped a green button above the two rocket-launch switches. "That one is for a sub-machine gun rigged up to the front of this baby." Lydia tapped the side of the truck.

"Well, there's a little bit of gunfire packed into this vehicle. But none of that'll be any good if they can hear us coming from a mile away."

"That's one of the hidden gems with this girl. She's silent. Zip. No one will hear you guys approach, nor will they pick you up if they have heat seekers running. If you must, you can take it off-road. You won't be limited with this one."

"Impressive," Emily said as she looked between the diagram and the controls. "Windows—are they bullet-proof? Armor protection?"

"Top of the range. You two will be safe in here. They'll have nothing on this one."

"Anything else we need to know?" Schultz asked.

"Do you know who you're going after?"

"Yeah. Fancy pants Ivan Kuzmich."

Lydia's face dropped, but her off expression quickly disappeared. "You do know who Ivan is, don't you?"

Emily and Schultz both shook their heads.

"It was a huge conspiracy at the time... it must be going on fourteen years now." Lydia paused for a moment, deep in thought. "It was all over the papers. Ivan was the favorite to win the presidential election. Three days prior to the closure of the candidate registration, his signature was replaced with someone else's."

"Is that even legal?" Emily asked.

"The outgoing president didn't address it, no one outside the party noticed, and the election continued to run with another candidate taking Ivan's spot running for president."

"Who took his spot?" Schultz asked.

"It was Ivan's close business colleague, the current president."

"So now Ivan's out for blood?"

"One would think so. Every year on the eve of the election date Ivan has a big press release and hoo-ha reminding the public he should be the one residing in the Kremlin."

"Right... So, what's so significant about tomorrow's date?"

"It's an anniversary marking the day his shot at presidency was taken from him, the day his candidacy was replaced."

"Great."

Emily turned to Schultz. "This only makes him more dangerous and unpredictable."

"You're right, Lydia. You wouldn't happen to have any personal protection in here? You know, in case we get split from our vehicle?"

"Check the back seat."

Emily peered around and saw a couple of bulletproof vests and an array of hand guns.

"Thanks. We'd better start making tracks."

"I'll contact the Kremlin, give them a heads-up. Get extra

reinforcements in place," Lydia said.

"No, don't." Emily held Lydia's hand.

Lydia pulled her hand away. "You're not meant to be here, are you?"

Emily glanced at Schultz, who nodded.

"We're not officially working."

"So the Kremlin does not know there's two foreign federal agents working on his soil?"

"One," Emily corrected her. "We were employees of a local company, helping them with their financial records, when we were both dragged into this."

Lydia studied them both, her arms crossed over her chest.

"What do you propose you're going to do? If I know Ivan, like I'm pretty sure I do, he'll have an army at the ready, all over western Russia."

"We'll do our best to stop them before they've even left the city perimeter, and with any luck the president won't know what went down. Ivan will fade into the night and the city will be back to normal come sunrise."

"I love your confidence, but it might not be enough."

"I've dismantled more than these wannabes in the past."

"You've got some stories to tell me once this is all over, then." Schultz sat back in his seat, taken aback.

"That makes two of us," Lydia piped in. "I don't feel comfortable about any of this but you two had better get moving. If you need anything, my number is in the glove box."

Emily wound the window down as Lydia shut her door.

"Actually, there is one thing." Emily thought. "Can you

rustle up any more men and truck power like this girl?" Emily tapped the door.

"I'll see what I can do. What did you have in mind?"

"If you can, get them to barricade the highways on the city outskirts. If Ivan has an army, the convoy will stand out."

"Be safe." Lydia tapped the door.

Schultz fired their new mode of transport up and slowly drove it out of the garage and into the desolate rear yard. Bouncing through puddles, they maneuvered through the tight entrance and back onto the street.

"What's our plan of attack?" Emily asked.

"We're going back to work."

"Why?"

Schultz pulled something from underneath his jacket and waved it in the air. Grabbing it from him, she studied the swipe card.

"What's this card—" Emily turned the card over and her mouth dropped open. Looking back at her was an image printed in the center in gold ink—a hammer and sickle.

"That card," Schultz took it back from her and slid it in his inside pocket, "is what will get us into the basement underneath our office."

Chapter 43

Ivan looked at his watch then around him. His men were still packing and loading crates onto the back of his trucks. Brian's computer system had left five minutes previously on its way to the port, to eventually disappear somewhere out in international waters.

"Come on, men. Twenty minutes before we need to roll," he yelled out.

The men continued at the same pace, in silence, and not one of them flinched at his orders.

Ivan clenched and loosened his fists. Closing his eyes, he took a deep breath. On opening his eyes, he felt a little more relaxed but the men were still going at their steady pace. Taking a position alongside them, he assisted with checking the contents of one of the many crates that still needed to be packed.

Around him, half of the basement floor was filled with rows of open crates. Each crate still needed to be inspected properly, ensuring the gun chambers operated properly, and magazines would load and unload effortlessly. All of the weapons needed to be in top working condition, otherwise they weren't going with them. Once each crate was at Ivan's high standard, it was repacked and loaded on the back of a truck.

Ivan had just secured his third crate when his cell's ringtone echoed through the emptying basement.

"Yes," he answered.

"It's been successful. X marked the spot."

Recognizing the voice, he said, "I thank you for your service tonight. You'll be rewarded shortly."

The caller disconnected the call. Tucking the phone back in his jacket pocket, he approached Brian.

"You still got access to the banking information on that handheld computer?"

Brian looked at him puzzled for a minute before following Ivan's eyesight to his hand. "Oh, the tablet. Yes, I do." He tapped the screen and handed it to Ivan.

"Your old colleague won't be a problem anymore."

Brian's mouth dropped open. Ivan walked towards the crates, punching in the bank transfer details. He didn't care about loss of life. Brian's old colleague was collateral in the revolution.

"What do you mean he won't be a problem anymore?" Brian asked as he approached Ivan.

"He was an obstruction to the revolution. It doesn't matter who you are. Anyone who's an obstacle will be erased. We have our mission. We're going to succeed at any cost."

"Any cost?"

"You deaf or something?"

"No." Brian lowered his head.

"Then stop repeating what I say and help load the trucks. We need to roll in less than fifteen minutes."

* * *

"How far away are we?" Schultz asked, glancing at Emily before returning his attention to the road.

Emily tapped on the onboard GPS screen. "Seventeen minutes."

Schultz accelerated, the light coating of snow on the road making their rear end drift out a little before he got their SUV back under control.

Emily hung onto her grip handle, her elbow banging against the window as they navigated the tight street corners.

"Can you see who that is?" He handed his cell to Emily. The caller identification was showing as a private number.

"Hello?" Emily answered.

"Lee?" a male voice answered.

"White?"

"Yes. Is Schultz there?"

Emily looked over at him. He shook his head. "He's just a little bit busy. Can I take a message?"

"I know he's there and I know you are both in Russia. Put me on loud speaker. Now."

Schultz shook his head. He ran his thumb in a straight line across his neck.

"Ah... You're breaking up. Sorry. Can't—"

"Lee, put the phone on loud speaker. Now."

"Hang it up." Schultz said and reached for his phone.

"Lee," she heard White yell into the phone.

Pulling the phone closer to the window, she blocked Schultz's arm with her shoulder and changed the phone's settings.

"White, you're on loud speaker."

"Schultz," White called out.

Schultz ignored him.

"I know you're there. Have you heard about Xander?"

Schultz kept his eyes on the road ahead. Emily didn't know where to look.

"He was killed tonight, but going by your silence you already knew that."

The silence was uncomfortable.

White continued. "What did you have him working on? I know it was nothing to do with any of his current cases."

"Schultz," Emily whispered, her voice pleading.

Schultz turned to her, his eyes red and watery. She nodded towards his phone.

"Yeah I know he's dead."

"Talk to me, please. What's going on? The boss is going batshit crazy." White lowered his voice. "X's computers have been smashed, the hard drives are all missing..."

"Not much going on." Schultz drifted around the next corner. "Just enjoying my holidays."

"In Russia? In winter? We both know you hate winters here, let alone there."

Schultz slammed the brakes on. Their SUV skidded and finally stopped a short distance away.

"What do you want me to tell you? I'm here enjoying my holidays, seeing the world while I have some time off."

"With Lee. And you're out and about in the middle of the night. I don't know what you've got yourself—"

Schultz grabbed the phone off Lee. "I'll call you back when I'm not tied up."

"I don't want to know what you two—"

"White, I've got to go." He disconnected the call.

"You're not blushing there, are you?"

Schultz pointed ahead. "White is the least of our problems."

"Great." Emily glanced over her shoulder. "We're trapped."

Schultz looked in both of his side mirrors.

"Which one of these switches..." Schultz moved his finger along the rows of switches and dials.

"What do you want it to do?"

"Blow some shit up."

Their cabin flooded with the onslaught of headlights extending from one side of the road to the other. A few seconds later, the blockade behind them turned their lights on, too.

"You got anything there? Sunglasses? Rocket launchers?"

"Still looking." Using her finger as a guide, she read the function of each switch.

"You'd better be quick. They're closing in on us."

Emily kept reading through the labels until her finger stopped on one. "Ooh, this sounds like a good one."

"Quick. Where is it?"

"This one here." She flicked the switch closest to her.

"What does that do?"

"Watch and learn."

The onboard navigation screen changed to a video stream of what was in front of them.

"That's a target on the screen." Schultz asked, his eyes fixed on the screen instead of the road.

"Things just got a little more exciting."

Emily grabbed the joystick positioned alongside the screen, the target on the screen following her movements.

Emily positioned the target off center and flicked the switch. The blast following her simple action was deafening.

Chapter 44

A gap in the blinding headlights emerged. Small flames were everywhere in the immediate blast zone. Looking above, Schultz saw the roof was lowering again. His ears hurt. He rubbed them but the ringing stayed.

Turning towards Lee, he saw her waving at the barricade, her mouth moving, but he couldn't hear what she was trying to say. Shrugging his shoulders, he looked out his side mirror and saw the back barricade closing in. In front of them, he saw the remaining men reforming, their guns pointing at them.

He felt Lee tug at his jacket. Turning, he said, "What?" But he couldn't hear his own voice. Using her finger, she scribbled something on the back of the dashboard layout card.

It took him a moment to realize what she was doing.

"G ... O?" Schultz hoped he was actually speaking.

Lee nodded and excitement was written all over her face.

She began etching the letters out on the card again, but Schultz didn't need reminding. She hadn't even finished the first letter when he moved the gear stick into first and launched their vehicle forwards, gaining momentum as they closed in on the front barricade.

Bullets bounced off their front windscreen and skimmed their vehicle. They were within two car lengths from the barricade when they came under fire from the rear, too. Gripping the steering wheel until his hands turned white, Schultz closed his eyes as he drove through the gap where one of the barricade vehicles had been parked just moments before.

Coming out the other side, Schultz opened one eye and saw they were clear. Opening the other eye, he looked in his side mirror. A single line of headlights followed him, the front vehicle passengers shooting at them.

"What else can this car do?" Schultz asked as he shifted up the gears.

"What did you have in mind?" he heard Lee's voice as if she was talking underwater. His hearing was coming back. If he'd been piloting a plane rather than this road-bound vehicle he'd have done a loop-de-loop.

"Anything to get them off our back," he said, enjoying the sound of his own voice.

She read through her chart, muttering, "You've got your

hearing back."

"Still a little ringing, but yeah, I can hear a bit better."

"Awesome..."

"What's awesome? My hearing returning?"

"No, this."

Lee stretched over to his side of the dashboard and pressed a green button.

"What does that do?"

At that moment, their SUV thrust forward. Schultz looked in his side mirror as a rocket careered into the convoy behind them.

"Nice."

"That should hold them for a few minutes."

"Let's hope so."

Schultz navigated the next two corners. The street behind them was still empty. Relaxing his clenched hands, he dropped his shoulders and flicked on the radio. All the stations seemed to be in Russian, so he flicked the radio off.

"How does it feel to be on the most wanted list?" Schultz asked Lee with a cheeky smile.

"Let's hope we get Ivan before anyone gets us."

Schultz chuckled as Lee squinted her eyes, trying to look frustrated but looking more tired than anything.

"You should have a power nap before we get to the office."

"I'll be all right." She raised her arms above her head and stretched her back.

"At least ten minutes?"

"That's not going to happen." Lee sat up. Staring straight

past him, her eyes widened.

Schultz looked out his window as he crossed an intersection. The adjoining street was filled with beams of white lights.

"They don't give up, do they?" Schultz put his foot down on the accelerator and their car's revs increased as it sped down the street.

"No, they don't. We're just under ten minutes away."

"We've made up a couple of minutes?"

"Yes, but we'll lose Ivan and his men if," she looked in her side mirror, "they hold us up."

Schultz navigated another turn just as the corner of a nearby building crumbled away. He swerved to avoid the debris but straightened their car fairly quickly and continued down the street.

"What was that?" he yelled.

"Let's hope this SUV is also rocket-proof. Quick, turn down that street."

Schultz looked to see where she was pointing.

"That one, quick." She pointed to an approaching street on his side.

He drifted the corner, sliding into the street.

"Re-calculating," their navigation system alerted them.

"I'd hope so," Schultz muttered.

"After this is all over, are you looking forward to returning to your federal job?"

"If I still have a job. Otherwise, I might have to join you on more assignments."

"I don't think so. You know I prefer to work alone."

Schultz chuckled; Lee had taken the bate as was expected. He glanced at his side mirror. Behind them, a black SUV had stopped in the middle of the street. "Hold on. Incoming."

"I've got a better idea."

She pressed the same green button as earlier. They were thrust forward again as another rocket was released.

"Schultz, put your foot down. We need to get out of here."

They were already traveling at a high speed. Schultz needed a plan B. Looking around, he spotted an intersection up ahead, but it was still half a block away.

Their SUV's rear end swung out as the impact of the explosion followed them down the street. He kept the accelerator pedal pushed against the floor.

"Did it hit?"

"Bit hard to tell with all the dust. When you turn the corner turn your headlights off and don't use your brakes."

"Driving blind?"

"There's street lights ahead and it's a dead-straight road."

"Seriously, I'm going to need a beer or two after this is all over."

"When we get through tonight."

Schultz grumbled as he turned into the next street. They were now back on track to their office. He flicked the headlights off.

"What got you into this business?" Schultz asked as he drove.

"That's a bit of a personal question."

"Well, if I'm putting my life on the line, I need to know about this side of you I didn't know existed."

"Fair enough. You can have the short version. I was fresh out of college when I was approached by two men who should've been retired with a lucrative offer. Young and naive, I took the job. And here I am, years later, with never a dull moment."

"Any regrets?"

"None. Some of the assignments end up like this, but honestly, most haven't."

"Fair enough."

"So, if I'm going to put my life on the line, why did you take this assignment?" Lee asked him.

"Don't you turn my words against me. I wasn't given an opportunity. You saw the message."

"Yes, and you didn't have to accept."

"That wasn't the only message I received from that number."

"What do you mean?"

"Did they threaten your family when you first started working for whoever hands out these assignments?"

"No. Did they threaten you?"

"Threaten might be too strong a word... more like blackmailed."

"What dirt do they have on you?" Lee turned around, her interest piqued.

Shaking his head, Schultz looked straight ahead. "Nothing."

"Come on, spill the beans. What do they have on you?"

"I don't know," he shrugged.

Looking out of the corner of his eye, he noticed she was trying to read him. Shifting in his seat, he rubbed the back of his neck.

"There's something there."

Lee grabbed his cell.

"Give it back." He reached over to get it but she moved the phone just out of reach, his arm brushing against her chest. They swerved.

"Watch out," Lee screamed, pushing his hand away.

Schultz sat up and straightened their car. Back on course, he held his hand out and clicked his fingers. "Please."

"Yeah. Nah. I'm busy."

"Busy, my ass."

Glancing between the road and Lee, Schultz felt more and more uncomfortable as she sat there with a smug look on her face, scrolling through what he assumed were his text messages. Suddenly her face dropped. She closed the phone and returned it to him.

"I see your predicament." She looked out her window.

"You now understand I didn't have a choice."

"Yes. There's got to be a reason why they were so hell-bent on getting you in on this case."

"I wouldn't worry about it. Fingers crossed, this time next week I'll cut my long-service leave short and return to my normal job."

"If there's still one there for you. Remember Xander. Not

to mention the small detail of working a case over here that isn't even in your jurisdiction."

"Thanks. Kill the only ray of optimism I had in this whole situation."

"Just saying it as it is."

Chapter 45

Ivan hauled the next crate into the back of one of his tarp-covered trucks. Stretching his back, he looked at his watch and shook his head.

"Hurry up," he yelled out as loud as his tiring throat allowed it. "We need to get moving in the next five minutes, otherwise the sun will be up before we even reach Moscow and all of this will have been for nothing."

"For nothing?" one of the men nearby asked. "You've busted your gut. Everything is planned down to the last details, except for the extra truckload of gunfire we're loading right now."

"Keep moving," Ivan instructed.

"You heard him. Double time. Now," the man yelled out

at the militias loading the truck.

All the men picked up their pace. Ivan nodded, impressed with one of his militias taking command.

Pulling him aside, he asked, "What's your name?"

"Tony."

"That's not very Russian. That doesn't matter. You'll accompany me in my vehicle. We have some issues to discuss."

"Have I done something wrong?"

"Quite the opposite. Keep the men working. We should've been rolling out of here ten minutes ago."

"Yes, sir." Tony saluted Ivan before turning his attention to the remaining militias and firing orders at them like an experienced officer.

Chapter 46

Locking the office building's front door behind her, Emily followed Schultz as he walked towards their office elevator, their footsteps echoing on the tiled floor.

"Where are we going?" Emily asked while keeping a few steps behind him.

Schultz walked past the elevator and Emily watched him pull the card he'd shown her earlier out of his inside coat pocket. An electronic beep sounded a moment later, and Schultz pushed the door open.

"You coming?" Schultz held the door open, waving her in.

"I'll entertain this for just a minute, then we need to find this so-called basement."

She walked past him, frowning at his Cheshire cat grin.

Brooms, mops and mop buckets greeted her. She turned to leave but Schultz stood in her way. He swirled his finger, indicating for her to turn back around, while flicking a switch with his other hand. The cleaners' closest was illuminated. Emily tried to move through the small gap between him and the doorway, but Schultz grabbed her shoulders and turned her around.

"What on earth is going on?"

"Look."

In front of her, beyond the mops and brooms, was a staircase. Emily checked it for any signs of spiderwebs, creepy crawlies, anything to give her an excuse to get out of there, but the staircase was immaculate. Like it was regularly used.

"These stairs don't exist on any of the building plans."

"Neither does the basement. We need to keep moving. We don't want them getting away." Schultz pushed her gently towards the stairs.

Hesitating at each step, they reached the bottom of the stairs and were greeted by another door with a few devices attached to the wall alongside it. Schultz leaned around Emily and swiped the card.

Nothing.

"What are you trying to do?" Emily looked between the door and Schultz.

"Franco said this card would get us into the basement."

"He's pulled a fast one on you. Unless you have a pin, fingerprint and eyeball that belongs to Ivan or one of his right hand men, we're screwed."

"Damn. This card was meant to get us in here."

"That card must be for another door. This door isn't going to budge without the added security that's been installed here."

"Shit."

"If you're certain Ivan has been running his operation from in there, we need to find another way in."

"Unless these devices have a failsafe." Schultz felt around the devices. "Shit, nothing."

"Right. We need to head around the back and see if there's another way in."

They took the stairs up, three and four at a time. Stepping into the foyer, they raced for the front door.

Emily fumbled with the keys and finally got the key turning in the lock. The door was barely unlocked before Schultz pushed them open and ran outside. Pulling the key out, she followed Schultz towards the rear of the building.

She'd caught up with him by the time they reached the corner. A street with just enough room to fit two cars alongside each other greeted them. Sparsely spread street lights lit the street. The first light was positioned halfway down the width of their office building.

Emily stopped and held her hand up.

"What is it?" Schultz whispered.

"Personal access door." Emily pointed at the rear of their office building. "Roller door alongside it. Lights are still on inside."

"They could still be in there."

They pulled out their handguns, and Emily stepped forward, her gun pointed at the roller door until she was alongside it. She crouched beside the door, which was rolled up a short distance, to just below her knees.

More than enough room to fit underneath, Emily thought.

She quickly glanced up the street, then over her shoulder. They were still alone. Emily turned back to the roller door.

"You ready?" Emily whispered.

"I've got your back," Schultz replied.

Emily placed both hands in front of her and extended her legs out behind. She lowered herself onto her stomach. Her gun pointing inside, she looked around. A large open area greeted them. Nothing. The room was empty.

"All clear. They're gone," Lee called out to Schultz.

Emily proceeded to crawl through the opening. Once inside, she stood up and tucked her gun away.

"They were here. I can still smell the diesel fumes," Schultz advised as he stood up.

"Same. Franco must've alerted Ivan."

"Not sure. When I left, he wasn't able to say too much."

"They weren't planning the takeover until tomorrow night. Why have they left now?" Emily asked herself as she walked around the vast room.

Studying the walls, she saw thumb tack holes and bits of sellotape partly adhered to the wall. By the corner, the wall cladding had been replaced with rows of screens.

"I think this area was the main hub," Emily yelled.

"Okay," Schultz yelled back. "I've got nothing over on this

side."

Emily turned to the adjoining wall, where an office chair was still underneath a table. Faint dust outlines where monitor stands once stood were the only hard evidence that someone had been in there recently. Leaning against the table, Emily looked around the basement. It was now an empty shell.

Pulling her phone out, Emily snapped a few photos of the basement, including the screens and the remaining office furniture.

"Why the photos?" Schultz asked, walking over to her.

"You got that swipe card?" She held her hand out for it.

He handed it over, and Emily snapped a photo of it too before handing it back.

"There's nothing here. We need to get moving." He tucked the card inside his jacket.

"In a moment. I just need to get these off to our case manager. This might explain, in part, the businesses high expenses."

"And it may not. Come on, we need to get out of here."

Emily felt deflated, a failure. This was the first assignment she wouldn't be able to complete. She looked around one last time then stopped in her tracks.

"Lee, we need to go," Schultz yelled from the roller door.

"Just a moment."

"Lee." His voice was irritated.

She ignored him and approached the table.

"There's nothing there," Schultz called out, but his

footsteps told her he was coming back in.

"Maybe not," she replied.

Squatting down, she balanced on the balls of her feet and reached under the table. She slid a piece of paper along the floor towards her.

"What you got there?" Schultz asked as he squatted beside her.

Emily jumped, almost losing her balance.

"Geez." She placed her hand over her pounding heart.

He grabbed the piece of paper from her. Unfolding it, he turned it over then back. "Hope your Russian is up to scratch." He handed it back to her.

Pulling up one of the office chairs, she placed the piece of paper on the table where they could both see it properly and took a photo of the page.

"Isn't that Stalin?" Schultz pointed to an illustration on the bottom half of the paper.

Emily studied it. A kind-looking but serious man in the center of the illustration was staring into the distance where rows of young women and children carried flowers and wide smiles. Behind him, groups of men were bearing guns and soviet flags, while old war planes flew overhead.

"Yes, I believe so." She sat back. "You don't think Ivan sees himself being like Stalin?"

"Who knows what he's thinking? Besides being nuts for trying to take on the Kremlin, whether it's rightfully his or not. What else does it say?"

"I'll need someone to help interpret this, but by what I can work out..." She ran her finger along the page. "This flyer is calling men to arms for a revolution."

"The one Ivan is planning?"

"I'd assume so, looking at the date and time. Midnight." She looked at the date on her phone. "Tomorrow night. Well, tonight, seeing as it's after midnight. Then, over the page," she flicked the flyer over, "is a map."

Schultz asked, "Do you think they're the designated routes to Moscow?"

"They appear to be." Emily snapped a photo of the back of the page. "I'll need someone to translate this for us, just so we can be certain. We can get X—"

"He can't help us anymore. And we don't have anyone—"

"Lydia." Emily jumped up, barely containing her excitement.

Schultz rubbed his ear.

"We could get her to help. She's out there positioning some assistance along the exits. This could help her strategize them properly while we approach from the rear."

"We barely know her. You trust her that much?"

"She's a contact from Xander. That must mean something. Doesn't it?"

"Okay, you got me there. They can't be that far ahead of us. Give her a call, but first we need to get moving. We don't know if the men who've been chasing us are Ivan's militias or someone else. What I do know is that it won't take them long to find us."

"Right." Emily looked around the room one last time

before rolling under the roller door.

Out in the street, she sent the photos of the flyer to Lydia's phone. As she caught up to Schultz, she called Lydia, putting the call on her phone's speakers.

Lydia answered on the second ring. "Hello?"

"Lydia, it's Emily. You should've received a couple of photos of a flyer we found."

"Something's just arrived. Hang on a minute while I check."

"Let's... keep moving," Schultz said as they rounded the corner.

His face was flustered and he was breathing heavily.

"Bit out of shape, are we?"

In between breaths, he managed to get out, "Look who's talking." He winked at her.

"I'm a lot fitter than I was in Melbourne. The freezing cold morning runs over here are paying off." Emily smiled and turned her head away from him.

"There's the girl I know."

"When you two lovers are finished quarrelling..."

Emily felt her ears burn up. "We're not lov—"

"Whatever," Lydia replied.

"Does the flyer say what I think it does?"

"It certainly does. With Ivan on the loose, I think it's time to call the Kremlin. At least give them time to get reinforcements deployed."

"Not yet. We still have just under twenty-four hours before their planned attack. How about the map?"

"They're routes to get from Saint Petersburg to Moscow."

"And I take it they're not taking the major roads?"

"Correct. Both minor and major roads. I have vehicles moving into position on the suggested routes. I'm guessing Ivan wasn't there when you got back?"

"Seems we've just missed him."

"My teams will be waiting for their arrival. They're not going to get out of here."

"Good. Without Xander to guide us, we need to go back to basics. We'll scope the streets on our way out. It shouldn't take us long to stop Ivan."

"Roger that." Lydia disconnected the call.

"You're confident we'll catch Ivan before his army reaches Moscow?" Schultz asked as they hopped in their SUV.

"Their chosen city exits will be surrounded. I'm confident they'll be stopped in their tracks before they even leave the outskirts of this city."

"It's good that one of us is confident." Schultz turned the ignition on.

"You're not? Confidence goes with your day job."

"True, that." He shifted the gear stick into first gear. "But it's a different story when heavy artillery is being fired your way in a foreign country by who knows what group that has a grudge against us."

"We'll stop Ivan before a drop of blood is spilled in Moscow then we can get on the next boat or plane out of this country. Deal?"

Chapter 47

On the outskirts of Saint Petersburg, Lydia pulled off the main highway to Moscow and rolled her armored SUV into a roadside truck stop. Besides the few parked-up trucks, there were only a handful of cars in the truck stop. Lydia looked around and noticed a nearby takeaway. She assumed the cars belonged to the staff who were closing up shop.

It'd been a while since she'd been involved in anything remotely like this. She wasn't going to take this one sitting down. No, there was too much propaganda filtering out onto the streets. Too many of Russia's youth had been caught up in this so-called revolution, including her little brother, who'd been killed in front of her by Ivan himself for refusing an order to shoot a fellow wannabe soldier who was caught stealing guns from Ivan.

"Holloway, what did you find?" she answered her phone as it connected to her car's Bluetooth system.

"Hey, babe, long time no hear. How's life treating you over there?" he answered, his voice sounding like he was toying with her.

"Cold. What you got?"

"Cut straight to the chase. No leading into it. That's a bit rough."

"No time for flirting. Not today."

She heard sniggers from the other three men in her car. Lydia turned and glared at them. The smirks were wiped off their faces. Lydia had known these men for a long time; they were like family to her. She trusted each of them to have her back tonight.

"Sure. I know you're blushing," Holloway toyed.

"She sure is," one of them piped up from the backseat, recognizing the voice belonging to Adrian Holloway.

Trying to keep a straight face, she replied, "Come on, Holloway, get on with it. What have you got?"

"I've got plenty."

Lydia coughed pointedly.

Holloway chuckled. "Oh, work. Right. We've located a convoy heading out of the city."

"Stop dragging it out. Which road are they on?"

"They're currently on the same road you're on, the M11."

"Great. Can you send the tracking feed through to my car?"

"Anything for you, babe. It's on its way. When are we going

to have that drink you promised me?"

"Bye, Holloway." She hit a button on her steering wheel and disconnected the call.

Pressing her comms earpiece into place, she was greeted by radio silence. The feed Holloway sent appeared on the screen of her tracking system.

"Alpha, are you in position?"

Radio silence.

"Alpha?" she repeated.

"Yes," a scratchy male's voice responded.

"They're rolling your way. Follow and observe. Action is a last resort. Do you copy?"

"Copy that."

Radio silence.

She pressed her earpiece again and the scratchy radio signal disappeared. Emily was next on her call list, and she answered on the first ring.

"They've been located heading east on the M11 highway."

"And that's the highway heading east out of Saint Petersburg direct to Moscow?"

"That's the one."

"Right. How far out on the M11 is the convoy?"

Lydia studied her tracking system. Ivan's leading convoy were fast approaching her location.

She cleared a lump in her throat before replying. "They entered the highway a couple of minutes ago. But Emily, there's too many in the convoy. You'll need more than what you've got."

"Seriously?"

"Deadly. Kuzmich has been building a following, an army full of young militias who aren't afraid to risk everything."

"And we're sure it's Ivan's convoy that's been located?"

"My source is trustworthy. The satellite footage he acquired shows a convoy of about half a dozen cars followed by ten army camouflage tarp-covered trucks heading out of the city. My source... He's better than Xander."

Tapping the screen, Lydia zoomed in the feed to about a six-block radius, watching them as they travelled along the M11.

"Ah. Change of plan. They've just split into three smaller convoys."

"They've split up?"

"One small group consisting of one SUV and six trucks have turned off the M11 and are heading south-east. While the remaining SUVs and trucks have remained on the M11 but have split into two smaller convoys."

"Which one is Ivan in?"

"No idea."

"You know Ivan a lot better than we do. Which convoy do you think he'll be in?"

Lydia's heart skipped a beat before she quickly refocused.

"If I were Ivan... I'd be in the main convoy heading south-east."

"South-east... what's down there? Another highway to Moscow?"

"There's the E95 highway which heads south-east out of

the city before swinging back on to the major highway directly to Moscow. It's out of the way but it's still a major road."

"Why would you suggest he's in that convoy? Wouldn't he be amongst the two smaller ones heading directly to Moscow on the M11?"

"The E95 is a quieter road. Less traffic, less chances of being spotted."

"Okay... Are there any smaller roads in between the M11 and the E95 highways?"

"Yeah, but you wouldn't drive on them, not in this weather. Besides, smaller roads are slow, and he won't want to be adding to their travel time. The longer they're on the road, the higher the risk of being stopped. If they get through my team, they could re-appear anywhere between here and Moscow."

"You're certain he'll be on the E95 tonight?"

"Uh, yeah... if I was in Ivan's shoes, I'd be making my way south and approaching Moscow from there."

Lydia studied the map. The larger convoy, which had split into two smaller convoys, were still travelling along the M11. The front one consisted of two SUV's with two tarp trucks right behind the SUV's. She still had time before they had to move into position at a nearby highway bus stop.

She felt something tap her arm. Her front passenger, Martin, was pointing out his window.

"Company," he whispered.

"Hang on a minute."

Lydia placed the call on hold and looked out Martin's

window. A set of headlights were entering the truck stop. Behind her, she heard the two men checking over their guns.

"Keep them out of sight until the last minute."

Her eyes on the approaching headlights, she pulled her trouser leg up a little. With her other hand she reached down and pulled her piece from her ankle holster. Lydia cocked the gun before placing it between her and her door.

"Don't make a move," Lydia whispered.

The approaching vehicle was two car lengths away from them. Lydia tightened her grip around her piece. The approaching vehicle slowed down as they drove past them then the headlights disappeared.

"All clear," Martin announced.

Lydia loosened her grip around her handgun. Her cell vibrated. Looking down she saw Emily was still on hold.

"Shit." She took the call off hold. "Sorry. Just thought we had company."

"You all right? Where are you?" Emily asked.

"All good. I'm... Where am I?" Lydia looked around. Bushes were shrouding her from the highway as she nestled in alongside them on the edge of a large parking lot, away from the resting truck drivers. Behind her was the takeaway. "I'm parked at a service station on the E95, just south-east of the city outskirts. You'll see my SUV parked out front. We're the only vehicle here."

"Right, we'll be there shortly."

The car speakers beeped, advising Lydia the call had been disconnected.

"We're not parked on the E95, nor is there a service station here." Martin turned around to face Lydia, his back against his door. "Why did you send them in the opposite direction?"

Lydia sank back into her seat, pulling her coat in around her as the cool night air seeped in through the windows. She watched the convoy on the screen as it headed her way.

"Because I don't need them getting in the way. Ivan is mine for the kill."

Chapter 48

Emily stared out her passenger window as they travelled along the Saint Petersburg Ring Road towards the M11, where shipping containers and low-lying industrial parks replaced the city skyline.

"You sure Ivan will be travelling on the M11? Lydia said she was parked at a service station on the E95." Emily looked up at the center poles that were positioned in the middle of the eight-lane highway.

"There was something in her voice I didn't trust... and this is the most direct route. He'll be doing everything he can to ensure he's the first one to arrive at their meeting point."

"Wouldn't he be worried about those cameras up there?" She pointed to poles in the center of the road.

"He's probably paid someone to turn a blind eye, or he may travel in between two trucks. He's smart. I'd say he's had this planned right down to the minute. Anyway, we're the most wanted, not him. We need to make sure we reach Ivan before we land ourselves in jail."

Travelling past a closed security checkpoint area, Emily caught a glimpse of a vehicle parked on the other side of the truck ramp. Moving forward in her seat, she looked out her side mirror.

"Schultz, did you see that truck parked back in that security checkpoint?"

"Probably someone catching some snooze."

"You sure about that? It looked like one of the trucks we blew up earlier."

"Those types of trucks would be common around here."

Emily looked around and ahead of them before returning to her side mirror. "We've got company."

"As long as we don't see red and blue lights flashing, we'll be fine."

"How about being high-beamed?" Emily shielded her eyes from the bright light shining through her side mirror.

"Crazy drivers, even at night. We'll see if this fixes it," Schultz said as he adjusted the side mirrors.

The high beams of the vehicle behind them remained on. Emily repositioned herself to see out her side mirror. The distance between them and the headlights behind them seemed to be increasing.

"What are you up to?" Emily asked the truck, as if it was

going to answer her.

Gunshots ricocheted off the rear of their SUV. Emily sat up. "Don't they ever give up?"

"How much ammunition does this car carry?"

"Not sure." Emily reached for the diagram sheet Lydia had given them earlier. "It isn't listed on here, and I don't remember if Lydia actually told us."

"Call her. Find out," he snapped.

Emily looked at Schultz, her mouth open, eyes wide.

He turned to her. "What are you waiting for?"

"I'm not the enemy here."

Shaking her head as she tried to comprehend the anger he was showing, she pulled out her cell.

"We don't have all day," Schultz snapped as more gun shots pelted their vehicle.

Emily dialed Lydia's number and she answered on the second ring.

"Hey, Lee. What's up?"

"We have company. How much heat have you packed in here?" She placed the call on her phone's speakers and held the phone between her and Schultz.

"What've you used so far?"

"A couple of side shells, a top one and some rapid ones."

"There's still plenty on board. But you do also have some grenades in the back. They'll pack a punch but if they've got anywhere near the protection you two have, they'll only put a small dint in their armor."

"That's pretty useless, then." Schultz shook his head as he

slowly increased his speed, being careful not to draw the attention of any CCTV operators watching the road.

"Lee," Lydia continued, ignoring Schultz. "You can access them via the back seat. Fold down the middle and left side seats and you'll be able to crawl into the trunk. I put some extra little surprises in there that may come in handy."

Emily hovered her finger over the disconnect call button.

"Thanks for that. We'll give anything a go to shake these guys off our back."

"I'll send a couple of my crew members to your location. They'll attack from the rear."

"Thanks."

Emily disconnected the call.

"She has our location?" Schultz asked as he navigated the curves off the ring road and onto the one straight to Moscow.

"Who knows what she's got?"

"Before we start pressing buttons, I need you to find something on that chart of yours that'll stop these pricks in their tracks," Schultz said.

"Looking now." Emily scanned over the page before stopping at an entry in the middle. Gunfire was still decorating their chassis. "Ooh, this one sounds good."

"We're off the main road now. I can't see any surveillance cameras. Whatever you're going to do, you'd better do it now."

Emily reached over to the center of the dash and pressed the middle button labelled *Shredder*.

"What's that going to do? I don't see any mutant rats around here."

"Very funny." Looking out her mirror, she said.

Behind them, underneath the back seats, a motor whirred to life, followed by what sounded like metal unwrapping at high speed.

"Come on, boys," she whispered as she leant forward.

Holding her breath, she watched through her side mirror. She saw their headlights swerve, and the gunfire ceased.

"Did you just land a tire spike?" Schultz asked.

"Yes. Let's hope it worked."

"I think it might have."

Chapter 49

Sitting in the rear passenger seat, Ivan had a good view of his driver and the road ahead. A glance at his watch confirmed his driver had put them back on schedule.

"We've still got a while to go," his driver said over his shoulder. "It'll be smooth driving for a while. Why don't you have a rest?"

Ivan stretched his shoulders and back. "We won't be safe until we're inside the Kremlin. Then, there'll be plenty of time for me to rest."

"You're not going to be any good to anyone if you're too tired to function," Tony stated from the front passenger seat.

Ivan crossed his arms and thought for a moment before replying, "Have you ever been held against your will?"

Tony shook his head.

"Tortured? Kept awake for days until they sucked what they wanted out of you?"

Tony shook his head, this time a little slower.

"A couple of days without sleep for an actual cause is a walk in the park compared to that. Thank you both for your concerns but I'll worry about my own fatigue."

Both the driver and Tony shrunk into their seats and they continued in silence. The city dwellings made way for wider roads and open spaces. Trees, shrubs and open fields were appearing along the roadside. Moscow and his position in the Kremlin were at the other end of the highway.

Leaning back into his seat, Ivan closed his eyes. His mind drifted to the other end of the road. What the coming days will hold for him and for the country that was close to his heart.

The thoughts were drifting further apart as sleep began to claim his mind, when a ringing tone startled him. It rang again. He quickly realized it was his cell phone.

It was a call he'd been waiting for. Taking a deep breath, he answered.

"Two asset carriers were destroyed. Five casualties," the caller stated.

Ivan relaxed his shoulders, recognizing the voice of his right-hand man, Nicholas.

Nicholas continued, "We're the only remaining asset and still on the agenda."

"Very well. Keep me posted. They've been a nuisance since

they arrived here. I want them BOTH out of my way. Understood?"

"Yes."

The call disconnected. Ivan was tucking his cell inside his jacket pocket when his driver clicked his fingers.

"What is it?" Ivan asked.

"We have company. Six o'clock."

"How many?" Ivan straightened his back.

Tony glanced over his shoulder and out the back window.

"Turn around now. Do not ever do that again."

Tony did as was requested and Ivan continued, "Your headrest is what little protection you have between that window and your head."

"It won't happen again."

"I don't care if you do it again. It's up to you to decide if you want to live through tonight or not."

Ivan turned his attention to the driver. "How many are back there?"

"At least one."

"See what happens when you slow down a little. I don't need to remind you not to put your foot on the brakes."

"Slowing down now."

Ivan felt his SUV slow. In his head, he counted the seconds since the last road marker. "Right, hold it at this speed."

It was a little slower than anticipated but not less than ten, maybe fifteen kilometers under the current speed limit.

"How's it looking back there?" Ivan asked.

Tony moved his head around when Ivan shot him an evil

glare and he shrunk back into his seat.

"They're maintaining their distance."

"Good. There's a slip lane ahead. We're going to make it appear we're turning off. We'll see what they do."

His driver carefully checked his mirrors before moving over the two lanes of traffic, pausing for a moment in between lane changes, before arriving at the outside lane.

"On cue, boss. They've changed lanes soon after we have."

"Right." Ivan turned to Brian. "Brian, see if you can figure out who's behind us."

Chapter 50

A set of headlights rounding the corner caught Emily's attention in her side mirror.

"We've got a problem." Emily turned to Schultz.

The bouncing headlights also caught his attention.

Emily continued, "They're closing in on us, quickly."

Bullets rained over their car once again.

"Tell me we've still got some firepower packed away in this girl somewhere." Schultz moved his gaze between his side mirror and the road ahead.

"We'll give this a go." Emily pressed a button along the top, amongst the other missile buttons and switches.

She held onto the door handle, her grip tight, and waited for the aftereffects of the missile being launched from their car.

Nothing.

Not a nudge. She reached over and pressed it again, leaving her finger hovering over the button.

Still nothing.

"Is it jammed? We need something now."

"I'm trying." She thumped the button a few more times.

Still nothing.

"Try something else," Schultz snapped as the continuous gunfire hammered their SUV.

Dropping her diagram, Emily began pressing all the buttons and switches.

"That's going to take too long. What else is in the back? Didn't Lydia mention there were some grenades back there? Give them a try. Anything is better than nothing."

"Do you want to swap? I'll drive and you can deal with all of this." Emily waved the diagram card in the air.

Schultz stared straight ahead, ignoring her. Shaking her head, Emily clambered into the back seat and pulled the seats down, exposing the trunk.

She fumbled around the trunk until her hand touched a wooden crate.

"What have we got here, Lydia?" Emily muttered.

She carefully pulled the crate towards her until it was on the back seat with her. Unlatching the lid, she removed it and peered inside. Her eyes lit up.

"Think we might have something." She pulled out one of the top cylinders.

"Whatever it is, do something. Now. They're right behind us."

Emily pulled the lid off the cylinder. A grenade sat quietly inside.

"With this bad boy we'll need some room. Can you put a little distance between us?"

Emily was pushed into the back seat as Schultz planted his foot down on the accelerator pedal. Their car's revs were high, almost at the point of needing another gear change.

She waited for the gear change. As she heard the revs quieten, she pulled the safety clip and wound her window down. Holding the safety lever down, she pulled the pull ring from the grenade.

"This enough distance?" Schultz yelled over the air gushing inside.

"Hold her steady."

Emily poked her head out the window. A good couple of truck lengths separated the two cars.

"Here goes." She eyed the pursuers' black SUV and threw the grenade.

Quickly pulling her head in, she wound her window up, braced against the seat, and waited. An explosion sounded behind them. A few seconds later the gunfire ceased.

"How did it go?" she asked.

She saw Schultz checking his mirror. "Whatever you hit, it wasn't them."

"Seriously?"

"Definitely. They're—"

Rapid gunfire pelted their car.

"Shit. Right."

Emily grabbed the next grenade and prepared it for launch. She wound her window down and, half hanging out the window, she threw it like a baseball. Ducking her head back in, she wound her window up again. Grabbing two more grenades, she jumped back into her seat alongside Schultz.

"Another miss. If we somehow get out of here alive, we need to work on your aim."

"It's not that bad."

"Why are they still on us?"

"They're stubborn." She looked out her side mirror, frustration brewing inside her.

"Pull the sun roof back." Schultz tapped the tinted sun roof above them.

Emily unlatched it and pulled it back. Another gush of freezing air hit her face.

"Shit."

"What's up?" Schultz sounded worried.

"Well, I'm definitely awake after that blast of cold air."

Schultz chuckled before replying, "Lee... Okay, serious now."

"Serious? Look who's talking."

Crouching on her seat, her focus on the vehicle behind them, she pulled the pin on the next one. There was a brief pause in the gunfire. She quickly stood up and threw it towards them. Ducking back inside, she pulled the sun roof closed.

Schultz peered out his mirror. "A little better but they're still on us."

Emily kept her eye on the black SUV behind through her side mirror when something in the distance caught her attention.

"We've got more company." Her attention was now on the second set of headlights, farther behind them.

"I see. Another black SUV. Let's hope they're the friendly ones."

The new vehicle quickly caught up and pulled up alongside the black SUV behind them. Renewed gunfire hit their car.

"Don't think so." Emily reached into the back and pulled out two more grenades. The box now felt empty.

"This is all we've got left?"

She held them up.

"Let's hope your aim improves now our target is wider.

"Confidence boost. Thanks." She winked at him as she opened the sun roof again.

Pulling the pin, she raised her arm through the sunroof and pitched the grenade at the convoy. She ducked back down and watched them through the rear window.

The vehicles both swerved to avoid most of the impact. She'd slowed them down for less than half a minute. They were quickly right behind them, firing on them again.

Schultz watched the two cars in his side mirror before returning his gaze to the road ahead of them.

"Last one." Emily raised herself up through the sun roof.

"Try and get one of them," Schultz yelled.

She was looking directly at the shooters. They began to raise their guns towards her. Pulling the last pin, she aimed and threw it at the second vehicle.

As she lowered herself back into their car, her eyes locked on the passenger in the SUV directly behind theirs. Their face was illuminated by the interior light.

"Nicholas," she whispered.

Not wanting to stick around for the aftermath, she quickly lowered herself and closed the sun roof as the shrapnel flew overhead.

"You got one." Schultz sounded like an excited child.

Looking out the back window, she caught sight of the erupting fireball.

She settled back into her seat and returned her attention to her side mirror. "Don't be so surprised. I don't know who was in that second SUV, but the one behind us right now is Nicholas."

"Ivan's man, Nicholas? The one who was there when the waitress was shot?"

"Same one."

"You sure?"

"Definitely. His eyes were focused on me like he was on a mission."

"Yeah, a mission to get his ass kicked. If we had more ammunition."

"We'll have to outmaneuver them."

"In a city we're not familiar with?"

Emily ignored him as she tried the buttons and switches

again, but nothing happened.

"What's the use of all these gadgets if they don't do anything? She thumped four of them at once as her fist connected with the controls.

"They're gaining on us."

Emily looked out the front window then into the rear, past the folded-down seats.

"Keep her steady. I'll see if there's any more ammunition in the trunk."

"You know I won't make promises I can't keep." Schultz winked at her.

Emily saw a smile emerging on Schultz's face when he quickly moved the steering wheel left then right. Their car swerved from one side of the lane to the other before straightening up.

She chuckled. "You'll keep."

Placing one hand on the center console and the other on her door handle, she braced herself as she pulled her legs up underneath her. Moving into a crouching position, Emily leant forward and looked skyward out her front window.

"What's that?" she asked.

"What? I don't see anything?" Schultz scanned the sky, too.

"Up there?"

"Probably a falling star."

"You'd better make a wish. A wish we get out of here alive."

"Very funny."

"No." She narrowed her eyes, hoping she'd be able to focus on the object more. "No, I don't think it is. It has red and green lights."

"It's probably just a plane."

"That low?"

She watched it as it traveled through the air towards them. Their headlights reflected on a white object, like wings with a dark center.

As it passed over them, Emily turned to Schultz. "That looked like a drone holding onto something. We need to get moving."

Chapter 51

Global Intelligence Agency
Switzerland Headquarters

Standing in the center of the control room, two elderly men watched over their computer technicians as they flew their latest top of the range drone over Saint Petersburg.

"Isn't this going against one of our core principles—that all agents need to complete their assignments on their own?"

"This is a little out of the ordinary. Don't you think, Leo?"

"You've changed your tune, Bert. Earlier you wouldn't allow me to intervene."

"This is a little different. This is her first time dealing with missiles and heavy gunfire. We haven't had the opportunity to fully train her on them yet."

"Twenty seconds from target," the technician seated in front of them announced as he tweaked the drone's flight path with a joystick.

"This will be the only one we'll help her with. After that, she'll be, like our other agents, on her own."

"Bert, it's time we commence stage two of her arms training."

"Yes. When she's out of there we'll get her started. She can complete the training in between assignments."

Video footage of two vehicles travelling along a highway out of the city appeared on a shared screen. The flares from bullets being fired at the front vehicle made both men uneasy.

"Circle around and gain some distance. We don't want our drone to fall into the wrong hands."

"Roger that." The technician pulled the drone around.

"Just make sure we don't hit that front SUV."

"They'd better make some distance."

"Disengage the targets electronics and computer systems."

"Done," another technician announced from the corner of the room. "Countdown re-commencing from thirty."

The men watched as the second vehicle crawled to a stop.

"Twenty seconds."

Bert crossed his arms over his stomach and clenched his jaw as he watched on.

Leo turned around. "I can't watch this."

"Ten."

The room was silent.

Chapter 52

"The drone's gone."

"Okay. Is our friend Nicholas on the move again?" Schultz kept his concentration on the road as he sped along the highway.

Emily looked in her side mirror. "No. It doesn't look like—Shit."

A large explosion followed closely by a fireball erupted behind them, and their car rocked and swayed with the force of the blast despite the distance.

"Hold on," Schultz advised.

Emily held on to the grip handle above her head with one hand and her seat with the other. She braced herself for worse yet to come. Looking over at Schultz, she saw his knuckles were turning white from his tight grip on the steering wheel.

Schultz straightened their vehicle up and continued down the road, gaining momentum.

Emily looked out her mirror. A huge fireball engulfed the middle of the highway.

"There's nothing left of them."

"Right. We're out of here before whatever that explosion was happens to us."

At that moment the drone flew over and lowered to just above the height of their car.

"Oh crap." Emily stared at the drone.

"It's all good. See the white underbelly?"

"Yeah."

"It's not hot. Hang on." He leaned over his steering wheel while keeping an eye on the road.

"What? What is it?"

"See those flashing colored lights?"

"Yeah."

"It looks like Morse code. L...e...e space y...o...u space a...r...e space s...a...f...e space f...o...r space n...o...w."

"I'm safe for now?"

"G...e...t   m...o...v...i...n...g   n...o...w   c...a...t...c...h I...v...a...n!"

Chapter 53

Since the drone incident, Emily had been using the time to get her head around the layout of the roads leading out of Saint Petersburg, in particular the E95 highway.

"Schultz, I don't want to be the one to admit this—"

"Come on, spit it out. What's on your mind?"

"Your instincts to go on the M11 were right."

Emily looked over and saw him doing a little jig in his seat. Choosing to ignore his excitement, she continued. "I've been scouring the E95 on my map application and there's no service station near or within fifty kilometers of the city perimeter."

"And your apps are up to date?"

"Yeah... I don't understand why Lydia said she's somewhere when the place doesn't exist."

Her cell phone beeped.

"Who is it?" Schultz glanced over at Emily.

"Ah." She opened the message. "It's Lydia."

"What's she got for us? Her correct location?"

"Not exactly." She looked over at Schultz. "You remember when we had the two SUVs chasing us?"

"Yeah. Nicholas was in the one behind us, wasn't he?"

"Yeah, and you remember I didn't know who was in the other car?"

"I assumed it was more of Ivan's militias."

"Well, Lydia's source has advised her that the occupants of that second car are believed to be connected to..."

She looked at the message again, shaking her head. Schultz clicked his fingers reaching for the phone but she pulled her phone away.

"They're allegedly connected to Fu."

"Your... ex-uncle?"

"Yes."

"I warned you last time you'd never escape him."

"That's not all. She's given me the details of her contact over in the States."

"Why would she do that? We guard those contacts with our life."

Emily checked the message details. "We must've been out of phone service when she sent this through. Apparently, hers was sent five minutes ago. You don't think something has happened to her?"

Emily felt the car's momentum push her into her seat as

their speed shot up.

"Lee, we're not going to start speculating."

As Schultz rounded a bend in the road, Emily spotted a vehicle to the side of the highway with its headlights off and doors wide open. Why would anyone be parked with all the doors open in the middle of an icy Russian night? As they approached, the interior lights shone on the front passenger. He was slumped against his window. Emily's heart skipped a beat when she recognized the vehicle.

"Stop up there." Emily pointed to the parked vehicle.

"Isn't that one of Lydia's vehicles?" Schultz slowed their vehicle down as they approached a bus stop.

"Yes, and that looks like another one, behind her car."

"Do we have any handguns in the back?" Schultz asked as he put their car in neutral.

"Nothing. We're empty."

"I don't like this."

Emily jumped out of their car and ran towards the front vehicle. In the front seat she saw a male passenger and the driver slumped over the steering wheel. Schultz was behind her, yelling, but she ignored him, instead focusing on the occupants.

There was blood everywhere around the front passenger. Peering into the back of the car, she saw two more men also slumped over and more blood everywhere. Emily turned her attention to the driver, whose face was hidden by long locks. She gently pulled the hair away.

"It's Lydia," Emily yelled over her shoulder.

Schultz was cautiously approaching, his hand positioned where his gun would usually be holstered.

"How is she?"

"It doesn't look good."

Emily turned back to Lydia. She was covered in blood from her head down to her waist. Her hand trembling, Emily extended her fingers towards Lydia's neck. She hesitated for a second before placing her fingers against Lydia's. Hoping and praying she felt a pulse. Nothing. A tear ran down Emily's cheek. She moved the position of her fingers. Still nothing.

She felt Schultz place his hand on her back.

"What a blood bath."

She ignored him, focusing on trying to find a pulse. Still nothing. Fighting back the tears, she closed Lydia's eyelids.

"She's gone."

Emily pulled herself away from Lydia's side. Stepping backwards, she pushed Schultz back and closed the door a little before stopping.

"What is it, Lee?"

"Not sure." She opened the door and ran her fingers along the inside of the window before continuing. "She knew her attacker."

"Why do you say that?"

"Look at this window." She closed the door enough so the interior light lit it. "Can you see where the bullets impacted the glass?" She didn't give Schultz a chance to reply before continuing. "The bullets didn't make it all the way through."

She opened the door and Schultz ran his fingers over some

of the bullet marks. He stood back and studied the car before replying. "What I don't understand is why would she open her door after her car was shot at? Why couldn't she get away?"

Emily looked around the car. It appeared to be leaning towards them. Kneeling down by the drivers' side front tire she ran her hand along the bottom half of the tire. Her fingers stopped at a thick fold of rubber.

"Flat tire."

She moved to the rear and felt the bottom of the tire.

"And another one."

"Okay, that explains why they couldn't get away. But I still don't know why she'd open her door when they were protected in there."

"Exactly. She must have known and trusted them." Emily walked back up to the driver's door. "While I check on the other occupants in this car, can you check the other car?"

"Onto it. And Lee..."

"Yeah."

"While you're in there, grab what you think we could use. Whoever did this can't be far ahead."

"Good thinking."

Emily opened the rear passenger door and felt for a pulse. Nothing. Leaning in she felt for a pulse on the other passenger. They were all gone. Guided by the interior light, Emily felt around for any ammunition or guns. Nothing. She moved back to Lydia's door.

"Anything?" Schultz asked as he stood beside Emily.

Emily jumped.

"Watch it, will you?"

"Sorry. They all had a similar fate but I have found a couple of guns and some rounds. How about you?"

Emily shook her head. "Nothing in the back. They've cleaned up after themselves."

"Anything in the front?"

"Still looking. I haven't checked the other side."

Schultz leant in through the front passenger door.

Emily looked around the dash. Empty. Not even a sat-nav.

"Anything under that scarf?" Schultz asked.

Emily looked at Schultz and saw him pointing to the center console. She looked down and saw a bundled-up woolen scarf where the center drink holders would be. She lifted the scarf up. A narrow black square device was resting on top of the drink holders.

"What have we here?" Emily asked as she pulled it out. "Looks like it could be a sat-nav."

"Is it working?" Schultz asked.

Emily tapped the screen. It remained black. She ran her finger around the narrow edge of the device until she found a button. When she depressed the button, the screen lit up.

"It is. But I don't think this is any ordinary sat-nav."

"Why's that?"

Emily turned the screen around to show Schultz, who was still looking around the passenger side.

"See the few dots moving along the road? Isn't that this road? It's tracking someone."

"I can't tell from here but we'll take it with us."

Emily studied the screen. Zooming the map out, she made three more bleeps appear on a nearby road.

"There's nothing on this side."

She heard Schultz shut the passenger door but she continued to watch the bleeps move along the roads.

"It can't be this simple, can it?"

"What's that?" Schultz asked as he approached.

"This couldn't be the location of Ivan's convoys, could it?"

Emily repositioned herself so Schultz could see the screen.

"Could be, or it could be Lydia's vehicles..."

"No. If it was her cars, there should be one somewhere behind us."

"Why do you say that?"

"Did you ever see the backup she was going to have attack from the rear?"

"Now that you say it, no, they never turned up."

"This could very well be Ivan and his vehicles. We'd better get back on the road."

A scratchy voice sounded inside the vehicle, somewhere in the footwell. Emily turned towards the sound.

"What was that?" Schultz asked.

The voice crackled again, this time a little louder.

"A radio." Emily felt around the floor, in and around Lydia's legs. Her hand stumbled on a small hard object with a narrow rod on one end.

"Got it," she yelled as she pulled it out.

"Tune it in. The rest of Lydia's crew are probably trying to contact her."

Closing the door, she turned the dial and the Russian voice came out clearer.

Emily translated the message as the voice repeated his message. "Team Alpha, do you have a copy?"

Emily looked to Schultz. He gestured towards the radio. "Answer him."

Emily pressed the side button. "We receive you loud and clear."

"Who's this? You're not Team Alpha."

Emily didn't know how to respond. Her eyes drifted to Lydia's lifeless form.

Schultz grabbed the radio off her. "Team Alpha is deceased."

"Deceased? Everyone?"

"We've only just arrived at the scene. Who's this?"

"Team Beta. The remaining crew."

"Can we switch to a secure line?"

"Trīgintā quīnque."

Recognizing the number in Latin, Schultz switched to channel thirty-five. Emily shook her head, in disbelief at this new trick Schultz had pulled out.

"Copy, Team Alpha?" the voice sounded over the radio.

"We have a copy," Schultz replied.

"Lydia? Is she gone, too?"

"Single shot to the temple. Sorry."

"Ivan and his men."

"You sure it was Ivan?"

"Yes. My team were on the other highway, the E95, when

they were attacked. She was one hell of a fighter. I take it you're one of the two Aussies we're helping."

"Yes, and we both thank you for everything you and your crew have done tonight. We'll take it alone from here."

"Like hell you are."

"We can't have any more innocent fatalities tonight."

"Who says we're innocent? We all knew what we were getting into when we agreed to help. I've got your vehicle on my tracker and I see you're not far behind the back of Ivan's convoy. Take the radio with you. I'll be in touch."

Radio silence.

"Has our vehicle got a tracker on it?" Emily asked as she looked at Lydia's device.

"No idea, but Ivan's convoy is just up that road and we need to catch them. Now." Schultz was already walking back to their car.

"Right behind you."

Standing by Lydia's door, Emily took one last look at her.

"Come on," Schultz yelled.

Glancing over her shoulder, Emily saw him gesture her towards the car. Holding her index finger up, Emily returned her gaze to Lydia, her eye drawn by something sparkling through the weave of her winter sweater. She reached in and pulled out a pendant dangling from a chain.

Schultz revved their car.

"Sorry," Emily whispered and yanked the chain from Lydia's neck.

"Now," Schultz yelled.

Chapter 54

Emily turned the pendant over in her hand, unable to understand why Lydia would be wearing it.

"What've you got there?" Schultz asked.

She held it up. "This was around her neck."

"Lydia's?"

"Yeah. But, why would she be wearing a golden hammer and sickle charm?"

"What I want to know is where are their guns and ammunition? I didn't see any full shells left behind. Did you?" Schultz asked.

Emily studied the charm, turning it over in her hand. "You don't think... No." She clutched it in her hand, shaking her head. "You... you don't think she was one of them? One of

Ivan's followers?"

"Then why give us this car? The gunpower?"

"She did give us an inferior vehicle. Half the buttons and switches don't work."

"True. When you put it like that... Why didn't I see the signs she was a double? It's my job, it's what I'm trained to pick up."

Emily reached over and placed her hand on his leg. "Don't beat yourself up. We're dealing with a highly organized group here who runs everything old-school. Something neither of us have seen for a while."

A small smile passed his lips as he patted her hand before quickly returning his hand to the steering wheel.

"We need another plan," Emily thought out loud. "We're the only ones who know there's an attack planned on the Kremlin in the next twenty-four hours."

"Us and the last of Lydia's crew."

"I can't rely on them, not now that I have my doubts about them. As far as I care, we're the only ones here who are actively trying to stop this maniac."

Emily grabbed the device and tinkered with its settings before loading the tracking screen again.

"Schultz..."

"What's up?"

"Lydia's been able to track us all night."

"What? That means she would've seen Nicholas behind us."

He glanced over. Emily angled the screen so they both

could see it and pointed to the dot at the bottom of the screen.

"Most likely. That's us, there."

"You sure?"

She raised an eyebrow.

"Sorry, I shouldn't doubt you." Schultz winked.

"One day you'll learn. Maybe."

"Those markers weren't on there before, were they?"

"No, I changed some settings. So..." She zoomed out.

"Up ahead we have markers, two groups. I'm still trying to locate team Beta."

"He said he was on the E95. Try zooming out and see if this device will pick them up."

Emily zoomed out. A cluster of markers appeared along the E95, not far out of the city.

"That could be the convoy that Lydia said broke off from the main one. And what do we have here? A single one a couple of kilometers back."

"Can you tell who is who?"

Emily tapped on some of the markers in the front cluster. Nothing. She tapped on the one marker out by itself. A small window appeared.

Emily read the pop-up window, "Team Beta."

"At least we know who's where."

"Did you see a handheld radio in Lydia's other car?"

"No, I didn't."

"That's weird."

"Schultz? Emily?" their handheld radio sounded.

Emily depressed the button on the radio. "Who's this?"

"I see you've found my present."

"Present?"

"Well, I'm talking to you, so that must mean you have Lydia's radio."

"Is that Ivan?" Schultz whispered.

Emily shrugged her shoulders and thought for a moment before responding.

"Why did you kill Lydia?"

"She was no longer needed. Not after Nicholas told me she'd supplied you with one of her cars. And Schultz, I've got some angry men, me included. We saw the evidence in the restroom at the club, of you taking out my best men."

Schultz chuckled, nodding. "Yeah, that's Ivan, and if they were his best men—"

"Go home while you can," Ivan said.

"Not happening."

"Have you seen the news? There's now a prize, on your heads... both of you. Dead. Or alive. Everyone will be looking out for you two, and the award for your capture will outweigh assisting your escape from this country. Do the smart thing. Give up."

Radio silence.

Emily switched the radio off.

"That bastard! He's going to die."

"How far away are we from them?"

"We're ten minutes behind them if we stick to the speed limit."

"We can't afford to attract any unwanted attention. Now

that there's money on our heads, who knows what they'd do with us if we're caught."

Emily went to interrupt but Schultz held up a finger and continued, "I think you'll agree that we need to stop this convoy before they reach Moscow and expose their lunacy. And I hope to hell we can clear our names the *right* way. May not be smart, but it will be right."

"The right way may well land us in jail."

"Do you have any better ideas?"

"Speed up and catch up with them?" Emily suggested.

"Come on. We need to be serious."

"Serious? I'm always serious, and comments like yours are why I prefer working alone."

"Ouch."

"It's true. I thought they would've learnt after the last five assignments never to allocate me another partner."

"The last five times?" Schultz's tone suddenly returned to his detective voice.

"Yeah. My partners were all killed," Emily added after a short pause.

Schultz pulled at his shirt. "Let's hope I'm the charmer that breaks the trend."

"And you tell me to be serious? When you spit out drivel like that?"

"It's not a rumor, then. You do lose your charm when you're tired."

Emily ignored him, instead checking the time on her watch. The time until this was all over and she could move on to her next assignment. Alone.

They drove in silence, the landscape widening under the moonlit sky. Emily kept an eye on the moving convoy.

"We have a problem. Either this device has stopped working," Emily thumped the screen, "or the convoy has stopped on the side of an intersection up past the next town."

"You what? Show me." Emily held it for him to see. "Hang on, I'll pull over."

Holding the device between them, Emily watched as Schultz edged the car over to the side of the highway and slowed to a stop.

"Let me have a look," Schultz asked as he placed the car in neutral.

Handing the device over, Emily watched as Schultz tinkered with it. She occasionally looked around, ahead and in her side mirror. There wasn't another soul on the road for miles in either direction.

"Don't know, but the other convoy on the E95 is still moving. So, the device isn't playing up. They've probably stopped."

Schultz monitored the screen while Emily scrolled through her messages. She stopped when she came across the one from Lydia. As the message opened, flashbacks tore at her. A young woman... dying alone, in the cold. Wiping a tear away, Emily took a deep breath.

"You alright?" Schultz asked.

"Yeah, fine." Holding her phone up, she asked, "Do you think we should ask for a helping hand?"

Shaking his head, Schultz replied, "I'm not sure. Xander was my go-to man. I don't know about using an outsider, someone we don't know. Someone who has a connection to Lydia and her little soviet pendant."

"What have we got to lose? There's a convoy full of weapons up ahead. Weapons we can't match. We really could do with a helping hand."

"Hang on a moment. We have action."

Schultz turned the device around so Emily could see it. Along a small road a dot was approaching the parked convoy.

"Another vehicle?"

Schultz tapped on the dot. "It's Team Beta."

"Team Beta—"

At that moment Emily's phone rang. The call identification was showing private number.

"Ignore it," Schultz ordered.

Her finger hovered over the accept call icon. The call ended and straight away rang again. Again, it showed private number.

She'd never been one to take orders. Lee answered the call. "Hello?"

Chapter 55

"Lee, is that you?" a smooth, young man's voice on the other end of the cell asked.

Emily thought he may have had a hint of a British accent.

"Who's this? How did you get this number?"

"Settle down. I got your number from Annab— sorry, I mean Lydia."

"And who are you?" Her tone was a smidgen softer.

"Put them on speaker," Schultz whispered.

"Yes, I need to talk to both of you."

"Right. You're on speaker phone." Emily pressed the speaker button on her screen. "Who are you and who is Annabelle?"

"Annabelle?" Schultz murmured, looking confused.

"How's ol' X going?"

Emily exchanged glances with Schultz.

"How do you know him?" Emily asked.

"X..." Schultz took a deep breath before continuing. "Xander's no longer with us."

"Shoot! Seriously?"

"Yes. How do you know him?" Emily asked, getting frustrated by the lack of answers coming from the caller.

"My apologies, I haven't introduced myself. I'm Holloway, but X may have mentioned me by Z."

Emily shook her head. "No, he never mentioned that handle name to me."

"That'll probably have to do with his gag order. There were four of us who would get together on weekends."

"Don't tell me, one of them is Y?"

"How did you know?"

"Lucky guess, I suppose."

"How long did you know Xander?" Emily asked.

"We need to get down to business. Your vehicle isn't firing any of the remaining firepower you have on board. I can't fix it remotely."

"How did you know?" Schultz asked.

Z ignored Schultz's question and continued. "Just past the next town, parked on a clearing alongside a private unsealed road, is a small convoy."

"Yeah we see it on this device," Schultz advised.

"It's Ivan and some of his men," Emily added.

"We need you to turn off at the next town. There'll be

backup waiting for you. From there you'll have firepower and some men hell-bent on getting revenge on Ivan... and Brian."

"Who's we?" Emily asked.

"That doesn't matter right now. When you get—"

"If you want us to trust you, we need to know exactly who we're working with."

"Very well. You're on your own then."

Her phone beeped and then was silent. Schultz thumped his fists on the steering wheel. Emily flinched.

Schultz shifted the gears into first and shook his head. "Our only lead to help us and you had to know everything."

"As soon as tonight's over, I'll try and make amends with Holloway. Deal?"

"You'll be doing a lot of groveling to get him back onside," Schultz mumbled.

"I heard that."

Chapter 56

Ivan moved around from the back of his parked SUV when his cell vibrated in his pocket. The screen read, *beta*.

Ivan answered his cell. "Simon. This'd better be good."

"We're not far out, just taking the shortcut from the E95 to your location."

"You were already meant to be here."

"There was a delay at your pick-up location. I couldn't get the additional ammunition you requested."

Ivan thumped the back of his SUV.

He yelled into his cell, "You didn't get anything? I needed those launches to take out the walls."

"I tried, but the location was hot. I only got out of there moments before the building was swarming in police."

"I'll work something else out. Keep your phone on you."

Ivan began walking around to the side of his SUV.

"Before you go. That Australian woman, Emily?"

Ivan stopped.

"I'm listening."

"Before you stopped, did you go past a town?"

"Continue."

"She's in Lydia's vehicle, and she's turned off and heading into town."

"Thanks for letting me know."

"I'll be there in a couple of minutes."

Ivan disconnected the call.

"This changes everything." He tapped his chin as he thought for a moment. "Right." He looked around until his eyes locked on the man he wanted. "Tony," he yelled out.

Tony walked out from behind a nearby truck and approached Ivan.

"Is everything alright, boss?"

"No. That, woman has been spotted."

"The Australian?"

"Yeah, her." Ivan spat on the ground. "The last town we've just travelled past. She's been seen taking the main road in. It's time for you to step up. Complete what Nicholas couldn't."

"Any means necessary?"

"Yes. Don't waste time. Only grab what you'll need."

"Onto it." Tony jogged back towards the truck. "Boys, we've got a job."

A group of three men walked over to Tony as he relayed the news.

What is she up to? Ivan thought as he watched everyone hop in one of his SUVs.

Tony pulled the SUV up alongside Ivan and wound his window down.

"We're all set, boss."

"Good. She's in a vehicle similar to Simon's. Catch up with them before they get any ideas, like disappearing."

Tony nodded.

"And... make sure you're not the next casualty tonight."

Tony spun the wheels as he drifted out onto the highway.

"Boss, we have company," one of Ivan's militias yelled out.

Ivan turned towards the voice to see all of his men looking down the road behind them, their guns drawn at the approaching vehicle.

"That was quick," Ivan muttered.

Crossing his arms, he walked to the main group of men as the vehicle approached, its lights on high beam. It wasn't until the approaching vehicle drove through a set of secure gates did it drop its lights to parkers.

"Lower your weapons."

"Boss? That's one of Lydia's cars," one of the men asked.

Ivan pushed his way through the men until he was standing a good five feet in front of them, watching as the approaching car crawled to a stop halfway between him and the gate.

The vehicle was stationary for a good half minute before the doors opened. Ivan's men took a step closer, every one of them with their guns still poised at the car. Their fingers hovered over the triggers.

A set of feet appeared beneath the passengers' side door. Ivan's men took another step closer.

"Wow, what a welcoming party," the man who got out yelled at the top of his voice.

He approached Ivan and his men, cupping his hands over his mouth and rubbing them together.

The armed men had now formed a circle around Ivan.

"How was the drive, Simon?" Ivan asked.

"All good. Your lead convoy on the E95 got through without any issues."

"Good, good. Very good."

Simon gestured towards his car for the occupants to emerge, and one by one they exited their vehicle. A couple had bags slung over their backs, others were carrying guns.

"And I believe Lydia is—"

"Dead? Yes. She was dead wood after she crossed us. She no longer served a purpose in our cause. Deal with that car." Ivan waved one of his soldiers towards Simon's car.

"Onto it." His soldier jogged over and waved his arm at his comrades. A couple of men joined him by the vehicle and together they did one final check.

Ivan and Simon watched as his soldiers pulled a couple of jerry cans out of the trunk of Simon's vehicle and handed them to the nearby men. The men immediately started splashing fuel over the dashboard, seats and the.

"Time to move out," Ivan bellowed.

Chapter 57

Travelling down the long road heading into town, Emily and Schultz passed a handful of single-level buildings. They appeared to be old, in desperate need of renovation. The sparse street lights lining their side of the road were the only sign of modern life on the stretch of road.

Under her coat, Emily could feel the hairs on her arms standing up.

"It's far from a tourist hotspot," Schultz said.

Checking her mirror, Emily saw a set of headlights behind them.

"What have we got here?" Emily asked rhetorically as she watched their follower. "You weren't around before."

"Could be anyone." Schultz shrugged it off.

"When we turned off there was not a single headlight on the highway. Now it's right there."

"Maybe they're in a hurry to get home. Now, remind me again, what's happening when we get into town?"

"There'll be some backup there, backup that is hell-bent on getting revenge, apparently."

"You know what, I'll call White, see if there's any intel over here. See if he can verify the backup option Holloway has lined up for us and tell me who it is."

"No, not after what happened to Xander. There'll be eyes on that office. Plus, whoever killed Xander will still be on the loose."

Schultz tapped his thumb on the steering wheel, hesitating before asking, "Do you think your Uncle Fu is over here, too?"

Emily glared at him.

"Where did that come from?"

"So sorry. He's been referred to as your uncle for a long time. What I meant is, clearly, his men are over here. Do you think he's here, too?"

Emily shook her head as she looked out her window. "No. He'll be lying low. Sending out others to do his dirty work."

"After this is all over you should re-consider protective custody. Fu won't be able to touch you then."

"The only thing that custody will stop is my career."

"Is your career still more important than your life?"

Emily turned to face him, her arms crossed.

"You've got dreams with the police department, climbing the ranks."

"Yeah, I do."

"How would you like to give up policing to go into

protective custody? To give up all those dreams and start from scratch again? Starting with a new identity, a new career you may not even like? A career that goes against your dreams and goals?"

"If it meant protecting my loved ones..."

Feeling her heart skip a beat, Emily put on a strong face before replying, "It's a good thing all mine are dead, then, isn't it?"

Straight away, she regretted what she'd said, and even more so when she caught a twinge of hurt on Schultz's face before he made it disappear.

"The offer still stands. Promise me you'll at least think about it."

She crossed her fingers before replying, "Yes."

"And you can uncross your fingers." He grinned as he shook his head. "You're unbelievable, trying to pull a fast one on me. One day you'll seriously consider the offer."

"We'll see. He was a great mate, wasn't he?"

"Who was?"

"Xander. Bending the rules to help us."

"Yeah, and if it wasn't for this assignment, he'd still be alive."

Emily's stomach twisted and churned at his harsh words. She looked away, her eyes welling up. She used the cuff of her coat to tap the corner of her eyes dry. She knew, deep down, that he was right.

Her thoughts drifted to her plans after this was all over. If they got out of here alive.

I'll sever all ties with the Bureau and Schultz. Go dark until I've corrected justice with Fu, she thought.

Emily cycled between looking in her side mirror and at her surroundings. A solitary troop carrier was parked along the side of the road. As they neared the vehicle, she noticed the rear windows were fogging up.

"You see it too?" Emily asked.

"Yes."

As they approached, she saw the driver's window was a little clearer, as if he'd been trying to clear his window. As they passed, Emily glanced back over her shoulder and saw a red glow behind the steering wheel, about chin height. The glow moved.

The parked troop carrier didn't move, so Emily sat back in her seat, relaxing her shoulders. Her eyes were beginning to feel heavier when a sudden bright light caused her to slam her eyes shut.

"What the—"

Schultz swerved sharply left then right then back to the center of their lane, obviously also taken by surprise by the overly bright lights. Placing her hand roughly where her mirror was, Emily slowly opened her eyes to see Schultz also shielding his side mirror.

"Son of a bitch, they're bright." Emily squinted.

The light beam behind them began to blend in with theirs. They were coming closer. Emily lowered her hand from the mirror, but the lights were still too bright.

The road was straightening when Schultz blasted the horn.

A troop carrier had turned out in front of them, and the driver didn't seem to be in much of a hurry. He drove straight on without the wave of a hand in apology.

Schultz moved to the left side of the road. The troop carrier in front also moved to the same side. Schultz moved to the other side and tried to overtake from there.

"Watch out," Emily yelled as she braced herself.

Schultz swerved a little. Looking out her window, they both watched as another troop carrier drove up alongside theirs.

"This isn't good," Schultz said.

Emily looked in her side mirror. The rear troop carrier was right behind them, their lights now dimmed. The troop carrier in front slowed down further.

"This has been staged." Emily shook her head. "Ivan's men."

"Why Ivan? We've seen his men in black SUVs and army camouflaged trucks."

Emily turned towards Schultz. "Think about it. Three vehicles from his convoy have been destroyed, and we're meant to be stopping them before they reach the Kremlin."

"But wouldn't he be more worried about getting to Moscow unnoticed?"

"With us on the loose? I don't think so."

Tap, tap.

"Lee..." Schultz stared at her, his eyes wide open.

"What's wrong? You're scaring me."

"Very slowly, you may want to look out your window."

Emily spun around.

"Slow—"

"Holy shit." Emily jumped in her seat. If it wasn't for her seatbelt she probably would've jumped into the backseat.

A gun barrel from the rear passenger seat of the troop carrier alongside them was poking out, pointed at her. The barrel tapped her window again, and the man holding it made little circles with his arm.

"You'd better do it," Schultz said as he concentrated on not hitting any of the troop carriers boxing them in.

Pulling her coat up around her ears, Emily wound down her window.

"Follow us or you'll be," he said in a heavily accented English, then he ran his thumb around his neck.

His face was barely visible between his fur hat, thick jacket and stubble growth that looked as bad as Schultz's five o'clock shadow if he left it unshaved for a week.

Winding her window back up, Emily studied the remaining occupants in the troop carrier. She couldn't see much with their windows fogging up, but as they passed under a street light, she saw three gun barrels, all sticking up in the air.

Turning to Schultz, she relayed their message. "Either we're dead if we follow them, or we're dead if we don't."

"Not many choices."

"No, but what are you thinking?" She could see Schultz was contemplating something, just by the way he was looking around. "Hmm. Where's that GPS of yours?"

"What? The map on my phone?"

"Yeah, that'll do. Where's the next intersection?"

Emily checked her phone.

"Just up ahead. Not far."

"Does that lead back to the highway?"

Emily zoomed out. "There's a few turns here and there. You'll need to go around the block to get back onto this road. I can only see one... two ways in and out of this town. But you can get back to the highway."

"Are there any more direct streets that'll get us there?"

Emily consulted her map again and shook her head. "No. This town is a maze. Full of dead-end streets and a river looping through the middle."

"The next one it'll be."

"You sure? You do realize that everyone in that troopy," she nodded towards the one travelling alongside them, "has guns?"

"Let's hope they're not semi-automatics, otherwise we don't stand much of a chance."

"Besides this car being bulletproof?"

"She's taken a beating already." Schultz rubbed the dashboard. "I'm thinking she's looking pretty sad on the outside, and our protection would then be second-grade."

"This is crazy." She glanced back at the troop carrier next to them. The passenger's window was still down, the gun pointed squarely at her. "And he's not backing down, either."

"It'll be all right. We'll be out of this town in a jiffy."

"I hope so."

They passed the last street light. The intersection was now just visible from their location. The troop carriers around them stuck really close. One wrong move and there'd be a four-car pileup in rural Russia in the middle of the night.

"You ready?" Schultz asked.

"Not really."

"Hold on."

The road widened to expose the intersection. Schultz yanked on the steering wheel. Their tires squealed as their car pulled around the corner.

"Car." Emily pointed to two cars blocking their way through.

Schultz pulled the steering wheel in the opposite direction. Their car began to swing around but they were still heading for the parked cars.

"We're going to hit them." Emily braced herself and closed her eyes until they were tightly shut.

Their car kept spinning around. They were now almost side-on with the parked troop carriers. Emily relaxed her shoulders as soon as their nose began to swing around back towards the road they'd just turned off.

A row of bright white lights hit them from the rear. The back of their car began to swing them around.

"Pricks," Schultz said.

Emily couldn't see anything but she felt their car stop. She heard Schultz's door open, quickly followed by hers. Someone grabbed her arm and tried to pull her out.

"Wait." She pulled her arm back.

The man maintained a strong grip around her arm and pulled again.

"Seatbelt." Emily pulled her seatbelt away from her body and raised her eyebrows, even though she could barely see.

"Quick," he said in English.

She kept her eyes on him while she unclipped her seatbelt, realizing he was the same man who'd tapped her window.

As she hopped out of the car, she asked, "Who are you? Did Ivan send you?"

Chapter 58

Emily turned her head from one side to the other. Everything was dark, not even a glimmer of light crept in through the black cloth bag they'd placed over her head. The knees of the men on either side of her knocked into her knee when they hit potholes. Memories of the kidnapping and the boat shed flooded back.

"Schultz?" she asked quietly as she tried to blot out the memories. "Schultz, you there?"

No answer except for a few sniggers from around her.

"Where is he, you bastards?" she screamed as she stamped her feet on the floor. "Where is my partner?"

"I'm sure someone is taking really good care of him."

More sniggers erupted around her.

"What do you want with me?"

The sniggers subsided. Then the same hand rubbed her leg again. "All in good time. All in good time," he told her.

"Well, you can tell Ivan, if he wanted me dead, he should've done it himself."

No one responded, and the remaining trip was made in silence. She tried memorizing the turns they made but quickly felt disorientated after a series of turns one after the other.

Then, in the still of the night, she thought she heard a scraping sound. Like steel rolling over the top of steel. They hit a sharp bump in the road, and the hum from the motor seemed to echo.

The car abruptly stopped and Emily lurched forward.

The engine was still running when she felt someone grab her by the arm and pull her out of the car.

Outside she heard the echo of another engine.

An echo? she thought as she swiped her foot around her.

The surface was smooth, like concrete. Her thoughts were interrupted by the sound of steel scraping along steel behind her.

"Where are we?" She turned towards the captor who held her arm.

Nothing.

The sound of a car engine drew closer. Then the scraping metal noise stopped. She felt the bag over her head move, then it was yanked off her. A bright light made Emily shield her eyes.

As her eyes adjusted, she slowly looked around. Her

remaining captors stood to the side. They were all sniggering, and either had their arms crossed, looking at her, or their guns were pointed at her.

Behind her was a large steel door on rollers, and above, a high bay light dangled from the center roof beam.

Locating the man who'd tapped her window, she stared at him and asked, "What have you done with my partner?"

"All in good time." He nodded to one of the men.

She turned to see the butt of a gun approach her head and ducked, but didn't see the second one coming from the other side. It found its mark, and Emily collapsed to the ground like a rag doll.

"Grab her," she heard one of the men instruct.

She felt her body being lifted as they grabbed her by her arm pits and dragged her across the length of the shed.

Her head throbbing, she squinted her eyes and slowly raised her head to see the men dragging her to a set of double doors positioned halfway along the shed wall. Turning her head to one side then the other, she saw only men dressed in full-length winter coats.

As the set of doors was looming, Emily couldn't help but feel that her head was about to be used as a battering ram. Two steps away from the door, two men stepped out from behind her and walked ahead to hold the doors open. Her shoulders were shoved up around her ears as they squeezed into a smaller office suite with a reception desk at the front, separated from the rest of the room by partition walls. Floor tiles that looked older than her, many either cracked or chipped, lined the floor. Some were missing, exposing the tile glue smeared over the cement slab.

Emily tried planting her feet into the floor but the men dragging her began moving quicker. They hauled her through the center of the room towards a wooden and frosted glass pane door. Words she couldn't quite catch in a simple, plain font had been painted in gold onto the glass pane.

The man on her right side let her go to open the office door ahead. She wriggled her other arm but the grip of her remaining captor tightened. On the next step, she brought her arm around, her closed fist aimed squarely for his knee.

Inches from the impact, her hand was stopped. Following the arm that held her fist, she found it belonged to the man who'd opened the door. In one swift movement he pulled her arms around and pinned them up against her back.

She flinched, gritting her teeth together and trying very hard not to show any sign of being uncomfortable from the sharp stretch that was running down her arm to her back.

Her captor pressed himself up against her back and whispered into her ear, "Stay looking ahead. One day this will make sense to you."

She felt a cool object being pressed into her palm and closed her hand around it. The object felt thin and round, like a coin or token.

He continued, "You have many followers waiting for the day when you rightfully take your place."

Noticing one of the men behind her, who was now holding the door open, had turned away, Emily turned her head slightly towards her captor. He grabbed the base of her head and gently turned it back around to the front.

Without moving her lips, she whispered, "You have mistaken me for someone else."

Emily felt her arms being pulled tighter as she was pushed into the office. The wall adjoining the door was floor to ceiling bookshelves. They contained a mixture of ornaments and books. A painting was hanging on the next white-plastered wall.

A large, dark wooden desk dominated the center area of the room. Halfway between the desk and the back wall, two simple plastic chairs sat opposite an oversized executive office chair on either side of the desk. The executive chair's back was turned to her. In the far corner behind the desk, a simple filing cabinet was positioned, with some sort of indoor plant on top of it. Behind the desk, a table sat against the wall, with an urn in the center. Beside the urn were three canisters labelled *sugar*, *tea* and *coffee*. In front of them were a set of teaspoons, cups and saucers.

The space between the desk and the wall alongside her was wide enough for at least two men to walk shoulder to shoulder.

Emily was pushed past the closest chair and shoved onto the second plastic chair. She brought her hands around and sat them in her lap, flexing her muscles and rotating her shoulders to loosen them up.

"Stay," her mysterious captor demanded.

Behind her she heard the door closing. A glance over her

shoulder confirmed two men remained in the room with her. Her "friendly" captor had taken up his position behind her, his gun aimed at her. He winked and placed a finger in front of his lips, his eyes moving between her and the desk.

The other man answered his cell phone and left the room without saying a word.

She glanced over her shoulder and whispered, "where's Schultz?"

But he didn't flinch. Looking back towards the desk, she saw she was still alone with her mysterious captor. She opened her fist when she felt a jab in her shoulder. Glancing over her shoulder, Emily saw her captor look between her hand and her eyes, shaking his head.

She closed her fist and he nodded. Turning around, she faced the desk, tucking the unknown object inside her coat and zipping the pocket shut.

A commotion on the other side of the office door drew her attention, and a second later the door opened. She heard a scuttle, someone resisting being brought in.

Turning around, she saw two men drag someone into the room. All she could see in between the men were a pair of pants and shoes. Men's shoes. The man closest to her knocked into the empty chair beside her as he tried to maneuver around it. She heard the chair scraping along the floor but couldn't see what was happening. A moment later there was silence and both men stepped away, taking their position around the room.

She turned towards the now occupied chair beside her.

Schultz was sitting in it, looking a little worse for wear, a few cuts on his face and a bruise forming under one eye.

"What have you done?" Emily asked.

"You're alive? And you've fared better than me?" he replied.

She ignored the note of incredulity in his voice. "Any idea what's going on?"

"I was going to ask the same thing. You're the one who directed me into this God-forsaken place they call a town."

"You're going to blame me for this? You're the one who decided to outmaneuver these maniacs."

Out of the corner of her eye, Emily saw the oversized office chair move, and a voice boomed from the other side, "Will you two just shut up!"

Chapter 59

As the arm rest of the oversized office chair came into view, Emily straightened her back until her shoulders were squared with her hips. She glanced at Schultz, but his expression remained unchanged—tired and exhausted. He ignored her. Not even a nerve flinched on his face.

The chair stopped moving. A black business-suited arm rested on its armrest, stretched along the length of it. A single finger tapped the curved edge.

Feet behind her stomped into a new position. Glancing over Schultz's shoulder, Emily saw the man guarding the door standing to attention.

Schultz gasped, his face showing traces of recognition.

"You know him?" she asked, looking between the business-suited man and Schultz.

The man in front of her brushed his finger through his thinning silver hair. He swept his hair from one side and over the top, covering a balding patch on the top of his head. His suit jacket was tight around his midsection, and his shoulders slumped.

He's not from the military or police. That's not where Schultz knows him from, she thought.

The two men stared at each other before a small smile appeared on the businessman's face.

Emily stood up. Placing her hands on her hips, she looked between the two men. "What's going on?"

"Sit down." The businessman glared at her.

"Not until you two tell me what's going on."

The man nodded, and before she realized what was going on, Emily felt pressure being applied to her shoulders and she was pushed back into her chair.

"Yes, I'd like to know that, too." Schultz crossed his arms. "What's going on?"

The man rubbed his stubbly chin. His eyes narrowed as he looked smugly at Schultz.

"Well, isn't this awkward?" He looked at Emily. "He hasn't told you about me? You don't know anything about me?"

"I know enough," she answered, bristling. "The man I see in front of me is uncomfortable in such fine clothing. By your awkwardness, right there, shifting your shoulders, I'd say you're trying to get comfortable. You don't wear suits very often, do you?"

319

He sat back and studied her. Emily stared back at him. He finally faltered and turned his attention to Schultz. "This one has some fire in her, hasn't she?"

A glance around the room confirmed all the men were standing with their shoulders relaxed and feet shoulder-width apart, their guns slung under their arms.

Standing up again, Emily pushed her chair back. The plastic feet skipping along the tiled floor. The guards lining the walls quickly pointed their guns at her.

"Tell me what's going on or we're walking."

The businessman pulled a long drag on his cigar before puffing smoke towards her. Emily held her breath, trying not to start coughing. He just sat there, staring at her.

"Fine." She walked towards the door. Two of the men kept their guns aimed at Emily, but she ignored them and kept going.

"You won't get far," the businessman finally replied.

Emily paused, inches away from the tip of one of the guards' gun barrels.

"The night is yet to reach its lowest temperature. Please sit back down."

"Give me one good reason." She crossed her arms and faced him.

"One of my men will put a hole in you." He drew on his smoke again.

Emily felt a sharp prod in her back, which jerked her forward. She tried to dig her feet into the floor but more prods of gun barrels pushed her off balance. Before she could regain her balance, she was dragged backwards and slammed back into her chair.

Blowing a puff of smoke towards them, the businessman continued, "You do realize the highways and backroads are going to experience increased traffic tonight. The closer to Moscow the worse it's going to get."

"Just like a normal city. What makes tonight so different?"

"You won't survive very long when one of the truck drivers sees you on the highway."

"What's so special about these trucks? They're just truckies going about their job, getting their loads unloaded or reloaded."

"You don't know?"

"Know what?"

"Your work colleague, Ivan Kuzmich. You know him, yeah?"

Emily looked at Schultz, who still hadn't said anything. He closed his eyes and moved his head up and down once.

"Yeah, what about him?" Emily returned her attention to the mysterious man in front of them.

"There's rumors he and his men are roaming the roads towards Moscow tonight."

"Which is it? Fact or rumors? I'm confused."

He sniggered before looking at Schultz. "Quick wit, this one."

Schultz managed a small nod.

"What were you doing out here in the middle of the night?"

"That is none of your business," Emily snapped.

"Oh, it is my business. You're trying to stop them single-handedly, aren't you?"

"I've got no idea what you're talking about."

He drew from his cigar, studying her face. The corner of her eye twitched.

Leaning his cigar against the ashtray, the man proceeded to stand up and walk around to the front of the desk. He sat on the edge of the desk, but leant in until she could smell the stale smoke on his breath.

"You can quit playing this game you're playing. We have received intel alerting us that you're more than aware of what's going down tonight. I also know you two have been running an undercover operation here without going through the proper channels. And what happened to operative Xander tonight."

Emily flinched but quickly refocused, her poker face returned. "I don't know where you got your information, but I'm over here on labor hire. Helping a local company in Saint Petersburg with their financial department." She turned to Schultz, pleading with her eyes. "Schultz, tell him what we're doing here." He lowered his head. "Schultz. Tell him." Her voice sounded despondent.

"Lee," Schultz said in a sheepish tone.

Emily felt her stomach churning. She didn't have a good feeling.

Schultz continued, "Meet former Deputy Commissioner Frank Wilde. Now a private detective for the rich and famous."

"Former... Deputy Commissioner?" Emily looked between the two men. "Of which force?"

"AFP."

Her mouthed dropped open while she tried to comprehend everything.

"You," she turned to Frank. "You were the one who had a... let's call it a disagreement... with the Commissioner?"

"The very one, here in the flesh." He held his arms wide open as if that was going to seal the real deal.

"What brings you here to Russia?"

Frank stood up and moved around to behind his desk. With his back to them, the clattering of metal on porcelain made Emily curious.

"Right. Now that we're all on the same page... Coffee, anyone?" Frank turned around, a metal spoon in one hand and an opened canister in the other, the aroma of coffee beans filled the room. Without waiting for a reply Frank turned around and continued making a coffee.

"No, I'll be all right," Emily snapped.

"Yes, please, Frank," Schultz replied.

Frank passed a filled cup to Schultz.

"You sure you don't want one?" Frank asked her again.

Emily sniffed. It smelled like the familiar coffee she and Schultz liked to drink.

"That standard police-issue coffee?" She nodded towards the coffee bag.

Frank chuckled. "No. No, it's not. It's just a fine brew. I

got Schultz onto that coffee. Here, have one. You could do with some warming up, and I know it's a coffee you two like to share."

He slid a filled cup over to her.

"I don't believe this." Emily slowly shook her head at Schultz. "First, I'm assigned a partner I don't need. Then, your old boss rocks up here in the middle of Russia."

"Well, not exactly the middle, let alone old," Frank interrupted.

"Have you checked your gray hairs lately?" Emily said before turning back to Schultz.

"You have your secrets, we have ours." Schultz averted his gaze from her.

"You can quit your quibbling. There'll be plenty of time for you two to sort out your differences later. Right now, there's more important things at hand."

Emily glared at Schultz as he sipped his coffee.

"What's with all the men and bringing us in at gunpoint?"

Frank also sipped his coffee before replying, "Have you not learnt anything while being here? You never know who's watching whom. Who's peeking out their windows, hiding behind bushes. We needed to make this look authentic... and I knew you wouldn't come willingly. Schultz warned me earlier today."

"The car following us off the highway..." Emily took a sip. "Was that one of your men?"

"No, that wasn't one of my men. You sure you were followed?"

"I'm not saying anything more until I know what you are doing here. I take it you're not here with the AFP."

"No, I'm not. I'm on a private assignment, just like you two."

"How private are we talking?"

"We were stationed here for another assignment, which doesn't concern you, when I received a call from Xander."

"You? Xander called you? Why would he do that? What is he to you?" Emily took another sip of her coffee, still not convinced by Frank's story.

"You want to know a lot, don't you? Is she always like this?"

"Lee likes to be well informed." Schultz faced Emily. "Frank is X's father."

"Seriously? My apologies, I didn't know."

Frank nodded before taking another sip of coffee.

"So, you're a little tech-savvy, then?" Emily asked, looking for any resemblance between Frank and Xander.

"No, I can't take credit for that. I can't even turn on the damn things. It blows my mind thinking about everything he was able to do with computers." Frank took another sip before continuing. "Xander contacted me soon after he uncovered what you two were up against and asked if I could help."

"Help, to what extent?" Emily asked.

"All in good time, my child."

She narrowed her eyes at him as he took another sip from his cup.

"Schultz, did you know about any of this?" Emily asked.

"No, he didn't. Xander did it on the quiet. He knew you

were in too deep. Ivan is a smart yet conniving businessman. He's out for blood, and that makes him even more dangerous and unpredictable."

"Well, if you think we're in too deep... What do you propose?"

"Leave, please," Frank snapped his fingers, his eyes still on her face.

"Done." Emily stood up and gestured for Schultz to do the same.

"Not you two. Everyone else, out."

Emily watched as all his guards walked out, the door closing behind the last one. She sat back down.

"Before Xander was—" Frank paused to collect his thoughts.

Looking down at his feet, Schultz asked, "Is he really..."

Frank nodded and Emily saw the corner of his eye well up.

"Unfortunately, his burial is something I'll need to deal with when I return home. Knowing the current Commissioner, no doubt he'll have questions about why one of his staff members was researching an unofficial investigation that was being undertaken on international soil. Are you prepared for that?"

"We'll worry about that when this is all over. Right now, we have a maniac we need to stop before the county wakes up."

"I don't envy you. Kuzmich can be a tough nut to crack. Anyway, Xander wasn't able to calculate the total number of men Ivan has on his payroll and how many of them are descending on Moscow tonight."

"Did he manage to get a rough estimate?" Schultz asked as he leant in and placed his empty cup and saucer on the desk.

"No. But he did find out that the money Kuzmich has been squandering away over the years is in the billions. By his quick sums after he subtracted the known expenditure, you're looking at possibly hundreds, if not thousands to tens of thousands of men. And quite a lot of firepower."

"Shit. That puts a different perspective on everything." Emily thought for a moment.

Frank continued, "Ivan will already have most of his men positioned around the Kremlin ready to take up arms in a matter of hours. This will be Ivan's weak point, a mistake in his strategy. By keeping a limited number of men with him in Saint Petersburg, he's left himself open to attack."

"And the convoys on the road tonight will be the last of his men?"

"And his larger firepower."

"Schultz, what we saw earlier on that device, that's only a small portion?"

"What device?" Frank asked.

"It was like a GPS tracking device we pulled from Lydia's car." Schultz ignored Emily's narrowed eyes and continued, "We've been using it to track the main convoy since leaving Saint Petersburg."

"Lydia? Who's Lydia?"

"We no longer know either, but earlier she was referred to as Annab before the transmission cut off."

"Annabelle?"

"No idea. Could be."

"Where is this device now?"

"Where is our car?" Schultz asked.

"James," Frank yelled out.

A few seconds later the captor who'd placed something in Emily's hand walked into the room.

"Yes, sir," he replied.

"Go find their car. There's a device in there tracking Kuzmich and his men. I need it."

Emily placed her hand over her inside pocket. So he did have a name, Emily thought as her hand ran over the peculiar object he'd strangely given her earlier. One end was rounded, ending in a long narrow bar. On the other end, an odd shape was attached to one side of the bar.

James coughed and Emily pulled her hand away quickly.

"Sorry, boss, cold air. I'm right on it," he responded before his heavy footsteps left the office.

"So, this device... You've received some help from some of the locals tonight, did you?"

Emily was going to argue but Frank raised a finger.

"X has already informed me."

Emily studied Frank before replying. "Yes, and she crossed us."

"How so?"

"So..." Emily leant back in her chair before continuing, "You don't know everything, then."

Digging into her pants pocket, she pulled out the star-studded pendant and slammed it on the desk.

"What is that?" Frank asked as he leant forward.

"It was found around her neck."

"Whose? Annabelle's?" He picked up the pendant. "That doesn't make any sense. Why would she be wearing this?"

Chapter 60

It was the second time that night Emily had heard that name mentioned. Well, the first time the name had been only partially mentioned by Holloway but enough was said for her to connect the dots.

"Lydia was one of them."

"Hmm, okay." He turned the pendant over. "I'd heard of a double agent working the grounds in Saint Petersburg. She was American-Russian, was she not?"

Schultz nodded and Emily shot a glare at him, but Schultz kept his eyes on Frank, ignoring her.

"She was an undercover agent for the Americans. Did you not see this?" Frank turned the pendant over. "Here she's got scribed on the back *for the American cause*. Quite nice craftwork, that engraving is. It's becoming rare to find any high-quality hand-engraving."

Emily leant in. The engraving was tiny but she could just make out the phrase. She shook her head; she couldn't believe she'd missed it.

"There were some rumors she'd gone dark some eighteen months ago," Frank continued. "She was refusing all calls from the American agencies. It got to the point where they issued a warrant for her arrest."

"That's a bit drastic, isn't it?" Emily asked.

"No. They were desperate to pull her out before it was uncovered the Americans had a spy on Russian soil."

"Oh, crap." Emily only now realized the full extent of Lydia's situation.

"Kuzmich must've learnt she was a spy and had her finished off tonight before she could put a stop to tonight's—as he calls it—revolution."

"Does the Kremlin know you and your men are here?" Schultz asked.

"No." Frank looked down at the desk as he dragged on his cigar. "As far as I'm aware, Xander was the only one who knew we are here."

"We? As in you and the men you ordered out of here?" Emily asked.

"Yes. We're a small but strong force. They're all retired from the elite or special forces."

"What do you propose, then? Our car still has firepower but it's refusing to fire."

"Yes, that vehicle was only a prototype. Annabelle hadn't sent it out on a trial run. Tonight was the first time it had been out of the workshop. It was probably full of glitches."

"So now we're the guinea pigs. Great." Emily stood up. "I've heard enough. Schultz, we're out of here."

"I can't stop you. But... his men will."

"My condolences for your son. He was a great techie... and a friend I could rely on. But you've held us up long enough. Ivan and his men will now have quite a decent lead on us."

Leaving the office area, Emily marched back into the shed where the three remaining troop carriers were parked in a line, all facing the exit. One was missing, the one James must have taken earlier. As she approached, they stood up and stepped in her way, their guns up in their hands.

Emily stopped in front of them, her face within inches of one of the men.

"Move," she demanded.

The man didn't say anything, just stared at her. She felt like he was searching her soul, trying to find any weaknesses in her.

She tried to push past him but he remained standing in his spot. The men on either side of him moved in, forming a human fence between her and the doors.

"We thought you were this big hotshot martial art Kung Fu kick-butt hero. But no, you're not. You're soft. At the first hint of things not going to your plan, you're out of here."

"You don't know anything about me." Emily placed her hands on her hips.

"Lee, don't. It's not worth it." Schultz tried to pull her by her shoulder away from the men, but she stood her ground.

"Let us through. Now."

The man pulled his gun around so the barrel pointed towards her stomach.

"You wanna know what I know about you?" His eyes narrowed as he looked at her first in the right eye, then her left. "Where do I start?"

Schultz placed his hand over the gun barrel and applied a little pressure. Looking between the two of them, he said, "Steve, Lee. Not here, guys."

"Do you know these guys too?" Emily asked.

"That doesn't matter. What does matter is that we need to work together to stop Ivan Kuzmich before he reaches Moscow."

Emily glared at Steve.

"Lee. Enough," Schultz snapped.

Schultz moved behind her, then she felt his hand on her back. The pressure increased until her feet began to move away from the men.

"Lee, stop fighting me."

Turning around, she took one last look over her shoulder before reluctantly walking back towards Frank's office.

"What I do know is that your uncle is on the wanted list, and you're following in his shadow over here," Steve yelled.

Emily veered around but Schultz grabbed her before she reached Steve, who was looking smug. She tried pulling out of Schultz's grasp, but his grip tightened the more she fought.

"Lee. He's taunting you. It's not worth it. They have guns. We don't."

"Mayday," a crackled voice sounded over the men's handheld radios. "We've recovered the device but we're under heavy fire."

Steve depressed the speaker button on his radio. "James?"

"Yes. We've got two down. Shit. Hang on. We're under heavy fire again."

Everyone in the shed fell silent. Even Emily stopped fighting Schultz and stood there, staring between Steve and his handheld radio. Waiting.

"This isn't good," Emily whispered as the silence drew on. "It's got to be one of Ivan's crew."

"Ms. Lee, where are you?" a new voice sounded over the radio.

Everyone looked at Emily, who shrugged her shoulders.

"Where are you hiding? Come out, come out and play."

Emily shrugged her shoulders. "I've got no idea who that is."

"I know you're around here somewhere. I'm all alone and want someone to play with."

"Who's this? What have you done to James?" Steve asked into his handheld radio.

"Are you James?" The voice over the radio sounded distant, like he was talking away from the radio.

Everyone in the shed was watching Steve's handheld radio. Waiting.

"Whatever he asks, don't do it. He's got a gun pressed to

my head."

Everyone exchanged glances as they recognized James distressed voice over the radio.

"If you're going to shoot me, hurry—"

"They've heard enough," the original voice over the radio returned.

"We need to get him out of there," Emily whispered to Frank.

"He's alive, for now," the original voice over the radio returned. "If you cooperate, your friend James will live."

"Here, hand me your radio." Emily held her hand out.

Steve shook his head. "It's exactly what he wants."

"I must thank you," the voice crackled over the radio again. "Was Ms. Lee not aware she was being followed?"

Everyone turned to look at Emily.

"Yes, I noticed someone behind us, but it was dark and they were too far away. All I could see were headlights."

"How long were they following you?" Frank asked.

"I saw the headlights when we turned off the highway. It could've been anyone."

"Not this time." Frank turned to Steve and nodded.

"Let me see... James demeanor leads me to believe he's defense force. Army? Ex-army, because I know there wouldn't be any active defense personnel over here. He wouldn't be out here alone with a bunch of civilians. That leads me to believe the rest of you would be ex-army too."

This time it was Steve's turn to shift uncomfortably as everyone in the shed waited for his reply.

"You're not going to defend yourself? Which must mean you're not even meant to be in this country. Hand over the two Australians and I'll let the rest of you go unharmed. You have my word."

"Hand me the radio." Frank stepped towards Steve and held his hand out.

Steve stepped out of formation, handing his handheld radio to Frank. Frank nodded as he grabbed the radio. Staring at Emily, Frank depressed the comm button.

"This is Xavier. How can I assist you?"

Emily looked confused.

"It's one of the aliases he uses," Schultz whispered into her ear.

"You have two Australians there. Do you not?"

"I have a few Australians here." Frank looked around at the men standing in front and to the side of him. "If I'm to help you, I'll need a bit more information."

"Two intruders. One male, one female."

Frank looked around. Emily turned her head and followed the circle around. The men were shaking their heads.

"Sorry," Frank replied. "No one here by that description. What have they done?"

"That doesn't matter. I need you to hand them over to me. Now."

"Manners." Frank stared at Emily.

Emily's heart skipped a beat before Frank smiled.

"If I could help you," Frank continued, "I would. Because you asked so nicely, if I do see them, how will I get in touch with you?"

"I'll be keeping your radio on me."

A single gunshot echoed from the radio through the shed.

"James?" Frank yelled into the radio.

"He won't be re-uniting with you," the crackling voice sounded over the radio. "Now, don't lie to me. Hand over the Australians."

Chapter 61

Emily followed Frank to a large trestle table that'd just been set up by his men at the rear of the lineup of troop carriers.

"You'd better be ready to dance," Frank said as a large map, almost the size of the table, was spread out.

"Muay Thai style? You bet."

"Muay what? You know what, it doesn't matter. You two had better be ready to step it up a notch. Ivan and his men, they're nothing compared with what's coming."

"You sure about that?" Emily asked.

Frank glared at her and her smile quickly disappeared.

"Right. There's less than six hundred kilometers to the Kremlin from here. That's a lot of ground to cover."

"Do we know if Ivan uses a cell phone?" Schultz asked.

"Even if we did," Frank turned to Schultz, "we don't have anyone on hand to track his signal." Frank studied the map, but Emily could easily see his mind was elsewhere.

Emily exchanged glances with Schultz. Taking a deep breath, she asked, "Do you, or anyone here, know of someone by the call sign Z?"

"Boy, I haven't heard that name in a long while. Not since..." Frank pondered for a moment. "Not since Xander joined the Federal Police."

"That's going on seven years," Schultz advised Emily.

"Frank, do you remember how close the two of them were?" Emily asked.

"I'm not senile. Not yet anyway. There were four of them. All very close. Until... until Xander was given the ultimatum. Jail or federal work. After that, as far as I'm aware, he never spoke to the other three again."

"Four?" Schultz asked, looking just as surprised as Emily was.

"Yeah. There was W, who also went by the name of Brian, I think it was. There was also Y—don't ask me what his real name was; I haven't the faintest."

"Interesting. Schultz, do any of those names sound familiar?"

"No, besides Brian and, before tonight, Z. No, I haven't heard Xander mention the other two hackers."

"Yes, Z seemed rather fond of Xander."

"He was." Frank's eyes glistened as he smiled. "He looked up to Xander like an older brother. Were you talking to Z tonight?" His face turned from happy to determined. "He can help us."

"I'm not sure about that." Emily looked down at her feet as she shuffled them. "I may have burnt that bridge."

"That'd be just about right." Steve smirked.

Emily looked at Steve, mortified, until he winked at her. Her eyebrows furrowed. A small smile appeared on Steve's face but quickly disappeared when Frank addressed them.

"One of you have his number? Yes?"

"I do," Schultz replied.

Emily turned to see Schultz tapping on his phone screen. "You do?" she asked.

"Still the same number?" Frank asked.

"Last number has changed," Schultz advised. "On its way to you now."

"Good, get him on the line."

Schultz didn't argue. He promptly dialed Z.

The call was answered on the first ring, "Holloway here, who's this?"

"Z, it's Schultz."

"Hi, Holloway," Frank yelled out.

"Ah Frank, it's good to hear your voice again."

"We need a favor, please," Schultz asked he he moved the conversation back to business.

"You'll be after a location on Ivan?"

"Yeah, what do you have?"

"I've been tracking him and his vehicles since they began moving again."

"Moving again?" Frank asked.

"Schultz can fill you in later. Right now, there's still two groups of vehicles heading along the highway."

"Which highway?" Frank interrupted.

"The M11, the highway closest to your location. First, you'll come across three SUVs. There'll be one in each lane and one following behind and all three travelling at the same speed. They're currently forty kilometers away from your current location. Further up another ten kilometers, there's another small group of two trucks. Again, one in each lane, both travelling at the same speed. Then another five kilometers up there's two trucks and an SUV. The SUV has one truck behind and one beside it. Ivan is in this front convoy."

"And you're certain Ivan is in the leading SUV?"

"Yes, Frank and... Brian is in the SUV with Ivan."

"Has Brian got a laptop with him?"

"That's how I was able to determine which vehicle he was in. Brian might be good, but he's not that good. I was able to hack into the tablet he's using and tapped into his inbuilt video camera."

"Nice."

"I trust your vehicles are ready and loaded?"

"Always. Keep us in the loop if anything changes with their location," Frank replied.

"Will do, boss."

Chapter 62

Ivan checked his watch, the tenth time in less than a minute.

"The time isn't going to go any quicker," Brian said.

"How is everyone tracking? I trust they're all on schedule," Ivan replied.

He watched Brian as he tapped his tablet. Leaning in, he saw a map zoom out. Saint Petersburg was labelled on the left, and Moscow on the bottom right corner.

"All going to plan. Do you see those dots moving?"

"Hmm... Hmm."

"That's your men."

"And Tony?"

Brian tapped at his keyboard, the map zooming in on a small town not far behind them.

"He's stationary."

"What does that mean?"

"It appears he's positioned himself near that Australian woman's location."

"It appears? Has he, or hasn't he?"

"Unless he has a rendezvous with someone else there. I'm fairly certain that's where she'll be hiding. Her car was tracked, and it's been parked for a little while now, a few blocks away from Tony's current location."

"I need to know why he's not already on his way back."

"Onto it."

Ivan watched Brian as he pulled up the satellite recording and began rewinding through the footage.

Watching Brian, he said, "And the Australian woman, she does have a name."

Brian stopped and stared at the screen.

Ivan continued, "I know about your past with her. In Melbourne? Don't play me for a fool. I did my research on you before you'd even stepped foot on that plane in Melbourne."

Brian slowly turned around until he was facing Ivan. "That woman... is nameless."

Ivan stared at him, neither men faltering.

"Obviously, there's more than what your file says."

"If there's something you want to ask, ask it now."

"All in good time."

"Very well. I have work to do. That is, if you want me to locate *that woman*."

Ivan's cell rang. It was a call he'd been anticipating.

"Very well." He waved Brian off.

Turning to look out of his car window, he answered his cell, "Yes."

"Are you on schedule?" the caller asked.

Ivan checked his watch before replying, "We may actually be ahead of schedule. Is everything in order, ready for our arrival?"

"All going to plan."

"He's staying on the grounds tomorrow night?"

"Yes, and tonight."

"Everything running normal there? No uncertainties, rumors, anything?"

"No, everything per normal."

"Good. Our access point?"

"It's all in order."

"Everything hedges on the access point being accessible."

"I'll be in touch if anything changes." The caller ended the call.

"All good, boss?" The driver quickly turned around to see Ivan tucking his cell away.

"Yes. Can we go any faster?"

"I can, but aren't you worried about catching the attention of the police?"

"They won't be annoying us tonight. You worry about driving faster, I'll worry about everything else."

Chapter 63

Emily heard a sound coming from the wall behind them. Straining her ears, she waited for the sound to return. Nothing. She took a couple of steps towards the shed wall.

"What is it, Lee?" Frank asked.

Emily turned around to see Schultz, Frank and his men around the trestle table, hands resting on the map, looking up at her.

"I thought I heard something outside."

"Sound?"

"Like someone or something was moving around out there."

"It's time to get moving. We're all on the same page?" Frank looked around at everyone.

Everyone in the room nodded as they looked down at the map, except for Emily.

"We only get one shot at this. If we fail, we won't see daylight again. We'll all be imprisoned—if we make it that far. Understood?"

Silence fell over the group as they nodded.

"Right." He folded up the map. "Everything ready to rock and roll?"

"We're ready to rock," Steve advised.

"Let's roll, then." He waved his hand in the air as he turned towards their parked troop carriers. "Lee, Schultz, you're travelling with me."

Everyone left the table towards their respective troop carrier and Emily joined Schultz at the back of the group.

"You all right?" Schultz asked.

She smiled, a forced one at that. "Yeah, all good. I think I'm just a bit tired."

"It'll be all over soon and you'll be able to sleep on the plane home."

"Sleep? Plane? Those two are polar opposites."

Schultz chuckled. "There's my girl."

Still in his joyful boyish mood, he reached his arm around her shoulders and pulled her in tight against him before releasing her.

"Come on, you two, get in." Frank held the rear door open on what looked like a ramped-up troop carrier.

As they approached, Emily saw Frank press a button on a small remote and the floor-to-ceiling sliding doors began to slowly grind open.

Following Schultz, she stepped up onto the rear step and grabbed the top of the vehicle. She stopped on the side step when the sound of glass smashing echoed through the shed. Looking around, she saw a metal canister hit the floor. Purple smoke was quickly emanating from one end of the canister.

"Get in quick." Frank pushed her in and threw himself inside the vehicle right after her, slamming the door shut behind him.

As he did so, Emily heard another window smash. Maneuvering past Schultz, who'd already positioned himself just inside the door and an assortment of guns lying on the floor, she took a seat alongside him.

"Roll, roll, roll. Let's get out of here. Now," Frank yelled out to the driver.

Their driver fired up the troop carrier, and their vehicle was the first of the three troop carriers to head towards the opening door.

Emily glanced around the interior, there were two bench seats ran along the length of the vehicle from behind the middle seats to the back door. The front half of the vehicle looked like a normal four-wheel drive. Steve was their driver, and the remaining four seats were occupied by a few of Frank's men.

Steve caught her looking at him and positioned the rear-view mirror until she could see his face. Then he winked at her.

"Eyes on the road, Steve," she called out, trying very hard

to remain serious despite her face warming up.

Frank was speaking fast into a handheld radio. "Headlights off until we're clear. We don't know what, or who, is out there. Be ready for anything."

Emily looked out the back window and saw the headlights on the other two troop carriers being switched off. There were now about three car lengths between the troop carrier she was in and the one behind her.

"How many men are in the other two troopies?"

"That doesn't concern you, does it?"

"Don't you think we should have our numbers evenly spread between all the vehicles? What happens if we're knocked out?"

"It's all good. The remaining troopies only have two or three men in each. They'll be the ones we'll send out to do surveillance or as a decoy. Here, you two will need these." Frank reached over and passed each of them a handgun.

Emily tucked hers inside her coat pocket.

"And... I'd find something to hold onto if I were you. Things might get a little rough."

Above her was a line of grab handles. She grabbed the one closest to her just as their vehicle moved over the shed's steel guide rails. The door opening was barely wide enough for them to fit through, but Steve revved the troop carrier a little more and they propelled out of the shed, landing on the road with a thud.

Emily looked over her shoulder and out towards the side she'd seen the canisters thrown from. Drifting out from behind the wall where it had clearly been parked was a black SUV that looked remarkably like one of Ivan's.

"Fire at that SUV," Emily pointed out the side window.

The SUV was now behind them, cutting them off from Frank's other men.

Chapter 64

"I've targeted the shed where the two Australians were hiding. They egot out, but I'm now in pursuit of their vehicle," Tony advised Ivan over their private radio channel.

"Fire back," Tony ordered to his passenger as gunfire rained on their SUV.

His passenger was quick to respond by returning fire.

"They got out? You'd better make sure they're stopped this time," Ivan instructed over the handheld radio, his voice scratchy.

"Onto it." Tony changed up through the gears, slowly closing in on the troop carrier.

Tony was less than four car lengths behind the leading troop carrier. He was still under constant gunfire when he flicked a switch. His overhead light bar lit up the street and front yards of the neighboring houses. The troop carrier in front of him swerved towards the edge of the road.

"Keep them hot." Tony pointed to the troop carrier in front of them.

"You want to me to take the Australians out right now? I can, and we'll stop the whole convoy," his passenger said.

"No, not here. We're too close to houses, and both of our parents live on this stretch of the road. We'll get them on the highway."

Tony glanced into his side mirror before swinging out and passing the leading troop carrier containing the Australians. Out of the corner of his eye, he noticed his passenger throw a light flare at the troop carrier as they passed. The shooters from the troop carrier ceased shooting at his SUV just long enough for him to gain some distance.

Tony looked in his rear and side mirrors but he couldn't see any of the troop carriers. He knew they were there, somewhere. He heard bullets hitting his SUV, but without their headlights on, he didn't know exactly where or how far behind they were.

This was the only time he didn't like how sparse the street lights were. In his teenage years, when he'd be sneaking home late, he used the lack of street lighting to his advantage, hiding in the shadows when vehicles approached. As far as he knew, he always arrived home undetected.

"Keep firing back," Tony ordered.

Not willing to take any chances, he pushed the accelerator

pedal down in a hope to put some distance between him and the troop carriers, heading directly to the highway.

"Update. Are they taken care of?" Ivan's voice came over the handheld radio.

Tony ignored him, his eyes focused instead on the road ahead, to the looming intersection.

"We'll ambush them up the highway. Away from our home town."

His passenger nodded.

"Tony, have you got a copy?" Ivan asked, this time anger replacing his calm manner.

Chapter 65

As they approached the highway, Emily leant on the back seat in between two of Frank's men.

"Sorry," she whispered to the one she'd just knocked with her hand as they hit a bump in the road.

Ahead, she saw the black SUV desperately trying to get away from them.

"Do we have anything stronger?" She glanced over her shoulder to Frank, to the guns on the floor then back out the front window.

"Not in here, we don't."

She turned around and gave him a strange look before tapping her foot on the bazooka.

"What about this one?" She kept her eyes on Frank,

studying his expression.

"Not in residential areas. Too much collateral."

"Too much collat—"

"There's a time and a place for everything. Look at him," Frank pointed out the front window. "He's desperate. He's a young yes-man who doesn't have the experience and patience we have. Don't worry, his time will come in a moment."

Emily looked at him, unsure how to compute what she'd just heard. Shaking her head, she looked back out the front window just in time to see the SUV drifting around the corner.

Out of the corner of her eye, she saw Frank pick up the handheld radio piece and advise, "Keep your headlights off."

The sparse street lights and a set of traffic lights ahead were their only guides onto the highway.

Emily sat back in her seat and waited.

"Here, help me," she heard Frank ask. "Men, incoming."

Looking over, she saw him trying to lift the bazooka she'd tapped moments before. Schultz was already lifting his end. Frank lifted the other end and rested it on the backrest of the row of seats in front of her. The men sitting there re-positioned themselves and assisted Frank in moving the bazooka into position.

"So, this is the time and the place, then?" Emily asked.

Schultz shrugged his shoulders and continued pushing his end towards the middle of the four-wheel drive.

"Wait and see," Steve yelled from the driver's seat.

She chose to ignore him, instead watching the men as they

positioned themselves. One of them opened and pulled back the sun roof. A gush of freezing night air swept in and straight to the back. Emily turned her coat collar up and wrapped her coat around her until her face was covered.

"Bit cold back there, are we?" Steve joked.

"All good," she yelled back and glanced back through the window.

Two troop carriers with no lights on turned onto the highway behind them. Up ahead, Emily saw a set of taillights.

"Is that him?" Frank asked, leaning over the middle seats and pointing forward.

"I'd say so," Steve replied. "We'll confirm first."

Emily saw a set of binoculars being handed from the middle to the front passenger seat. Everyone was silent, holding their breaths, waiting for confirmation.

"Well?" Frank asked, growing impatient.

"We are set to go," the front passenger announced. "I repeat, we are good to go."

"Boys, you know what you need to do." Frank nodded to the three men sitting in front of them.

The man in the middle stood up and propped himself against the car as the other two men guided the bazooka up to him. When it'd disappeared through the sun roof, the two other men held onto the shooter's legs.

"Steady up," the shooter yelled out.

Steve slowed down their vehicle as they entered the straight highway. A set of taillights were visible a few hundred meters in front of them.

Emily felt Schultz breathing down her neck. She turned to see him trying to look out the front windshield. She moved a little so he was able to get a better view.

"Thank you," he whispered into her ear.

His breath sent a shiver down her back.

They were almost at a crawl when a loud explosion sounded above her. The bazooka was handed down and the shooter took his position back in the middle, while one of the other men closed the sun roof.

A fireball erupted ahead of them.

"We have impact with the target," the front passenger announced.

"Speed up." Frank ordered over the radio. We need to ensure no one escapes that car."

"I don't think anyone could've escaped that," Emily said.

"We don't act on thoughts. We act on facts."

"Well, that's where we differ, then."

"Yes. The sooner you're out of this country the better. I'm sure Schultz has suggested protective custody a number of times."

"Not you too." She reached for the grab handle above her as their troop carrier sped up.

"He does have a point. This is dangerous territory. It's not some Kung Fu punch-up on the corner streets of Melbourne."

Emily turned towards the front of the troop carrier, away from Frank.

Their vehicle was slowing. Emily looked out the front window to the approaching fireball that had been one of Ivan's

SUVs. The skeleton of the SUV was showing through the flickers of flames.

No way could anyone have survive that, she thought.

"Team two, check the site. Extinguish the fire and report back on your findings," Frank advised over the handheld radio.

They slowly drove past, the heat radiating through her window, warming her face. Emily searched the wreckage, but the flames were too fierce for her to be able to see anything or anyone inside.

"Pretty grim, isn't it?" Schultz asked, watching her face.

"Huh?" She took a moment to comprehend what Schultz had asked then quickly covered her shock, smiling it off. "No, it's not that. It was just the intensity of the heat; it took me by surprise. I wasn't expecting it."

"First time witnessing something like that?" Frank asked as he picked up one of the guns from the floor.

"Kind of."

She watched him as he checked the gun's mechanism.

"You'll see a lot more than that tonight." Frank didn't look up as he spoke.

"As long as it's well before the walls of the Kremlin."

"That's the plan." Frank looked directly at her as he made the loading mechanism click.

Chapter 66

Ivan checked his watch. It'd been ten minutes since the last radio communication.

"Anything?" Ivan asked his driver.

Keeping his eyes on the road ahead, the driver shook his head.

"Try again."

"You got a copy, Tony?"

Radio silence.

"Tony, you got a copy?"

Ten seconds passed, and no response.

Pulling out his cell, Ivan brought up his recent call list and dialed Tony's number. It rang out.

"Brian, check his tracker."

Brian typed on his tablet then paused, shaking his head.

"No signal."

"No signal?"

"His signal has gone offline. I don't have a way to track him."

"I'm not a dumbass. I know what offline means." Ivan looked out of his window, his elbow resting on the armrest and his hand cupping his chin.

"You want me to swing back around?" his driver asked.

Ivan checked his watch again, not to know the time but purely from habit, to appear to his men that he cared for them.

"No, we don't have time. We need to keep moving forward. I'll deal with him later."

"Just a thought..." Brian's voice trailed off as he appeared to be carefully choosing his next words. "Could we send one of the other vehicles back around?"

"How about you check your surveillance? Backtrack his movements. Do what you need to do to find him."

"Was just a thought." Brian returned to his tablet, sounding deflated.

"You worry about the computer side of the operation and I'll worry about the rest, including how I manage my men."

Ivan leant forward and tapped his driver on the shoulder. "Keep pushing forward. Stay focused. Nothing can derail us. Not when we've worked so hard to get here and we're so close. Understood?"

His driver nodded and Ivan leant back in his seat. He rubbed his forehead. A headache was brewing. Closing his eyes, he relaxed his shoulders into his seat's backrest.

"I've picked him up at the shed," Brian advised.

Groggy, Ivan cracked open one eye. "Huh?"

"I've got him tracked to the shed."

"I'm not deaf." He rubbed his head. "That doesn't tell me if he's alive or not."

"I should have something for you shortly." Brian returned to his screen.

"You came with blazing referrals. I'm not seeing that person."

Brian ignored him. Sighing, Ivan looked out of his window.

He hadn't realized his fee included babysitting someone who should be more astute than the kid who was sitting alongside him, he thought.

"Holy crap."

Ivan turned to see what all the fuss was about now, only to see Brian staring at his screen, mouth and eyes wide open.

"What is it?"

"I'll just rewind it."

A few seconds later Brian turned the tablet around.

"What is it?" Ivan asked.

"I've used your satellite feed to monitor your convoys tonight."

"Get on with it. What do you have there?" Ivan nodded to the screen.

"I've also been monitoring Tony's SUV since he left us back up the highway. He's already taken care of a James."

Ivan shrugged, not recognizing the name.

Brian continued, "You really need to see this."

Brian leant over and hit the play button.

The surveillance footage started to play. Ivan saw an SUV approaching the highway.

"Tony?" He pointed to the SUV.

Brian nodded but kept looking at the floor.

"Who's in the other vehicles? Are they troop carriers?"

"Keep watching."

Ivan didn't argue. He kept his eyes on the screen and watched as Tony turned onto the highway. At that moment he lost sight of the chasing vehicles. He leant in towards the screen.

"They've turned their lights off."

"What are they up to?" Ivan voiced his thoughts out loud.

On the highway now, he saw Tony was making some distance. Ivan calculated he must be almost at top speed.

"Okay, so he got away." Ivan leant back. "So, where did he go next?"

A white light flare filled the screen. Ivan jumped back. Rubbing his eyes, he slowly opened them as the night footage returned to normal, all except for a fireball on the highway.

"What in the world was that?"

"It's what you think it is."

"Survivors?"

"From this recording, there's been no movement."

"And we're certain Tony was in that vehicle?" Ivan pointed to the fireball on the screen.

"Unfortunately, yes."

"So, who caused this?"

Brian paused the video surveillance as the chasing convoy drove past the wreckage. Zooming in, he turned the screen around.

"Am I meant to recognize it?" Ivan asked.

Brian clicked through a few open programs, stopping on one that looked like more video recordings. Pressing a few buttons, he enlarged the still image—an entrance to a shed on the far-right side and three cars leaving.

"Right. This is the surveillance from Tony's SUV. Recognize anyone?" Brian asked.

Ivan looked at the paused image, a male, mid-thirties, sitting in the front, and two more men close together behind the front seat. Another three people were sitting in the back, along the back windows.

Shaking his head, he asked, "Who are they?"

"That there is our growing Australian convoy."

"You sure they're Australians? They look like one of us."

"I've reviewed Tony's radio communication. They've," he pointed to the men, "admitted they're Australians."

"Okay..."

Brian resumed the video and paused it a few seconds later, zooming in on the paused image.

"That bitch." Ivan thumped his door's armrest.

Brian moved the image along. "And that man there, you know him. He's the Australian cop, Schultz."

Ivan pushed the tablet away from him and stared out of his window, his chin resting on his hand.

"All three troop carriers were able to get out of the shed before Tony's canisters fully exploded. I've listened to the audio. It all matches everything we heard earlier over the radio."

"And they're the ones who killed Tony?"

"Yes."

"Right. Change of plans."

Chapter 67

Looking around, it dawned on Emily it'd been some time since there'd been any traffic on the road. The last car she'd seen was about ten minutes after they re-entered the highway, after they blew up one of Ivan's SUV. Since then, it'd just been them and their convoy still chasing Ivan and his men down. There hadn't even been a hint of taillights on the horizon.

"Steve, can this thing go any faster?" she asked.

"Boss?" Steve looked in his rear-view mirror at them.

Emily looked between the two of them. Frank sat there looking torn.

"It's the middle of the night. There's no one about."

Frank just sat there; his expression unchanged.

Emily continued, "Do you want to catch them before or

after they take over the Kremlin?"

"It's Z." Frank tapped a couple of buttons on his cell and answered, "You're on speaker."

"I'd better behave, then."

"How far out are we from catching Ivan?" Emily asked.

"Frank, you need to really push that troopy of yours if you want any chance of catching Ivan's convoys. You guys are still fifteen minutes, at least, behind them."

"Steve," Frank yelled. "Put your foot down. We've got some ground to cover."

"Boss..." Steve glanced through his rear-view mirror. "Aren't you trying to avoid attention?"

"That's the least of our worries right now. Besides Ivan and his men, we're the only ones who are aware of what's going down."

"Right-o boss." Steve increased the speed of their troop carrier.

"Z, thanks for the update."

Frank disconnected the call. He'd barely disconnected the call to Z when Emily's cell phone buzzed. It was a message from Ivan.

Brian, that bastard! she thought as she opened the message. It read:

> *Back off now and Schultz will live.*

At that moment, bright lights were approaching from a side road and didn't appear to be slowing down. Emily looked over her shoulder. A steel median barrier was running down the middle of the highway. She looked back at the approaching intersection. The oncoming vehicle wasn't slowing down.

Emily yelled out, "Hold on, everyone."

"I see them. They've come out of nowhere," Steve shouted as he yanked on the brakes.

Steve pulled their troop carrier to a complete stop. The approaching vehicle hit their front corner panel and spun around multiple times before coming to a stop, facing their troop carrier.

"Where did they come from?" Frank asked.

Emily looked out the front window and saw it was an SUV. It had hit the median barrier, leaving its impression in the steel before bouncing off and coming to a stop.

Waving at Steve, Emily yelled out, "Move. Now."

Their tires squealed as they began to move. Emily saw a second set of headlights approaching from the side road.

They cleared the intersection as the second SUV entered it. The sound of metal grinding on metal echoed through the night. Emily turned around. A crumpled mess greeted her.

Out of the corner of her eye she saw Frank pick up the handheld radio and ask, "Troopy two, you got a copy?"

Emily turned to Frank to see his eyes glued to the carnage behind them. She felt their troop carrier slow down.

"Keep going!" Frank yelled as he picked up the handheld radio and asked again, "Troopy two. Have you got a copy?"

There was a pause before a crackly voice was heard over the radio. "This is troopy three. Troopy two is out. I repeat, troopy two is out. No movement. We're going in to check."

Chapter 68

Ivan answered his cell. "Update."

"Lead vehicle only received a nudge and are on their way towards you. Second target has been demobilized. No movement seen, probable fatalities."

There was a pause. Ivan tried to ignore the caller's heavy breathing and focus on the background. Gunshots? Lots of them, some nearby.

The caller returned. "Got to go. We're under heavy fire from the last vehicle in their convoy."

The cell beeped in Ivan's ear.

"Shit." Ivan threw the phone down.

He stared out his window, his breathing heavy as his frustrations brewed inside. After a minute of reflection, he turned to the men in his car.

"That's the last of my vehicles that woman is going to take out tonight." His nose turned up at the thought of her name.

Mumbles came from everyone else in the car, all avoiding eye contact with him. Picking his cell up off the floor, Ivan made a call.

"Move into position," he advised as soon as the call was answered.

"Understood."

* * *

"Have you got a copy, Frank?"

"Loud and clear. What've you got?" Frank replied into his radio receiver.

"No survivors on impact."

"Just ours, or theirs too?"

"Theirs too. The occupants in the second SUV, the one that took out your second troopy were Ivan's militias. They were loaded with guns and ammunition."

"And the first SUV that hit us?"

"More of Ivan's militias. There was some resistance but they'll no longer be a problem."

"You've searched our men and their troopy?"

"We've taken care of it," he said, his tone somber. "There's no trace left in the troopy that'll connect us to them."

"We all knew that if we were to find ourselves in a situation like this, all our identification would be stripped from us."

"Agree. Just... the reality."

"Keep focus. We're nearly done."

"And our fallen?"

"I'll get our men home, some way. How much damage did your troopy receive?"

"Extensive."

"Drivable?"

"No. We've already cleared it of any identification, just applying accelerant."

"You know the drill?"

"Yes, we'll meet you back in Melbourne."

Chapter 69

They were passing another quaint town when Ivan started to drift to sleep but was interrupted by another phone call. He didn't read the caller ID before answering.

"This had better be good," he snapped.

"Sorry if I woke you. I have news on the president."

"Who's this?" Ivan glanced at his phone but the caller ID was blocked.

"Ivan, it's Asjay."

"Oh, Asjay. Sorry, your name didn't appear on my screen."

"I've had to get a burn phone. The president's private security detail have tapped my work one."

"Have you been compromised?" Ivan glanced around at the occupants in his car only to see them all quickly turn away.

"Possibly. Too hard to tell. Either way, this will be my last call. I'll be disappearing for a while."

"Be safe."

"Will do. Good luck. Bye—"

"Hold on. What news did you have?"

"Oh, sorry. Ah, yes, that's right. The president has made an unscheduled stop at Veliky Novgorod."

"How unscheduled?"

"Unofficial matters requiring his attendance there tomorrow."

"That will change what we do." Ivan pondered for a couple of seconds before continuing, "Everything still good to go at the Kremlin?"

"Yes."

"Can I ask you to complete one last favor?"

"I really must go." The woman was almost whispering.

"I need to move my plans to tonight."

"Tonight?"

"Can you do it?"

"I really don't know."

"I'll see to it that you're set up financially."

"I... I don't know."

"One last time?"

"Alright. I've got to go now."

"As soon as you can, I need you to send through to me the president's exact location tonight. And Asjay?"

"Yes."

"Thank you for all of your hard work. Stay safe out there."

Ivan ended the call.

"What do you need me to do?" Brian asked.

"Nothing. You keep monitoring the crews."

"Boss, what's happening?" His driver looked at Ivan through his rear-view mirror.

"We're still heading towards Moscow."

The driver nodded.

"Tomorrow morning the citizens will wake up to a new president."

"We're going in tonight?" the driver asked.

"That's what I said. There'll be no stopping until we arrive at the Kremlin. Understood?"

"Yes."

"Everyone else?"

Brian and his front passenger both acknowledged Ivan.

"Good. You two," he pointed to Brian and the front passenger, "start your preparations."

When he saw them getting organized, he made another call.

"Zane, there's been a change of plans."

"How much change are we talking?"

"I need you to redirect your convoy to Veliky Novgorod."

He turned to Brian, covered the cell's microphone and whispered, "How far out is he?"

Brian tapped on the keyboard. "They'll be the first convoy to arrive there."

"They don't need to backtrack?"

"No."

"Good." His phone vibrated. It was a message from an unknown number. The messaged started with *Veliky Novgorod*. A small smile appeared on his face; she'd come through. "Right. You there, Zane?"

"Yes. We've checked on our end. We're not far from there. What do you want us to do when we get there?"

"Hold tight, prepare, stay undetected. I'll be sending the remaining four convoys from down south to you."

"O-kay. Who's our target?"

"You need to ensure the president doesn't leave his current location."

"The president? Isn't he—"

"I'll send through the coordinates in a moment."

"Are you joining us there?"

"No, we're continuing as planned. Use whatever force you deem necessary. I'll be in contact again once we've taken control of the Kremlin."

Ivan made another four phone calls, advising the convoy leaders of the new plan.

"Zane and his convoy are on target. The remaining four have re-directed to their new route," Brian advised as Ivan tucked his cell phone away.

"Good, good." He dragged his hands down his pants to his knees, where he clenched his fists.

"You having doubts?" Brian asked.

"No. I've been preparing for this night, to get in there and do the job I was meant to be doing."

Chapter 70

Frank and his crew were starting to gain some serious ground on Ivan when he peered out the front window and saw a set of taillights, a few hundred meters up the highway.

"Steve, you see what I see?"

"Two sets?"

"Yeah. Slow down a little. We'll see what they're up to."

"You think it's them?" Emily asked as she peered out the front window.

"Not sure. I suppose we'll find out soon enough."

"Have they stopped? In the middle of the road?"

"I'd say if they haven't stopped it's pretty close to it. Steve—"

Steve slowed their troop carrier down even more. "Already

on it."

"What are you two up to?" Frank murmured.

They were now within one hundred meters and still gaining.

"See if you can take them on the shoulder."

Steve moved their troop carrier towards the edge of the road. The two SUVs ahead remained in their lanes. Steve sped up.

They were now two car lengths behind the roadblock. Steve moved their vehicle a little farther over. They were now off the road.

"Hold on," Steve yelled as stones flicked out from under their tires.

Their hood was now alongside the back of the vehicle in the right lane.

"They're moving over," Emily yelled.

The SUV in front of them moved over towards the shoulder. Steve applied the brakes and moved back in behind the roadblock.

Frank felt his troop carrier speed up and slow down as Steve varied his speed. Each time, the two vehicles ahead of them followed suit.

"Steve, up ahead is a break in the middle traffic barrier. Take them on their left. You'll then be on the wrong side of the road but it's only for a few kilometers, until the next break in the barrier."

"Roger that."

"Keep behind them until the last second," Emily advised.

"Emily."

"Yeah."

"I know how to drive."

Before she could respond, Steve swerved out onto the wrong side of the highway. The black SUV in the left lane joined them, pushing them out onto the shoulder on the far side of the road. Their tires flicked stones everywhere.

"Guns!" Emily pointed to the SUV next to them.

Frank looked out the window to the three barrels pointed at them. He turned to his men, but they were already grabbing their guns.

"They're Ivan's so-called militias," Emily yelled.

"You sure?"

"Definitely. They're wearing the same uniform as Nicholas."

Steve slowed down until they were able to slide in behind Ivan's militias. One of Frank's men popped out through the sun roof and opened fire. Gunfire was returned.

"We have double trouble."

Frank turned around to see Schultz pointing to the other vehicle, on the other side of the highway.

"Men, all hands on deck and let's show them some fireworks."

A gun dropped down from the sun roof, and the two other men handed their comrade a loaded RPG. They wound their windows down and returned fire.

"I've had enough of his clown." Frank turned away from the shooting and dialed Z on his cell phone.

"I didn't expect to hear from you again so soon," Z answered.

"I need a favor."

Frank jumped at the sound of a loud explosion beside him. Looking over his shoulder, he saw a fireball erupting right behind them.

One down, one to go, Frank thought.

"All good there?"

"Yeah, sorry." Frank turned away again. "Just some friendly locals."

"Sounds like it."

"Can you run a trace on Ivan's bank accounts?"

"What are you looking for?"

"Money. Whatever he's got."

"O-kay," Z answered, unsure.

"Send all his funds elsewhere."

"I'm not sure... I don't like—"

"Brian's involved."

"Well, then, that changes everything. Did you have anywhere in mind?"

"Charities. The ones that could actually do with a good cash injection. Remember, all transactions need to be untraceable."

Chapter 71

Looking down their side of the highway, Emily was relieved to see there weren't any headlights flashing them. On the opposite side of the highway, they still had one more SUV to stop.

"Boys, they've pulled out the big guns."

Emily couldn't move as she stared at the gun pointed at her.

Boom.

A deafening explosion erupted in front of her. Emily pressed her hands to her ears and bent over until her elbows touched her knees. The sound of metal being torn apart and various flammable substances exploding brought her very little comfort.

Emily felt a light tap on her shoulder as quiet was returned to the empty highway.

"Lee, it's all over now."

A burning mass of twisted metal greeted her as she looked up and out the window. The fire dwindled in the distance as they continued moving.

"Is this starting to become too much for you?"

Frank's stare was uncomfortable.

"No, not at all. I'm just going be glad when I finally come face to face with Ivan and Brian."

"How so?"

"I want to be the last person they see before they're locked up."

"Those are some bold words. You'd better be careful what you wish for."

It wasn't long until they were back on the right side of the highway and knocking down the kilometers.

Chapter 72

"Z, you're on loud speaker," Frank advised as soon as he answered his cell phone.

"Hi, everyone."

"What've you got?"

"I've been analyzing your speed tonight and, at your current speed, you're not going to reach Ivan and his convoy before they reach Moscow's suburbia."

"Seriously?" Frank glanced between Emily and Schultz.

Emily was looking up at the roof, watching Frank in her peripheral vision, and Schultz just shrugged his shoulders.

"He's right. We need to increase our speed again or hope they have an unforeseen delay," Emily said. She could have told him that without a complex speed analysis.

"Z, are there any other options? Trains? There's got to be one travelling past soon."

"Even if there were, you have in your company two of the country's top most wanted, and you and your men have been banned from entering Russia. How you lot entered without leaving a trace is beyond me."

"That doesn't matter. We're here now, and we have to stop that man."

"You do know it's not too late. I can have a plane waiting for you. You can still get out of there before the authorities catch up with you."

"No," Emily interrupted them. "I need to see this through to the end."

"Schultz, think about your career. This could end it."

"Z, I thank you for your concerns but Lee and I know what we need to do."

"You guys may not be aware of this," Emily snapped, "but earlier tonight I was taken into a forest. The sedan I was in was shot at. I was kidnapped, taken to some island. I had to fight my way out. And Schultz was also attacked by some of Ivan's men at a local nightclub. So, no, we can't back out. I don't want to speak for anyone else in here but with what he's put us through tonight, I'm seeing this through to the end. I'm going to be the last person Ivan and Brian see before they lose their freedom."

Dumbfounded, Frank stared at Emily, eyes wide and mouth open. Emily raised an eyebrow, showing him exactly what she thought of his dumb expression. Murmurings of agreement from the remaining passengers brought their attention back to the conversation.

"There's the fighter I thought was in you," Steve called out from his driver's seat.

"Well then, I wish you all the best of luck tonight." Z disconnected the call.

Emily and Schultz stared at Frank, waiting for him to comprehend just who he was dealing with.

"So, leader, now that you know we're not about to roll over and let Ivan get his way, what do you propose we do? What are our options?" Schultz leaned back and crossed his arms.

"I... I..." Frank couldn't hold his gaze. His eyes slid to a dirty spot on his shoe. "If we don't catch him soon. It might be a good time for all of us to think about parting ways. Take Z's option and get out of this country while we still have half a chance."

"So..." Schultz paused as if he was contemplating his next few words. "You want to bail out on us?"

"I didn't say that. We just need to look at our options and seriously consider them. All."

Chapter 73

"Why are we pulling over?" Ivan asked.

"You don't hear that?" His driver asked as he placed Ivan's SUV in neutral, pulled the handbrake on and turned the ignition off.

Ivan shook his head. "No, I didn't hear anything."

His driver and front passenger both hopped out of the SUV and walked around to the back. Ivan looked at Brian, who just gave him a dumb look. Then Brian's door opened, and before he could draw his gun, his driver poked his head in. "I need both of you out."

Brian, with his tablet, removed himself from the SUV without hesitation, too absorbed with the screen.

"There'd better be a good reason for this." Ivan opened his door and placed one leg outside. "We're almost there."

Stepping out, he closed the door behind him. He looked around. They were in a deserted area, open paddocks on either side. He felt reassured by the lack of lights on the highway.

His remaining convoy were parked around him, providing some protection while he was vulnerable. His soldiers were positioned around the parked convoy, their guns poised outwards. Ivan moved around to the rear of his SUV. All the contents of the back were being piled up on the side of the road.

"What's going on here?" he asked.

No one answered.

He stalked around to the other side, where two men were huddled over the rear tire.

He stood behind them. "What's going on?"

One man was positioning a jack under his vehicle while his driver was attempting to loosen the wheel nuts.

"Just," the man strained as he pushed down on the wrench, the wheel nut barely moving, "a flat tire. Don't worry, we'll be..." he pushed on the wrench again, "moving again as soon... as... we've got this changed."

"Right. Use what men you need to. I need us back on the road in less than five minutes. Understood?"

His driver nodded as he pushed down on the wrench. The wrench wouldn't budge. Ivan's driver tried again. Nothing.

"Is there a problem?" Ivan asked, looking on as his driver tried another wheel nut.

"These are on tight. There's no way this wrench will remove the wheel nuts." His driver stood up before continuing. "I need an airhose and impact wrench to get this tire changed. Have you got them in the back of one of your trucks?"

"Check the toolboxes on both trucks. If I have one, they should be in there."

"Onto it," his driver replied as he walked towards the trucks.

Ivan looked around for Brian and saw him leaning over the SUV's hood, his face illuminated, he suspected, by the tablet's screen.

"We're so close now I can almost smell it. Can you smell it, Brian?" Ivan asked as he approached.

"Huh?" His dazed eyes met Ivan's. "Yeah..."

"In a few short hours, my Russian people will be waking up to the news that their rightful leader is finally in his spot. Nothing is going to stop us now. Are you ready for what's going to happen tonight?"

Brian finally gave Ivan his full attention. "What do you mean? Have the plans changed? I was of the understanding I was being taken to the airport."

"You'll be taken to the airport when I'm ready to send you there."

"I've already got the ticket."

"You are still needed."

"I don't know what more you require from me. I have completed everything you hired me for."

"There's a few more things I need you to do."

"What's that?"

"First one is, I need you to send one hundred thousand US dollars to Asjay."

"Now?"

"Yes."

"Her banking information?" Brian began tapping on the tablet.

"It's all in there." Ivan peered over and saw Brian was already accessing the system. "You just need to complete the transfer. I don't need to remind you to make it untraceable. Understood?"

Brian nodded as he entered in the transfer.

"Uh, boss... We have a problem."

"What is it?" Ivan leant over and Brian turned the screen around until he could see it.

"Son of a—" Ivan stood back, placing his hands on his hip. "How did that happen?"

"I... I don't know."

"Find out, fast. And if I find out you've embezzled, I promise you that you're a dead man."

Brian didn't acknowledge him but his stumbling fingers and the corner of his mouth trembling told Ivan that the techie had heard him clearly enough.

"You find anything?" Ivan tried to peer at the screen.

"It'll take longer than twenty seconds to run the trace on the transactions."

"There's more than one?"

"Yes. There's at least one hundred, if not more. It's going to take me some time. I really need my computer set up to process these searches quicker."

"Well, that can't happen. Do you know any hacker who will be able to do what I need done?"

Brian recoiled. Ivan was certain that no one before had ever requested, let alone to his face, another hacker's expertise over his.

"No, I'm a one-man show," he finally said. "There's me or me."

"Well, you're not going to be any good to me if you don't find out who accessed my account." Ivan tapped his jacket over his holster.

Brian gulped. "I'll do my best," he said and returned to his screen.

Chapter 74

They were hurtling along the highway when Emily spotted up ahead two sets of taillights, one in each lane. Taillights up high and down low. Trucks. The gap between their troop carrier and the two trucks was closing.

"Steve, slow down," Emily advised. "You guys still got the binoculars up there?"

The momentum in their troop carrier immediately slowed down.

"Sure do. Coming over."

Emily reached over the sleepy occupants in the middle and grabbed the binoculars from Steve.

"Two trucks, up ahead." Emily nodded towards the front window.

"Could be anyone."

Sitting back down, she zoomed in on her targets.

"Could be, but we need to check."

She looked over the truck in the right lane first. The back of the truck was covered by a tarp. Moving down to the number plate area, she adjusted the zoom until she was able to read it. Standard Moscow number plate, but that was not all. The hammer and sickle symbol glowed under the number plate light.

She checked the other truck. Same Moscow number plate and matching symbol on the right side of the number plate.

"We have two of Ivan's trucks," Emily yelled.

"Time to light them up." Frank handed the RPG over to the men in the middle of the troop carrier. "Take out the one on the left side first."

The three men nodded, now fully alert. Cold air gushed in as the sun roof was opened.

"Steve, keep it steady," Frank yelled.

"Right-o," Steve replied.

The one in the middle hoisted himself up onto his seat and up through the sun roof. The man in front of Emily lifted the RPG up to the shooter.

In the blink of an eye, the truck in the left lane exploded into a fireball. The truck in the next lane swerved but quickly straightened up.

"We need to get the next truck before it goes around the next bend." Frank handed another grenade over to his men.

The grenade was passed up through the sunroof.

Emily watched Frank as he placed a semi-automatic gun

on the seat alongside him before picking up another one from the floor and checking it over.

"Here, you two, we'll need these." Frank handed them each a semi-automatic gun.

"Thanks." Emily placed her gun over her knee, her attention remaining on their target ahead.

"Now we're talking," Schultz said.

A fireball erupted out the front. A perfect hit. A moment later the RPG and shooter dropped in through the sun roof.

"Steve, time to get out of here," Frank yelled out.

Without a word, Steve accelerated their troop carrier down the highway, maneuvering around the two fireballs.

Frank's cell phone rang. Tapping a couple of buttons on his cell, he answered, "Z it's so good to hear from you. You're on speaker."

"I have another update on Ivan's location. You guys are going to like this one," Z replied.

"Where are they?" Emily asked.

"They've pulled up on the side of the road just up around the next bend on the highway."

"They've pulled over?" Schultz asked.

"Yeah, car troubles. The boot of the SUV is open."

"Flat tire?" Emily looked between Frank and Schultz.

"It isn't much of a convoy," Z continued. "Two trucks and one SUV. The SUV is parked on the shoulder of the highway, while one truck is parked behind it and the other is alongside the SUV in the outside lane. If you're going to take Ivan down, now's the time."

"Thanks for that, Z," Frank replied.

Disconnecting the call, he yelled out to Steve, "Did you get that?"

"Three red eyes parked up ahead?"

"Everyone else, you all had better be armed and ready for action. You have less than two minutes until we enter that bend."

Frank and his men silently checked over their firearms.

"It all comes down to this." Emily's grip tightened around the binoculars.

"Not long now," Schultz replied.

She felt his hand on her knee, gently squeezing it. Emily turned to him. He ran his hand down the side of her face and whispered, "Not long now."

She managed a small smile when she felt their troop carrier slow as they entered the corner.

"Three red eyes ahead," Steve announced.

Emily snapped around to the front of the troop carrier and looked through her binoculars, zooming in on the convoy. They were stationary and parked just as Z had advised. She zoomed in on the number plate of the truck parked in the emergency lane and saw the now familiar symbol.

"Time to light 'em up," Emily announced.

Chapter 75

Frank and his men were getting into position as Steve charged their troop carrier towards Ivan's parked convoy. Cold air gushed in through the open sun roof. Emily scanned her surroundings. Open paddocks were beside them, and a mini forest on the opposite side of the highway. Looking out their back window, she saw a set of headlights a couple of hundred meters behind them. Emily looked through the binoculars, focusing on what she thought was an approaching vehicle, but the headlights had disappeared.

Emily scanned both lanes. Nothing. As she lowered the binoculars, the headlights re-appeared. This time they appeared a lot closer, not even a hundred meters behind them, and were quickly gaining on their troop carrier.

"Schultz. SUV fast approaching."

"Friendly?" Schultz asked.

Emily zoomed in on the number plate. Nothing.

"There's no sign of who they are but they're not slowing down."

"Frank, you'd better get ready for some friendly fire," Schultz advised.

Their troop carrier's taillights illuminated for a second the front of an approaching black SUV. Emily's eyes widened.

The approaching SUV was less than five meters behind them when they turned their lights on high beam. Emily flinched away from the blinding white light.

"Brace for impact," Emily yelled.

Emily's side slammed into the back of the middle seat.

She closed her eyes and waited. Around her, she heard a few moans, but nothing from Frank or Schultz.

Then she heard the SUV rev its engine and ram the back of their troop carrier again. Shards of metal sparked along the road as their troop carrier tipped over and screeched along the asphalt.

Emily opened her eyes and couldn't see the headlights out the back window.

"Schultz. Frank. You guys alright?" Emily asked.

Groans sounded from Frank and a few of the other occupants. Nothing from Schultz. She searched through the tangle of people and debris and saw Schultz was lying on the floor against the length of her seat.

"Schultz." She prodded him with her foot. "Schultz, wake up." He groaned. "Schultz, wake up. Now."

She edged her way over to Schultz, who was trying to get up. Emily grabbed his arm and helped him up.

"You injured?" Emily knelt in front of him.

"Just a sore head."

"We need to get out of here. You right to walk?"

"It'll take more than a sore head to keep me down." Schultz chuckled.

Looking around, Emily saw Frank and his men were all beginning to move, a few still groaning. Emily was relieved to see that everyone had survived.

"Everyone alright?" Emily asked.

"Yeah," they all groaned.

Emily looked around her, grabbing a couple of guns.

"Good." She handed a gun to Schultz. "So, unless you guys like being sitting ducks, grab what you need and move. Now."

Emily ignored the groans as she edged towards the sun roof. Her gun poised, she looked around, surveying the area, watching for movement. Nothing. She inched her boot out until it found the asphalt road. Emily surveyed the area before crouching through the sunroof. Stepping outside, she looked down the highway. The convoy was still parked.

Emily moved around to the back of their troop carrier. Crouching beside the back tire, she peered around the corner. The SUV who'd pushed them off the road had careered into the median barrier. Behind her she heard the men groan as they exited the troop carrier.

"What have we got, Emily?" Steve asked as he crouched beside her.

In the moonlit night, Emily saw movement inside the SUV.

"We have two inside the SUV—"

"Lee," Schultz whispered.

Emily turned to see Schultz and Frank at the other end of their troop carrier with three of Frank's men. Schultz pointed towards the SUV and whispered, "Three people in back seat."

"That's at least five wannabe soldiers," Emily whispered.

Gunfire erupted—first from the other side of the SUV that had rammed them, then behind her. She spotted the driver's window and then the passenger window being wound down. Two-gun barrels appeared. Emily opened fire on the driver. Hitting her first target, she moved her gun to the next opened window and lined up the back passenger.

A bullet from one of Ivan's wannabe soldiers found its mark on their troop carrier, less than a foot from Emily. She opened fire on the SUV. The passenger returned rapid fire.

"Here, let me take position," Steve said.

"I've got it." Emily returned fire. Her gun wasn't keeping up with the rapid fire that was pummeling their troop carrier.

"Lee," Schultz whispered into her ear. He placed his hand around her arm. "Let Steve take position. We need to work out our plan of attack on Ivan."

Emily lowered her gun and turned to Steve.

"Can your piece keep up with their rapid fire?"

"Better than yours. No offence."

"None taken. I just grabbed the first ones I saw."

"Don't feel bad. We've all done the same earlier in our careers. Now, we'll take care of these muppets. You two plan how we're going to take out Ivan."

Emily looked back towards the SUV. The passenger had his door open. Schultz gently pulled her arm back. Feeling defeated and knowing her gun didn't stand a chance against the rapid gunfire, Emily pulled her gun in and edged away from the back of the troop carrier.

"All yours. Driver's side passenger door open."

Steve quickly took his position and opened rapid fire on the SUV.

Taking cover behind their upturned troop carrier, Emily and Schultz moved down the length of the vehicle, stopping at the sun roof.

Squatting on the road, Emily peered through the sun roof and out the front window. She felt some comfort seeing the convoy was still motionless up ahead.

She looked around the debris inside the troop carrier.

"What are you looking for?"

"The binoculars." Her face dropped. "They're inside."

She patted her pockets all over. "And my phone."

Crouching, Emily moved her hand inside the troop carrier.

Schultz grabbed her arm. "No, it's too dangerous. I believe you."

"My phone. It has all my personal contacts, my assignments. My whole work life is on it."

"Lee. Look at me."

His voice was stern, and she had no choice but to look up at him. He held her head in his hands. "We'll get your information secured."

"How? We don't have anyone now that X is no longer with us."

"We'll work it out. Right now, I need you to refocus. Where's my strong woman?"

Knowing all too well it was too dangerous to re-enter their vehicle, she nodded, and he loosened his grip. Crouching in front of Schultz, she looked around. On their side of the highway were open paddocks, no protection. She couldn't see what lay on the other side of the dual lane highway.

Emily moved up to Steve and whispered, "Steve, what cover have we got on the other side of the highway?"

"The highway's exposed—dual lanes with only a steel guardrail marking the center. Across the road, I can just make out low-lying shrubs and trees.

"We'll be too vulnerable." She thought for a moment, looking between Steve and Ivan's trucks up ahead. "How many shooters are left in the SUV?"

"One. I should have him taken care of in a few minutes. You got a plan?"

"Before Ivan gets any ideas of escaping, we need to demobilize his two trucks."

"And the SUV?"

Emily glanced over her shoulder, she smiled.

"That's not going anywhere. I'd say they're having issues with their wheel nuts."

"True, that." Steve looked around before spotting Frank. "Oy, Frank, did you guys grab the bazooka out of the troopy?" Steve called out.

Crouched over, Frank approached bazooka in arm. "What you thinking?"

"We need to demobilize Ivan's trucks."

"Well, this will definitely do that. But, tell me. Aren't you worried we could also take Ivan down at the same time?" Frank asked.

"If we don't do something now, he'll be in one those trucks and out of here."

"Don't need to tell me twice. Get the lads to cover me."

Steve nodded and signaled his men.

"Lee, you and Schultz cover me from the front. If gunfire erupts from any of those trucks, you fire back," Frank ordered.

"Done."

Emily moved back to Schultz and relayed the change of plans.

"It's a good thing I grabbed this, then."

Emily's eyes widened.

"You crafty little bugger."

She reached over and grabbed her phone from him.

"No thanks?"

"Thank you, thank you, thank you." She leant in and gave him a little peck on his cheek before quickly turning her attention to her phone.

"There's a small crack across the screen," Schultz said.

"That doesn't matter," she replied as she tucked her phone

inside her boot.

"Good, now let's get the maniac." Schultz lined his gun up with the parked convoy.

"You two ready?" Frank asked.

Emily raised her gun and scanned the convoy.

"Ready," Emily replied, her focus still on Ivan's trucks.

"Firing in three, two..."

Chapter 76

The truck at the back of Ivan's convoy erupted in a fireball. Emily scanned around the last truck, watching, waiting for movement, her finger hovering over her trigger, when she spotted five men emerge from behind the flame.

"Here we go," Emily whispered.

Behind her she heard Frank load the bazooka when gunfire erupted from Ivan's men. Emily and Schultz returned fire. The bullets being fired from Ivan's militias were falling short of Emily and Schultz's position.

"Firing in three... two... one."

A moment later gunfire from Ivan's men ceased as they scrambled to escape the approaching doom. Three of the men were thrown in the air, clothes on fire, as the last truck exploded. As Ivan's men landed on the road, two of them began rolling around, screaming in agony as they tried to extinguish the flames. The third man wasn't moving. Where his remains lay, a fire flickered in the night.

"Two of Ivan's men escaped the blast. One deceased. Two dying in agony," Emily reported.

"Steve," Frank yelled.

"Yes, boss." Steve approached, his gun resting in his hands.

"That SUV," Frank nodded towards the SUV that'd destroyed his troop carrier.

"The last one gave us a bit of resistance but he finally succumbed to our stealth maneuvers. We grabbed one of his radios."

Steve handed a small handheld radio over to Emily.

"This could come in handy." Emily turned the radio over in her hand.

"Any survivors?" Steve nodded towards the two fireballs and asked.

"We have three down. At least two escaped the blasts. I haven't seen Ivan or Brian," Emily advised.

"So at least two to four remaining?" Steve asked.

"Yes. We're going to be exposed as we approach Ivan's SUV."

"We'll approach first. Those last two wannabe soldiers have nothing on us. They'll be dead before they see us."

"What do you want us to do?" Schultz asked.

"You and Lee follow behind. You'll have our backs."

"And you'll leave Ivan for me take care of?" Emily asked.

"Unless he shoots at us first. Then my men will return fire."

A voice on the other end of the handheld radio began talking and kept up a continuous string of chatter, barely stopping for a breath.

"Ivan?" she asked as she looked up to Schultz.

"Yeah, sounds like him."

"Listen to the tone in his voice," Schultz said.

Ivan's voice came over the radio again, still in Russian.

Schultz continued, "He's worried. He knows something is wrong. If you don't talk to him, I will."

Emily looked between Schultz and the fireball of Ivan's two trucks.

She pressed down the button on the handheld piece. "Your men can't come to the radio right now."

"Who's this?"

"Oh, I'm disappointed. You don't recognize my voice? You should."

"What have you done with my men?"

"Don't worry," Emily glanced back at the SUV that'd pushed them off the road, "they're at peace now. Asleep."

"Emily?"

"The one and only. Now, are you going to surrender like a civilized person?"

"Not a hope."

"You must be down to only a couple of men and... what, no usable vehicles?"

"I still have my army here."

"Army of four or five, and that includes Brian," Emily whispered.

"Turn the radio off. Radio silence from here on out," Frank ordered.

Emily turned the radio off and slipped it on her belt hook.

Frank continued, "You all know the drill. Stay alert."

In the glow of the fire, Emily could see Frank's men nodding.

"Right, time to move in. Move into formation," Frank ordered.

Steve and Frank's men lead the group down the highway towards the remains of Ivan's convoy while Frank, Emily and Schultz brought up the rear, surveying beside and behind them.

They were about twenty meters down the highway when she spotted three soldiers march out in front of the burning trucks. Steve spotted them at the same time and raised his hand. His gun aimed ahead, he lowered himself until he was kneeling on the road. His colleagues on either side of him also knelt down.

Gunfire erupted from beside the fireballs.

Frank's men returned fire.

Emily lined up the first of the three militias, the one standing closest to the two burning trucks. She released her trigger. He fell.

The other two fell.

"Man down, man down," Steve yelled as he crouched over the comrade alongside him.

Emily looked over to see Frank had already moved up to the front. Emily inched closer. Steve had his hand pressed against his comrade's chest.

"We need to keep moving. Kane, stay here. You know what you need to do."

A man from behind Steve repositioned himself beside his fallen comrade.

"Steve, time to go."

Steve didn't move until Frank pulled him.

"Everyone, move, quick time," Frank ordered.

The small party were on the move again with Frank taking the lead alongside Steve. Everyone paused for a couple of seconds as they walked past their fallen comrade. When Emily walked past, she refused to look down. His struggling gasps of breath were enough to tell her he was dying a slow and agonizing death.

Frank's men spread out as they approached the convoy. Some moved out towards the roadside, ready to approach the SUV from the outside. Emily and Schultz followed Frank and one of his men as they approached the convoy from the inside lane of the highway.

Gunfire erupted once more.

Everyone returned fire. Emily continued shooting as she tried to locate the shooter, but he had good cover. She spotted Frank continuing to shoot as he approached the convoy. Following his lead, she fired rounds in the direction where she suspected the shooter was hiding as she moved closer to the convoy.

Gunfire from Ivan's convoy ceased.

Frank held his hand up. Everyone ceased shooting. Emily glanced over her left shoulder then her right.

"Schultz," she whispered.

Nothing.

Looking behind her, she saw him laying unmoving on the road.

Ignoring the possible repercussions from Frank, let alone Ivan and his men, she screamed, "Schultz."

Nothing, not even a stir.

She looked towards the convoy and muttered, "You bastards."

Blind with fury, Emily marched towards the burnings trucks but Frank grabbed her arm.

"You can't just go marching in there. We don't know what's waiting for us on the other side."

Emily turned side on to Frank and pointed towards Schultz. "He's not moving."

Frank glanced over her shoulder. He clicked his fingers and a couple of his men ran towards Schultz, their guns aimed at what was left of the convoy.

"They'll look after him. You ready?"

Emily nodded.

"Right, keep focused," Frank advised.

Her gun poised, Emily checked her surroundings while taking a wide berth around the burning truck, Frank right beside her.

She stopped, cocking her ear up the highway.

Sirens, and lots of them. They were getting louder. Towards Moscow, the road was dark.

"They're still some distance away," she whispered.

"We should get out of here while we can."

"Not until I see Ivan and Brian. In the flesh."

"If there's any part of them left," Frank whispered.

Emily ignored him and looked around, taking in the burning piles scattered over the road, some bigger and longer, others smaller. The heat from the trucks on fire warmed the side of her face. Despite the arctic night, it was a little too much heat.

She pushed towards the SUV. From what she could see, the SUV appeared to have weathered the blast fairly well compared to its companions. A few small burning piles of debris lay scattered beside the SUV but the vehicle itself was still intact. The sirens were getting louder as she walked around to its other side.

"I don't like this. Those sirens are getting too close. I'm out of here." With a jolt to the stomach, Emily realized Frank's voice had dropped a bit farther behind her.

"Fine, be a sissy. Doesn't worry me."

"Ivan and Brian aren't worth it. They're not worth risking your life or your freedom for."

She heard hurried steps then Frank grabbed her arm.

Turning around, she looked pointedly from his hand to him then back to his hand. He let go.

"Yeah, they are. Brian is an employee of my father's brother."

"So, your uncle?"

"He's no uncle of mine. If Brian is here, Fu will already know I'm here."

"I don't know what issues you have with your family but don't make this personal."

"Too late."

Bang.

Emily ducked at the sound of a gun being fired. She turned to see Frank fall to the road, clutching his shoulder.

"Son of a—"

"Go. Get the bastards," he grunted, waving her off.

Another shot rang out.

Emily crouched behind the SUV. More shots flew directly over her head. She waved for Frank to move but he lay there, turning his head away from her.

With shots still flying over her, Emily hurried to the rear tire. She slowly stood up until she could peer in through the tinted back window. Ducking back down again, she shuffled around the rear of the SUV. Peering around the side, she spotted them. Two men, one of them armed and leaning against the roof of the SUV, while the other crouched a little farther back and didn't appear to be armed.

"Brian?" she whispered.

The unarmed man faced her.

"To your right," Brian yelled out and scrambled behind the gunman.

"Come out, come out wherever you are," the gunman taunted her.

The taunting voice was Ivan's. Emily stepped out from behind the SUV, her gun aimed at him. Ivan turned towards her, his gun pointed at her.

"Ivan, we meet again. Your men haven't fared well tonight."

"It's not over yet."

Emily fired a single shot at the rear tire of the SUV.

"Well, this SUV isn't going to get you to Moscow." She aimed her gun back on Ivan.

"I have other plans."

"This is the end of the line, Ivan. Surrender and I won't shoot you."

"Like hell I'll be doing that. There's an empty seat in the Kremlin that needs filling."

"What do you mean? What have you done?"

"Shoot me and you won't find out." He sported a smirk as he lowered his gun.

Emily kept hers pointed at him.

"What have you done to the president?"

"Isn't your government going to enjoy hearing how two of its people are terrorizing my country?!"

"This isn't your country."

"You seem to forget that you are the most wanted person in Russia. Yes?" He stepped towards Emily.

"Stop right there," she yelled. "Do not take another step."

Ivan raised his arms until they were level with his head but took another step towards her.

"Come quietly." She stepped backwards. "I'll ensure you'll

go to a pleasant jail. And if you cooperate, I may even get your sentence reduced."

"Like hell you will. You're the criminal here, not me."

"There's only one criminal here, and I'm looking at him."

"I'm only doing what the people asked for but never got."

"By unlawfully booting the president out."

In the reflection of the back window of the SUV, she saw the blue and red lights approaching.

Not long now, she thought.

Ivan chuckled. "If you think they're going to help you, you'd better think again. I'm sure the police will frown on a tourist operating a firearm."

"Stop moving, or I'll shoot."

"If you were going to, you'd have already done it. Now hand the gun over."

Emily took a couple of steps back.

"Before I do, I want to know one thing."

"Continue."

"The money you used to fund this... what are you calling it? A revolution? How long did you think you'd get away with it before questions were asked?"

"I still am. You're the only one left who knows about my paper trail. Or should I say 'knew'?"

Emily felt a gun barrel being pushed into the middle of her back.

"Lower your gun," a woman's voice behind her demanded.

"Katinka?"

Chapter 77

"Lower your gun," the woman's voice demanded again.

Emily peered around. Flashing red and blue lights lit up the night. Police were scampering behind their vehicles, guns aimed at Emily and Ivan.

"All right, all right. I'm putting it down." Looking straight at Ivan, she added, "He's armed, too."

As she lowered her gun, she felt the pressure of the gun in her back lessen. Kneeling down, she placed the gun on the road. A quick look around confirmed she was surrounded. Police cars had stopped randomly behind and in front of them, blocking both sides of the road.

Bang, bang.

Shots rang out. The gun in her back was gone and the

police returned fire. No time to grab her gun, Emily ran towards some nearby bushes. The gunfire intensified. The bushes didn't provide much camouflage. Looking at the convoy, she saw Ivan was alone.

"Where's Brian—"

Her eyes quickly found him. Brian was running away from the scene towards her when his body fell to the ground. He stretched his arm towards her. She stepped back away from the bush, a twig cracking under the weight of her foot.

A bloodcurdling scream echoed through the night. Emily looked up to see Ivan fall. But who'd shot him?

A flashlight was bobbing towards her.

"Emily. Come out. It's over," the same woman called out.

"Katinka, is that you?"

"Yes. Now, please, come out before the others get here."

Emily stepped out from behind the bush, her hands in the air.

"What's going on? You're my assistant, not a police woman. I don't understand."

Katinka approached her. Grabbing the closest wrist, she pulled Emily's arm back.

"Ouch." Emily flinched.

Snapping a handcuff on Emily's wrist, Katinka said, "You're under arrest. Anything you say," she pulled the other arm around and snapped the other handcuff on, "can and will be used against you as evidence."

Emily shook her head. "Where are you taking me?"

"To Moscow for processing."

"Ivan and Brian. I want to see them. Please."

Emily was now surrounded by police officers, their guns all pointing at her.

"It's all right, she won't be any trouble. Will you?"

"No. I'm the innocent one here."

"Innocence doesn't exist. We all have something to hide. Don't we?" an officer directly in front of her said, his gun pointed at her head.

"Do you?"

She saw the officer's eyes twitch before he lowered his gun.

"This way." Katinka pushed her back. "They're over here."

Glancing over her shoulder, Emily glimpsed officers moving around quickly and heard orders flying everywhere.

She stopped and looked Katinka up and down before asking, "What's all this?"

"I was undercover. There were rumors this was going down. It was just a matter of when. But then you got involved and everything escalated."

"You knew about all this?"

"I couldn't blow my cover."

"Well, you had me fooled. The device you put under my desk? I know it was used to extract data from Ivan's organization."

"Ah, you saw that?"

"No, Ivan's men did. They showed me the video surveillance."

"I needed the data to help secure his arrest."

"Is there a problem here?" A male officer approached them.

"No, all's good."

He stared at Emily until she looked away.

"Get her out of here. We need to get this highway re-opened."

"Yes, sir. This way." Katinka guided Emily away.

"Schultz? Is he okay? He wasn't moving earlier."

"He'll be fine. Just a little graze. He'll live to see his day in court and serve time for his alleged crimes."

As they approached Ivan, she could hear muffled groans. Katinka kicked his gun away while Emily stood over him.

"Lots of noise for a single gunshot wound. Your arm will be fine."

"You're still alive? I sent my finest men to finish you off."

"They couldn't take care of one woman and you thought they were good enough to set off a revolution. What can I say? You just can't get good staff anymore." Turning around to Katinka, Emily said, "Let's go."

Ivan grabbed her leg. She looked down to see him wincing.

"I'd be watching your every move," he hissed through his clenched teeth. "You just don't know who could be hiding in the shadows."

"Is that a threat?"

"No, it's a promise." He laughed through the pain.

"Right, that's enough," Katinka ordered.

Ivan grunted as Katinka stood on his injured arm. He released his grip.

"Emily, over here." Katinka guided Emily away and yelled to a nearby officer, "This one's alive and still has some fight about him."

Two officers ran over, one radioing in what Emily suspected was the ambulance, while the other one checked Ivan's pulse.

"Don't know why you're doing that. You won't feel anything. That man doesn't have a heart," Emily said.

"Funny," Ivan said through clenched his teeth.

"Brian fell over there." Katinka guided Emily towards him.

Brian was still lying face down to the ground. Emily kicked his feet. Nothing. Moving around, Emily used her foot to push Brian onto his back.

Emily stared down at his empty eyes and felt nothing.

Katinka leant down and placed a finger on his neck. "He's gone."

"Good."

"Bit of bad blood there?" Katina asked.

"What did your research tell you?"

"Who is he?" Katinka nodded towards the body.

"He goes by Brian. He's a hacker."

Katinka shook her head. "That's the missing piece of the puzzle. He hid his trail. We couldn't work out how Ivan was getting his information out undetected. Now I know how. With his help."

"Yes, he was good at that. He and a friend of mine were arrested. The charges against this animal disappeared, while my friend received a criminal record."

"I'm sorry but they need to take you in now."

Chapter 78

They'd been weaving through Moscow when the police car Emily was traveling in crawled to a stop in front of a boom gate with a small guard cubicle beside it. An officer stepped out and waved them through as the gate was rising.

Emily looked around. The building complex they were entering was like the rest of what she'd seen of Russia, an older style, with no signs or hints of what was hidden behind the walls.

Their police car had barely stopped when the officer in the passenger seat jumped out and opened her door.

He ordered something to her in Russian.

Emily shrugged her shoulders. "English?"

The driver looked at her via his rear-view mirror. "Out.

Now," he said, his English barley understandable.

"This is going to be interesting," Emily mumbled as she swung her legs out of the car.

She'd barely put her feet on the ground when the officer grabbed her arm and pulled her out. The other officer, now standing beside her, grabbed her other arm. Together they marched her up the small flight of stairs and inside.

As they walked through an area barely the size of a standard bedroom, Emily saw an elevator in the middle of the wall ahead, with a set of frosted glass-paned doors on either side of it.

After swiping an access card, the officers pushed her through the glass-paned door to the left of the elevator and into a room filled with desks and police officers who continued working. To her side, she saw that the other door led into the same area.

The officers pushed her down the long line of desks where she received a few sideway glances. Holding her head high, she continued walking deeper into the labyrinth of desks.

"Turn here," the officer who had been their driver held an arm out, gesturing for her to turn.

Four solid doors along the wall greeted them. They guided her towards the one straight ahead, the only one with its door ajar. Pushing her inside, the non-English speaking officer approached her, grabbed her handcuffs and unlocked them, while the other officer stood in the doorway, his arms crossed.

"Stay," the officer said as he closed the door behind them.

She was in a simple room. Four solid walls surrounded her

and a single fluorescent light provided her only source of light. Emily noticed a camera up in the corner. A simple table with a chair on either side sat in the middle of the room.

Walking up to the door, Emily pulled down on the handle and gave the door a tug. It didn't move.

"Great."

She slumped in the chair facing the door. "At least I'm not dead. Yet."

* * *

A creak of the door woke Emily up. Lifting her head up from the table, where it had slumped as she'd fallen asleep, she watched through groggy eyes a figure walk in before the door closed again.

Rubbing her eyes, she focused on the figure and recognized who was now sitting opposite her.

"Schultz. What are you doing in here?"

His arm was in a sling. "Thanks for the welcome, Lee. How long have they had you in here?"

Stretching her shoulders and back, she thought about it. "Too long. What's going on out there?"

"Don't know."

"Even with your credentials, they didn't enlighten you?"

Schultz chuckled before wincing. "Don't make me laugh. It hurts."

"I'll try if you want me to."

"By the daggers I felt earlier when I ran the gauntlet out

there," he nodded towards the door, "I'm not going to be receiving any extra privileges."

"Up there." Emily rolled her eyes up to the corner. "Camera."

Schultz nodded and placed his hand against the side of his face, blocking his mouth from the camera. "Did you know Katinka is a fellow officer?" he whispered.

Emily nodded. She also used her hand to cover her mouth from the camera. "I didn't see that one coming."

"You're as surprised as me then. Have they questioned you yet?"

Emily shook her head. "You?"

"Yeah, for about an hour. Two doors down."

"What did they want to know?"

"Not much, just information on Ivan. Probably just cross-checking the information they already have."

"Why have they got us in the same room? Don't you guys usually keep everyone separated?"

"Back home, yeah, we do. Here, I don't know. Maybe they want to see what else we'll spill in here."

Sitting back in her chair, Emily crossed her arms and glared at the camera.

"How long are you going to keep that up for?" Schultz asked.

"Until they grow tired of me watching them."

Schultz shook his head. "You'll last two minutes before you grow tired of it."

Beep.

They both looked towards the door as it swung open. An older man in a black business suit and greying hair stood in the doorway, one hand in his pocket and the other one pointing out into the labyrinth.

"You're free to go," he advised.

Emily and Schultz exchanged confused glances.

"What do you mean?" Emily asked.

"The president has given you both a full pardon."

"I know you're not Russian. Scandinavian, maybe? Who are you?"

"Leo." He smiled as he pulled his hand out of his pocket.

A chain dangled from his hand. He held his hand up revealing a small pendant in his palm. A chain was threaded through a small hole in the top of the pendant.

"What's with the old coin?" Emily asked.

"Have you not seen this before?"

Emily shrugged her shoulders and replied, "Should I?"

He studied her for a moment before slipping it back into his pocket.

"Very well then. There's a lot we need to explain to you."

"Seriously, what are you talking about?"

"All you need to know right now is that you're both in safe hands. But we really must start moving."

Leo stepped inside and held an arm out, gesturing for them to leave first.

"One thing I don't understand," said Emily. "Why were we held in here for so long?"

"Would you rather be arrested and not see the light of day

again?"

"No, of course not." Standing up, she shrugged and shook her head.

"I'm sorry, Leo." Schultz placed his hands on Emily's shoulders. "She always needs to know everything. Lee, let's get moving." He gave her a gentle nudge.

"That's not... entirely... true." Emily shrugged off his hold and remained where she was.

"It's all right. I'm a stranger, and I'm sure you both have lots of questions. I've called some favors that were owed to me. But that doesn't matter right now. I've been ordered to take you both straight to the airport."

"I need to know something before we leave. Do you have an update on Brian, Ivan, or Frank?" Emily asked.

"As you know, Brian—"

"Dead on the scene."

"Correct. Ivan is under police custody. He'll be a bit sore for a while but he'll live. Frank and his men are currently getting their wounds attended to at the hospital. Once they've cleared, they'll also be on the next plane out of here. The president assures me there'll be no evidence they were ever here. He's also given his personal guarantee that everyone who helped tonight will be taken care of."

"Exactly what does that mean?"

"If we get you two out of here now, the local officers cannot press charges against you. I don't need to remind you that last night you two performed various offences spanning the length of at least a page. We need to get you on that next plane before anyone changes their minds."

"All right, then. Let's go home." Emily stepped out of the office, finding it hard to believe her luck.

They quickly weaved their way past the desks. Emily noticed a few of the police officers nodding to their group, while smiles crept on a few faces.

Ahead, their exit was nearing. Her heart racing, Emily quickened her pace. The door was within reach. Pressing the handle down, she pushed the door open. She stood there, unable to move. Blocking her exit, two officers were fighting to hold on to a handcuffed Ivan, who was acting like a wild animal. He was thrusting his shoulders every which way and snarling at the officers. A third officer stood behind the trio, his eyes firmly planted on Ivan.

The officers guided Ivan away from Emily and towards the other entrance. The officer at the rear moved around the trio, nodding to Emily, before opening the other door. Emily remained where she was, waiting for them to move.

One officer was through when Ivan looked up and saw her standing opposite him. His snarling and thrusts stopped. The officers followed his gaze, then looked back to Ivan.

Emily shuffled her feet.

Come on, get moving, she thought.

"You haven't stopped anything. You've heard it here first. The revolution is only just beginning." An evil laugh erupted from Ivan as he threw his head back.

Emily quickly stepped out of the room and walked straight towards the double doors at the entrance.

"You all right?" Schultz placed his arm around her.

Her chest was racing and her hands shaking. Emily tucked her hands under her armpits. Turning towards Schultz, she managed a weak smile. "I'm all good. Let's get out of here."

Chapter 79

Sitting in the middle of the airport lounge, waiting for their plane ride home, Emily stretched her neck. A few passengers nearby were pointing at them, smirking.

"Why don't you take a photo? It'll last longer," she said to them.

They quickly looked the other way.

"Seriously." Emily turned to Schultz. "You'd think they haven't seen anyone bruised and battered, hey?"

Schultz grunted, his head in his phone.

"Anything interesting?"

"Just work."

"Seriously?"

"I'll know when I get home. All I know is that as soon as

I'm off the plane I'll be escorted straight to HQ."

"Nice, a welcoming committee."

"Yeah, probably not the sort I'm after."

"Who knows, it might not be as bad as you think it'll be."

"Doubt it. But I can't do much about it now besides enjoy the on-flight entertainment. Anyway, what are you going to be doing when we arrive home?"

"I need to travel on to Adelaide, to the Barossa Valley."

"Ooh, nice. Apparently, there's some nice wineries there."

"I won't be going there to enjoy the wine. A childhood friend, Jack Sinclair, has passed away."

"I'm so sorry."

Emily smiled but her mind had already drifted to her Golden Retriever, Koko, who loved licking peanut butter straight from the spoon. Her career was sending her away frequently and she was unable to care for Koko so Jack had offered to take her in. The last time she'd seen Koko was when she drove away that morning. Barely halfway down the drive, she spotted Koko already off, racing the trainers and horses as they went through their morning training.

"We'll see." She patted his knee before standing up and stretching her back.

Walking over to the airport lounge windows, she placed her hands in her coat pockets and felt a small round object. She quickly realised it was the object James had secretly given her. Pulling it out, she turned it over in her hand. One side was silver, with a single curved line going from one side to the other. Turning it over, she saw the image of what looked like a mountain with a small blackened area in the middle, like an opening, a cave. Around the circumference, a series of small symbols were printed.

She pulled her cell phone out of her back pocket. Her phone alerted her the battery was almost flat. Disregarding the notification, she took a photo of the coin, dropped the photo into her search engine.

A coin appeared at the top of the search results, looking like hers only more tarnished. She checked the image description. It read: GIA-C.

"GIA-C?" she whispered.

Scrolling through the next couple of search results, she stumbled on another:

Global Intelligence Agency: Wikipedia
Update: Tensions still rife in the GIA
GIA News

Curious, she clicked the first one. There was only one line on the page. It read:

The information from this page is unavailable.

Returning to her search results, she tried the next one. The page was blacked out and required a user name and password. Backing out, she clicked on the next entry. It also returned the same log-in requirements.

Turning the pendant over in her hand, she whispered,

"You're giving me more questions than answers."

"You talking to yourself again?" Schultz whispered into her ear.

Emily jumped, her shoulders almost connecting with his jaw. Sliding her hand into her pocket, she released the coin as she turned around. "Don't scare me like that."

"Sorry. They're ready to board us."

Looking out into the airport lounge, she observed a group of men and women sitting on a row of seats, two rows back. Each one of them was staring at her, their faces expressionless. Looking closer, she noticed they all had one headphone placed in their ear, their lips pursed open, barely moving as they talked. She stopped at the man sitting in the middle of the group. He blew her a kiss then chuckled.

Turning away, Emily braced herself against the glass. Her heart racing. "We should take the next flight. It's only a two-hour delay, with an extra stop over. What do you say?"

Schultz placed an arm around Emily's shoulders and asked, "What's spooked you?"

"Behind us, two rows back. A group of men and women, all staring this way. The man in the middle, he was one of the captors on the island."

Schultz turn his head around slightly.

"There's no one there."

"What?" Emily turned around. "They were just—"

The seats were empty. She scanned around the lounge, looked at every person lining up to board the plane... but nothing.

"They were there." She pointed to the seats they had occupied.

Schultz stood in front of her. Placing his hands around her, he pulled her in tight.

"I believe you. We'll be home soon," he whispered into her hair.

Emily pulled away, her eyes red and welling up, she managed a small smile. Wiping her eyes, she turned towards the boarding gates. A female airline employee was approaching them. The woman's nametag indicated she was their flight attendant.

The woman looked between Emily and Schultz. A small smile appeared on her face as she said, "We're ready for you to board now."

Follow the Author

If you'd like to be kept up to date on new releases please subscribe to K.A. Bragonje's email list at:

www.kabragonje.com.

You can also find K.A. Bragonje on the following platforms:

Amazon www.amazon.com/author/kabragonje

Facebook www.facebook.com/kabragonje

Instagram www.instagram.com/kabragonje

Books by the Author

If you haven't already read book one in the Emily Lee series, The Analyst, you can request a copy from your local bookshop, online book retailer or a signed copy can be purchased direct from myself.

If you'd prefer eBook format, it's currently exclusive with Amazon on most of their marketplaces.

Acknowledgments

Writing is often a solitary craft, countless hours alone with just the characters. But not far away is my awesome team.

First and foremost, I'd like to thank you for choosing to read this instalment in the Emily Less series.

Next, I'd like to thank my personal cheer squad, my family and friends. Their support, and asking when the next book was going to be coming out, has kept me motivated to finish this book. Thank you all for continuing to believe in me and the stories I'm telling, and for the one's I'm yet to write.

I'd like my editor Ella who stuck with me as this book went through the rounds of editing. I've learnt a lot, and continue to do so to this day about the world of editing.

Thank you to my cover artist, Olivia, you've made the

whole process enjoyable.

Last, but not least, thank you to the writing and indie groups I'm proud to be a member of. If you didn't share your experiences, I would still be dreaming about one day being a published author.

Do not ever underestimate the power your heartfelt encouragement will have on someone.

www.ingramcontent.com/pod-product-compliance
Lightning Source LLC
Chambersburg PA
CBHW020008120726
47903CB00004B/1183